MW01115840

Book 3

HOUSTON HARE
Tallstrunt Press LLC

Sprig
Book 3
Copyright © 2024 Houston Hare
Tallstrunt Press LLC
https://Sprig.HoustonHare.com

First Paperback Edition 2024
Paperback ISBN: 978-1-7342980-7-9
Hardcover ISBN: 978-1-7342980-8-6

Art by: Houston Hare

Published by Tallstrunt Press LLC

tallstrunt press

TallstruntPress.com

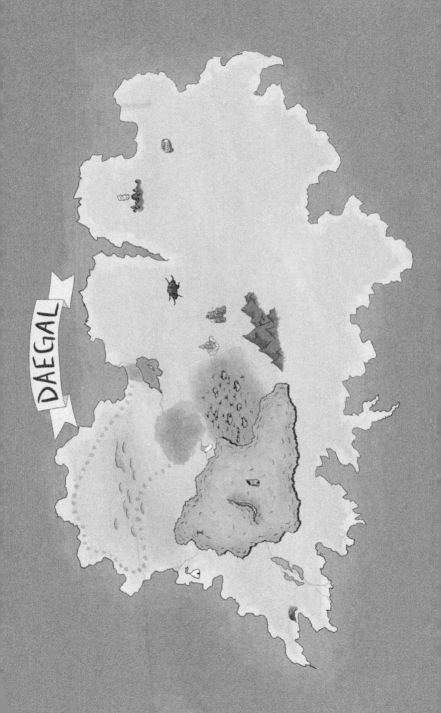

16: Cypress

16.1 Cypress

We climbed over the rubble toward the noise. I walked in a daze, unable to process our current situation. Unable to believe that Zef was actually dead. After all we had been through.

The world carried on around me as I focused on walking. One foot after another, rock after rock. I didn't have the capacity to care about anything more than that.

We reached the source of the noise. Marv stood in rock form with tears streaming down his face. In his arms was a limp girl.

No! I ran to him. I had already lost Zef. I couldn't afford to lose Abigail too, someone who shared so much of my own story.

Abigail laid in her father's arms with a red gash across her forehead. Other than that, she still looked intact.

"Tigala, can you check her?"

Tigala was already stretching out a hand. The orange glow radiated from her hand and spread across Abigail's skin. Then it faded again. Tigala withdrew her hand.

"I think she's going to be okay," said Tigala. "Maybe a concussion?"

Marv and I both breathed a sigh of relief.

Behind him, there was screaming coming through cracks in the rubble. Marv looked down at his daughter and then in the direction of the noise. He was more capable than most of digging through the rubble with Crag helping.

He looked down at Abigail again. "I can't lose her again." Then he looked back toward the noise. "But others need my help." He lifted his rock arms toward Tigala. "Can you please take care of her in the meantime?"

It was a different Marv than the one I had met in the jail cell. It was a different Marv even than the one that entered the mountain of Dwarven slaves. He had been overprotective and unwilling to let Abigail help. Now she was hurt, and he was strong enough to accept it and help others.

Marv and Crag stomped over to a large rock sticking out of the rubble. He grabbed it and squatted as he tore it from the ground, revealing an overhang where ten or so people I didn't recognize were huddled. They must have been a group of the original colonists. They looked at Marv in fear.

"It's okay. I'm trying to help," said Marv, holding the large rock up. "Now come out so I can put this down." His voice was sad, but there was a hint of confidence. He knew what he was capable of. He knew why we were here and it was good to have him on the team.

A few gave him thanks as they ran out from the opening onto the higher ground. Once the last of them climbed out, Marv slammed the rock back down in the rubble. The colonists looked around like lost dogs. They probably needed someone to step up and explain. They at least needed reassurance that we were going to get out of here. I couldn't offer either. I didn't have it in me.

Marv returned to Tigala to check on Abigail again. "Is there anything I need to do? How do I help her?"

"Just let her rest and bandage her head. Her body should do the rest," she said, handing the girl back. Marv let Crag crumble off of him and turn back into his small rock form. Marv laid his daughter on the rocks and knelt over her. Crag joined him with a sad glowing face. Marv glanced back at me with tears in his eyes. "We'll be alright." he said, in a gentle dismissal.

I gave him a half smile and turned to Tigala. "Have you seen our group? Do you know if they made it out?"

She shook her head. "We should go check."

I nodded.

We headed for the staircase that led to the room where we were cornered by the Arcus. Was our group still in there or did the fight continue elsewhere? I hoped they were okay too, but at this point, I expected the worst. Out of all of the tragedies we had suffered at the colony, this was the worst. Not only did we fail to stop a monster big enough to destroy a town in seconds, but we lost many of the few people that survived the dragon attack. We probably lost most of the people who had been enslaved too.

Before we got to the room of the fight with the Arcus, I found a Saurian body. It was Ferek. There were only a few small rocks on his back, but the black mark at the back of his head led me to believe that Wikith or Brendell had killed him. Just beyond Ferek was another Saurian, half-buried in rocks. I recognized the blue scales as Garlar, the first Saurian to give me a chance.

I looked away.

There was a scrape of shifting rock nearby. An Elven hood poked up from the rubble near the wall. His face looked our way as the rocks sloughed off of him.

3

"Lolan!" I yelled, so happy to see that he had made it out. He was beaten up. He had burns on his jacket and scrapes across his face. Dried blood mixed with rock dust flaked off of his cheek.

He gave a weary smile as he reached behind him. He heaved a body out of the rubble. I was scared to find out who it might be. Lolan lifted the body over one shoulder as he struggled to his feet, and I saw the yellow robes of the Arcus. It was a smaller body than Wikith's. It had to be Brendell.

"Is he okay?" I asked, picking up my pace as I approached.

Lolan looked up with weariness on his face. "I don't know."

As I got closer I noticed that the robes didn't fully extend down one arm. The black lining faded to black and red— burned flesh.

"Did you do that?" asked Tigala.

Lolan took a deep breath and nodded, breaking eye contact.

"Geez," said Tigala.

"Is he breathing?" I asked. "How did you knock him out? With the fire?"

Lolan nodded again. "He's breathing. And yeah. If I didn't, he would have killed me, and probably others." The pink glow still burned bright on Brendell's temples. It must have been a terrible call to make.

"I'm sorry you had to do that," I said.

"Me too," he said. He looked behind us and then back at me. "Zef?"

I couldn't form the words and instead shook my head as tears welled up again.

He breathed a huff as he fell to his knees.

"He died saving people," said Tigala.

Lolan didn't cry. He looked like he was out of tears.

"We got to say goodbye," I said. "He's buried beneath the tree if you want to pay your respects."

Lolan didn't say anything and just slammed a fist into the ground. It was more emotion than I had seen from him in the past. Was he going to be okay? We waited for him to gain his composure and then helped him up, with Brendell still slung over his shoulders.

"We still have each other," I said. "I'm with you guys no matter what."

Lolan winced at the statement. He looked at me with so much pain in his expression. "No matter what."

"I'll carry him," said Tigala, seeing how worn out Lolan was. She grabbed the Elf and slung him over her own shoulders.

"What do we do now?" said Lolan.

"I don't know," I said. "Zef said it was up to us now. I'm not sure I feel up to anything, but I guess we can at least look for survivors."

"How do we stop that thing?" said Lolan. "Did you see it? It was able to see outside of the cavern with its feet flat on the floor of it."

"I don't know how we could," I said. "It would kill us in an instant." We were close to the room where we had fought Wikith. I couldn't see much, but I did see a body with long blonde hair on the ledge outside the door. I ran forward and up the broken staircase to her.

Tallesia laid there unconscious. She had scrapes on her arms and face, but she was breathing at a normal pace. I leaned over her and shook her arm. She woke up and spoke softly. "What?"

"Are you okay? Are the others—"

She cut me off. "Don't go in there," she said. "It was a blood bath."

"Wh—what?" I said, unsure of how to process the words she spoke.

"Wikith only kept the rest of us occupied when he lost track of you," she said. Her voice was airy and weak. "Once the creature woke up, he stopped holding back. I think he only spared me because I'm an Elf."

"Who?" I said.

"Kricoo. Ferek. Wallace. Seth. I don't know about the others. Some got pushed out of the fight. They were the lucky ones."

"No!" I said. I looked at the room. The dark doorway stared back at me menacingly. "Where is Wikith?" I asked with my jaw set.

"He escaped," she said.

I looked up to the sky showing through the shattered roof of the cavern hoping I might see him exiting the cavern. No such luck. He was gone.

"What do you need?" asked Lolan. "Are you hurt?"

"He hit me with a strong current," she said. "But I should be fine. I was able to redirect some of it."

"Can I help you up?" said Lolan.

"Yes, please," said Tallesia.

Lolan stooped down and wrapped her arm over his shoulder. She stood slowly with most of her weight on Lolan.

"Have you found any of the others? How many survived?" she said.

"We're not sure yet," said Tigala. "Not many so far."

There were dead people all around us. The cavern was in shambles. The colony was charred and ruined. Half of the colonists were still recovering from the dragon attack. And now a giant monster sleeping in the heart of the island awoke. *What is this place? Why did I even come here?* I broke down again. This time it wasn't because of the people I had lost. It wasn't that I still mourned the loss of my parents. It wasn't that I wished people would just look past each other's differences.

I broke down because I was completely and utterly lost. There was no hope. There was no way forward, and there was no reason to even look for a way forward. It was all in shambles. It was all hopeless. And I was tired. Tired of fighting, and tired of losing every step of the way.

I sat on the ledge outside of the room, while Lolan escorted Tallesia down the stairs. I didn't cry. I was all out of tears. I sat in silence and stared out at the expanse.

More people were now moving around the rubble, searching for people who had been buried and moving rocks. Tigala sat next to me.

"You okay?" she asked.

"No!" I said. "Are you?"

She hesitated. "No."

"I don't understand what we're supposed to do with this. I thought we were doing good here. I thought we were actually bringing change and showing people that we don't need to be constantly at each other's throats. And every time I feel like we're making progress, the stakes are raised. First trolls and a dangerous forest, then a dragon, now... this"

Tigala was slow to respond. "Yeah. It's a dangerous island. But at least in all of the other examples, we adapted. More people were willing to help us each time."

"Does it even matter now?" I said. "We can adapt all we want, but nothing is going to change the outcome of us going

7

up against *that* thing." I pointed at the cavern wall where gashes taller than trees marked the swipe of one of the monster's claws.

"I don't know." She didn't say anything else. She sat next to me for a time and we watched the other groups. Lolan had a conversation with another Elf and ended up passing Tallesia off to the stranger, probably for medical care.

I didn't have anything more to say. I just sat and thought through the cycle of hopelessness in my head. Then, on the far end of the rubble, I saw something that piqued my interest. A green glow marked the use of nature magic. Some of the Treeks had survived!

It was the first thing to give me some form of hope since the ceiling collapsed.

"I need to go talk to some people," I said to Tigala. "Do you mind giving me some space?"

Tigala looked a bit distraught at the request. But I needed space. I needed to talk to them on my own. I needed to know anything they would tell me, and they might not if Tigala was there. I also just needed to talk to people like me. I had fought the segregation for so long, and look where it got us. Maybe I *needed* some segregation.

Tigala nodded. "Just come back. Okay?" she said.

"Yeah," I said. I lifted myself up and walked over the rubble to the Treeks.

16.2 Cypress

I approached the group of Treeks with my heart pounding in my chest. I didn't know what to expect. I didn't want to expect anything, given my last run-in with a Treek, but I couldn't keep myself from dreaming about the family I could find.

They were *my* people. I hadn't been around other Treeks since I lived with Mother and Father in the forest. Would they speak differently than me? Would they have their own cultural norms that I knew nothing about? Or did the war wipe the world clean of Treek customs?

But even more importantly, had they heard of my parents? It was a fool's errand, but I still didn't have a solid answer. Malcolm had said that he killed them. Maybe he had. Or maybe he was just trying to provoke me—hurt me in more ways than just physical pain. If they *were* still alive, it would give me hope. And if they weren't, it would be the final page of that book. Even if they were gone, the Treeks might be able to tell me about them—fill in gaps in my memory, or remind me of what it is to be a Treek.

They saw me coming as I approached deep in thought with my head down.

"Can you help?" one of them yelled. It was a tall muscular Treek. His bark-like skin formed ridged muscles on

9

his upper arms and chest. His shirt was off, and he wore only a loincloth to cover himself.

"Yeah," I said. I ran forward and joined a half-circle next to a very old Treek with branches growing out of his hair, and a small boy. The three worked in tandem, like mirrors of each other. Their magic fed and pulled a root the width of a tree trunk as it struggled to lift an oblong boulder leaning against the cave wall.

"Careful," said the old Treek. "Light movements. We can't hurt him." I followed the instructions and focused mostly on the upper part of the root, leaving the more granular control to the others.

"Okay," said the muscular Treek. "Hold."

We all stopped the root where it was. Then with a small push from the muscular Treek, the end of the root curled down and grabbed at the ground. It pulled back with something large and furry wrapped up inside of it.

The muscular Treek brought the vine near and then unfurled it in front of us. A deer or something like it rolled out of the massive root's grasp. It laid there unconscious.

"Bubba!" said the old Treek, running to the creature's side once it was clear of the rocks. He looked Bubba up and down for injuries of any kind. Then, he grew a plant beside it, crushed it in his hand, and pushed it into the animal's mouth.

While the old Treek revived the large animal, the muscular Treek approached me. "I'm Kadero," he said, "and this is my son, Coran."

I nodded, with my eyes half on the Treek with the animal. "Nice to meet you," I said.

"That's Palem," he said gesturing toward the old Treek. "And his elk, Bubba. He got hurt in the collapse."

"Yeah, it seems like a lot of people did." I saw his expression stiffen. Had he lost someone? I looked at the boy. His eyes were red.

Kadero spoke solemnly, "My wife, Creda, among them."

"I'm so sorry," I said.

"Me too." he said without much emotion at all. "She will be missed, but we will survive. It's what we do." He gave me a slight smile.

How he had the fortitude to look past his wife's death just moments after was beyond me. I glanced at the boy again and saw him trying to keep up the same facade.

"Where did you come from?" asked Kadero. "Did you come to free us?" He paused. "How long has it been since this started anyway? My memory is still blurry."

"Yeah, uh." I was having trouble forming words. I was still hurting in so many ways and hadn't dealt with any of it. "You've probably been here for a few months. It was about two months ago when the colony formed to find you—"

"A colony formed to find us? There are that many Treeks left?"

I shook my head. "No. I was the only Treek there. The colony was a temporary truce formed to figure out what was happening on this island. It wasn't just your group that went missing. All of the colonies on Daegal at the time vanished in an instant. I guess you were all abducted at once."

"Hmm. And how long did it take for the truce to be broken?"

"It depends on what you count as it being broken. I was there for a few days before I was attacked without any kind of consequence. But it never fully broke down. Many of us are here now. Many of us died in the collapse too. We worked together to find you and free you."

He scoffed. "That's ridiculous. It's only a matter of time until they stab you in the back. Treeks will always be taken advantage of if given the opportunity."

I sighed and glanced back at the others. I could see Tigala lifting large rocks that the small folk weren't able to move. Marv was in rock form breaking through a boulder. I saw small flames from Rodrigo as he knelt with Lolan next to Brendell—cauterizing his wounds or something.

"I'm not sure if that's true," I said. "All of this fighting, it only makes the world a worse place to live in. More dangerous. If we could just look past it..."

"Trust me. You're never better off with other races. There will come a time where they are weak or hurt, and they won't look past it. They can't. You're a Treek. It's as plain as the texture of your skin. They will never fully know what you have been through, what you've done to survive this long, or what was taken from us."

He was right. I was a Treek. And no matter how much I cared about those people, we weren't the same. There were always going to be differences.

But did that mean that cooperation led to destruction? Zef believed the opposite. I thought that Tigala and Lolan were of a same mind. I just wasn't sure anymore. There had been so much destruction since I came to Daegal. I had been lucky to not lose anyone close to me in the chaos until now.

I looked at the group of Treeks. They had the same bark-like skin as me. They knew the same type of magic. They had been hated their entire lives and on the run. I didn't have to ask to know it was true. And they knew it was the same for me.

"You need help, Palem?" Kadero asked.

Palem sighed and sputtered before deciding on what to say. "I don't know. I think he's okay, but... Yes, could you help me move him? Somewhere more out of sight than here?"

We were on the field of rocks, the same level as many of the other survivors who were rummaging through the rubble. I wasn't sure why he wanted seclusion though. These people were trying to help. At least the ones I could see were.

Kadero was already approaching the elk. It was huge, and I wasn't sure the two of them could lift it. I almost spoke up to offer my own strength, but before I did I saw that they were using their combined nature magic to create a bed of plants to make Bubba glide across the ground as new plants pushed up from the ground and leaned in the direction they walked. I had never thought of doing that before. I would have to keep that in mind for the future.

I looked down at the boy who stood next to me and watched them move the elk. He had been quiet, and based on his expression, I was pretty sure I knew why.

"Did you know other Treeks before you came here?" I asked.

The boy glanced up at me, and then back at the ground. "Yeah." He paused as if gathering his thoughts. "We met others here too. There was one that might have been a little older than you. His name was Riak."

"Riak. Yes, I ran into him actually. They had him working with the Dwarves."

"Is... is he okay?" Coran asked, glancing back at me again.

"I don't know," I said. "The last time I saw him was in a similar situation actually. He ran before the rocks fell."

Coran nodded. "There was a girl too." He said. "She was my age."

"You haven't seen her since you were abducted?" I asked.

"Since before that," he said. "A group of Saurians found our camp on Daegal." He shook his head. "She was weak. Like you."

It caught me off guard. "What?"

"None of them have a heart. None of them care about you. They'll all turn on you sooner or later."

"I don't th—"

"They killed her because she wanted to spare an injured Saurian. If we had killed the Saurian when we had the chance, she'd still be here. The same will happen to you if think that you can work with those monsters."

I didn't know what to say. He had obviously been through a lot. And the sentiment sounded like Kadero's feelings toward other races. I had also been through a lot, and as bad as it sounded, I understood where he was coming from. I wasn't sure if I fully disagreed with him.

Is this all there is for me? I thought. *Death and heartbreak?*

I kept quiet while I thought about it. I got the sense he didn't like me very much anyway. Which was a shame. Even among the Treeks I had a hard time fitting in. But would that be different if I stopped trying to work with the other races— if I chose to only trust them?

After a few moments, I finally responded. "I'm sorry for your losses. Every Treek death hurts." I didn't try to talk to him anymore after that. We followed Kadero, Palem, and Bubba in silence.

They moved slowly, but their method of moving the animal didn't seem to tax their magic very heavily. I imagined they probably could have kept it up for a while if they needed to, but our destination came quickly.

There was a ditch along the edge of the cavern where an overhang prevented rocks from settling. The rocks sloped down beneath it and formed a small cave-like area. The Treeks continued down the slope and set the elk up against the wall to rest.

Palem sat next to the animal watching over him.

Kadero looked back at me. "You're welcome to stay with us. You're a Treek, a dying race." The smile he gave didn't have any joy to it.

"Thanks," I said. This was weird. I still wasn't sure what I was doing here. But I wasn't sure what I was doing anywhere else either.

I chose to avoid prying too much yet about possible connections to my parents and joined Palem next to the Elk.

"Is he a pet?" I asked.

"You could say that. I think of him more as a friend though." He said. "My name is Palem, by the—"

I nudged my head toward Kadero and said, "Yeah, he already introduced you. I'm Kaia."

"Kaia, it's nice to meet you. Where had you been before all of this? I don't see many new Treek faces. I figured our colony was the last of us." He looked at the others and his face saddened. "And now that has been reduced as well."

"I'm sorry," I said and gave an apologetic look. "I lived in Brighton for a while. I hid and stole what I needed.. I was alone." I thought of Chipry, my only friend. I didn't even have him anymore. It dug the pain in my chest even deeper.

"Before that, I lived with my parents in the Tellstoy forest. We kept from being captured for a long time but were eventually found out. I think they're dead now." If there was

15

any hope left in me, saying the words out loud killed it. I hung my head.

"I'm sorry to hear that." He looked at the others again. "It's a story we're all too familiar with."

"Yeah," I said. He didn't need to explain. It was part of our story as a people. We were exterminated, and it left the few of us remaining with a lot of loss. I might have been lucky to have *only* lost my parents.

I looked back up at him. "Did you know other Treeks?" I asked.

"I knew a lot of Treeks," he said with a sympathetic smile.

16.3 Cypress

Really?" I said, a little too hopeful. "My father's name was Lyndon, and my mother was Marigold."

Palem's eyebrows rose. "Oh, um. Hmm. The names don't ring a bell. Was there anything else notable about them?"

Notable? I wasn't sure what that would mean. And spending my formative years hiding from anyone else didn't really lead to me seeing them interact with others in a notable way.

"My father was a good hunter. I think it was something he did back in the town we came from."

"Do you remember which town that would have been?"

"Wilderwood."

"Ah, Wilderwood. Yes, I know the town. Their skin, it was similar to yours?" he asked gesturing at my arm.

"Yes," I said. I thought back and tried to remember the specifics. It had been so long that I wasn't sure about much. I hated that I was forgetting the people who made me who I am. "I think so at least. My father might have had a darker tone to his. My mother wore her hair in dark dreads."

"Ah, yes. I do remember them. They were leaders in the town. Strong people. Seems like you got some of that in you."

"Can you tell me anything else you know about them?" I asked. "I have been dying to learn more and to find out if they are still alive."

"I'm sorry, but I don't know if they're alive or dead. If I haven't seen them in person, I assume the worst these days." He gave me an apologetic look. "I do know the people though. That town focused a lot on animating plants. With enough of them using their magic, they could create armies of plant monsters. Mushroom warriors, twig soldiers, and even treants."

"Treants?" I asked

"Trees that can walk and attack for them," he said, gesturing at the tree in the distance that stretched out of the cavern floor.

"Oh," I said. "That explains a lot."

"What do you mean?"

"I kind of created a wandering forest on Daegal using some veins of nature magic."

He gave me a confused look. "I thought you were the only Treek on Daegal besides us."

"I am," I said, unsure of what he meant.

"Then how did you animate an entire forest? That should take a whole Treek village to do."

"Oh. The veins—they were some kind of magical reserve. I tapped into them and lost control, but it made whatever I did a hundred times more powerful."

He winced. "I hope there aren't more of those. Sounds like the kind of thing others will use as a weapon."

"There's more," I said. "But it may not matter with that thing wandering around."

Palem looked up at the sky, pondering the thought. Then he continued. "Well, I think you probably have some of those genes in you. We pass down our magical strengths to our descendants."

"We do?" I asked. "I've never heard that before."

"Sure," he said. "When you use parts of your magic less, your descendants are likely to be less naturally talented with it and vice versa. If your parents were skilled animators, and it sounds like they were, you probably have that in you too. It will come easier to you."

"Cool," I said. "Is there any way to get better at it? I've heard other magics come easier if you're in a certain state of mind. Do we have that?"

Palem smiled. I got the sense that he was enjoying coaching a young Treek. I wondered if Coran talked to him about this stuff as well or if he stuck with his father.

"Yes," said Palem. "Nature magic is a hopeful magic. Each plant is a celebration. It's a new life coming into existence. Our magic works the same. If you can get yourself to look past the evils of the world and focus on hopes and growth, it will make the plants much easier to grow."

"Huh," I thought back through my recent usage of magic. Most of it had been from a place of desperation, trying so hard to scrape by and save us from the current threat. I was excited to try it out.

"Come sit, Kaia," said Kadero. He was leaned against the wall of the small alcove a short distance from us. I gave Palem a quick smile and went to join Kadero.

He was breaking small twigs and placing them in a teepee formation on the ground. He grew a few vines, one much smaller than the others, and made a miniature bow, like Lolan's. He wrapped the bow's string around a stick. With a rock to hold the top of the stick upright on a plank of wood, his other hand moved the bow back and forth in a sawing motion and the thin vine served to spin the upright stick. Like a wooden drill, the stick spun on the plank, creating friction.

I looked at Palem to see if he was going to join. He nodded and groaned as he stood to his feet. We sat around the pile of sticks while Kadero drilled away. Already, the plank of wood beneath the drill was starting to blacken from the friction.

"So," said Kadero. "What are you best at with your magic?" I hadn't thought too much about it before. I didn't really have anyone to compare to, so everything I did was what I was good at I guess. "I prefer vines mostly," I said.

"Ah, yes," said Kadero. "They are a very versatile weapon."

"Palem was also just telling me I might be skilled with animated plants. I've made a few on purpose, and a lot by accident."

Kadero raised an eyebrow, and even Coran perked up where he sat next to his father. "Can you show us?" asked Kadero.

"Uh, sure," I said. "But first, how are you able to grow so much down here. I'm finding mostly rocks, no fertile soil."

"Ah," said Palem. "That would be me. I was working on attracting some ants that formed piles of dirt. They're stored in the pack on Bubba."

"Oh, so you brought dirt with you?"

"Right. It helps when you're out of your element," said Palem.

I couldn't believe it hadn't occurred to me before. I guess that was one of the downsides of not knowing anyone of your own race.

"Do you mind if I grab some?" I asked.

Palem smiled and stretched out a hand toward Bubba. I approached the beast. It was a big animal. It was still laying on its side, its grey-furred chest rose and fell. I reached into the pack at his side and grabbed a mound of dirt in my two hands. I brought it over to the campfire and set it down in front of me.

"Okay, we'll see how this goes." I said. "I don't have a lot of practice with it."

"Take your time," said Kadero.

I focused on the small mound. It was a sticky kind of dirt, holding its shape in a clump fairly well. I poured my magic into it. The green glow emanated out and I pushed the sprout up. It stretched and leaves unfurled.

I tried to keep what Palem had said in my mind. I needed to be hopeful and focused on growth. I tried to think of something hopeful. I imagined the group around me somewhere else. We were in the woods, building houses out of trees and vines. We had a Treek colony of our own.

While I imagined I pushed the plant further, willing it to grow and take a shape that could grab the root ball.

I imagined the people of our village. It was small. There weren't many of us left. I tried to imagine our relationships. Coran hadn't liked me much, but maybe he would grow to. And Palem seemed to like me enough. So did Kadero. But for some reason, it felt hollow—empty. Was that really it? A colony of the last of us holding out as long as we could? Was surviving around people like me really all that I wanted?

The plant slowed. The growth looked unhealthy and spindly, and a couple of the leaves turned black. Maybe I wasn't as hopeful about that as I had once been. But why not? These were my people. This was what I had always wanted, to be with other Treeks, and now imagining our future together was making my magic unusable? I didn't understand.

I looked at the other Treeks and gave an apologetic smile.

Maybe I just shouldn't think about anything at all, like previous times I had grown plant monsters.

The plant picked up a little, growing new leaves to replace the damaged ones. I focused on new growths of the stem instead of the original main stem. It did grow, but it was still slower and more forced than before. What was different? Was it just that I had the knowledge now?

I thought about the previous times I had done it. I grew plant creatures when testing my capabilities with Lolan, Tigala, and Zef. I did it again with them before I created the wandering forest. Every one of those times I was with my search party.

I thought about them, and the plant began to grow faster. It strengthened, growing a sturdy stem. New branches came out of it and I almost couldn't keep up with the magic.

I thought of Tigala, and the change we had brought. I thought of her faith in me. I thought of Lolan, and how he took a chance on me, defending me from an ogre, and many monsters since. I thought of his willingness to grit his teeth and keep pushing forward no matter what. I thought of Zef— how he died to save others and believed in me to carry on his legacy.

Without putting much focus on it at all, the plant reached down, grabbed its root ball, and folded itself into a humanoid shape. The little plant monster had bark that hung down from its chin in what looked like a long wooden beard. A tail hung off of its lower back.

"Bravo," said Kadero. "I wasn't sure if you were going to pull it off at first, but that is very well made."

I looked away. "Thanks."

"Can you make it do anything?" asked Coran, forgetting about his distaste for me.

"Uh, yeah." I moved my hand in a circular motion and the tree monster waved at the three of them. "Can you guys not do this?"

"No," said Kadero. "I am very skilled with trees and offensive abilities, but I never could create things like that."

"I've always wanted to learn," said Coran.

I looked at Palem. He smiled and nodded at me. Could he tell how that exercise made me feel? I still wasn't sure what I thought of it myself.

Kadero almost had a flame now. He had stopped the spinning for a moment while I called my plant creature into being. Smoke was starting to pour out of the wood plank now.

"What do you plan to do next, Kaia," Kadero asked while gritting his teeth as he drilled.

"I don't know?" I said. "You mean you want me to grow something else?"

"No, I mean, now that you've found us. This is what you came here for right?"

"Oh, yeah. It was." I hadn't thought too much about it. "What are *you* planning on doing now?"

"We'll get as far away from here as possible," he said. "We'll leave as soon as Bubba is back up and ready. Probably at night to avoid getting ambushed by the others out there." He nodded his head toward the rest of the cavern.

"I don't think anyone is going to ambush you after that," I said, referring to the giant monster that just crawled out of the earth. "You don't want to help? That thing is going to kill thousands of people if we let it go."

"That's their problem," he said, looking toward the rest of the cavern again. "One of the benefits of being a small group is that it's easier to move around—easier to hide. As long as it's focused on other people, we're safe."

"We're talking worse than the Treek plague," I said.

"Don't call it that," said Kadero as the kindling he had collected burst into flame. He buried it in the pile of sticks and blew on it. The sticks caught fire and the flame grew. "That wasn't us. If it was, we were set up. And if it's going to be worse than that, then they'll get what they deserve for massacring our people."

He looked at me with anger in his eyes now. The flames formed shadows on his cheeks and the bridge of his nose.

We had suffered a lot of losses, and Kadero had just lost his wife. But I still wasn't sure if I could follow his thinking. That monster was sure to massacre thousands of people, and he wanted to do nothing—to hide while the world burns.

More importantly, was I okay with that? To go with them was to ignore everything we had accomplished on Daegal. It meant walking away from the friends I had made. It meant ignoring what Zef died for.

"I—I can't do that," I said.

"Can't do what?" he asked.

"I can't leave the rest of the world to die while I could have done something to stop it."

"You can't stop that. It's enormous. And you can't help if you're dead."

"You also can't help if you don't try," I said. I glared back at him now. I knew that people hated other races. I knew that the Treeks were slaughtered all throughout the world, but did that really extend so far that we could watch the same happen to others without feeling remorse? Although these people were Treeks, I couldn't bring myself to stay with them.

I couldn't believe what I was considering. All of my dreams, and fantasies of finally being back with the Treeks. Learning from them, growing old with them, maybe falling in love with one, it wouldn't happen. If I walked away, I wasn't just walking away from a few angry people of the same race. I was walking away from my heritage, my culture, my history. Could I really do that to help people who wouldn't do the same for me?

"You'd have to be a fool to think any of them will change," said Kadero. The fire was in full force now, creating dancing shadows against the cavern wall.

I stood and took a deep breath. "I'd rather be a fool than a coward."

With a wave of my hand, my tree creature jumped into the fire. I watched it burn for a moment, and then turned and walked up the slope and out of their hiding place.

16.4 Cypress

"I left the Treeks behind me, climbing the rubble up to the level where the others searched—helping others that were buried and injured. I wasn't sure what to do. I could help, but I didn't have the piles of dirt that Palem and Kadero did. I didn't have the Treeks, and I wasn't ready to face Lolan and Tigala.

I knew I couldn't turn my back on this. I knew I couldn't just let more people die, but I was so tired. I was tired of losing people I cared about. I was tired of fighting. I was tired of everyone being against me every step of the way.

I looked around the cavern and noticed a pile of rocks that I had seen earlier. Previously, it had just looked like more stone, but from my current angle, I could see that it was actually the stalactite that hung down over the cavern—the command center. The bottom half of it had broken off and crumbled in the commotion.

I walked to it with no particular goal in mind. Maybe I'd find something, but I had no clue what that something might be.

The room leaned sideways on the pile of rubble. Glass was shattered about the rocks, and the flat floor of the room stood upright out of the pile.

I climbed up the pile and kept my eyes peeled for anything interesting. I saw the table that held the map we were looking at. It was cracked in half. The map was torn and pinned under some rocks. I uncovered it and rolled it up before putting it in my bag.

As I dug I heard footsteps approach.

"Kaia," said Geralt as chipper as ever. "Are you okay?"

"Yeah," I said. "Just looking for something to help us, I guess." I didn't look up at him.

"Well, I can help!" he said like he was excited about it. His voice was a little shakier, but maybe that was still just shock from the collapse.

"I think I just want to be alone," I said.

"No problem," he said. "You won't even notice I'm here." Not the response I was hoping for.

"You know, we were lucky to get to the room in time," he said, ignoring my request for solitude. "I think that we—"

"Geralt," I said. I wanted him to stop, but I was trying my best not to be so blunt as to tell him that. I didn't know how to say it. Instead, I went with: "Why are you always so confident."

"Because. I'm a hero of the people!" he said, cocking his chin to the sky.

"Cut the act," I said. "It's just us. You can't seriously be like that all of the time." He was taken aback at that. His eyes scanned the rubble, and then his head dropped.

"You're right," he said. "I'm not confident. I—I want to be, so I act like I am. Fake it until you make it, right?" He gave a half-hearted smile and spoke like the I had knocked the wind out of him. "Wallace and Seth are dead," he said, no longer pushing the rubble around.

"Oh, I'm so sorry," I said wishing I hadn't been so harsh. "Did you know them well?"

"Seth was my friend from childhood. He believed in me. Or at least, he put up with me. I didn't know Wallace very well. He kept himself at a distance, being a hired hand. But I think he was starting to like us."

"I'm sorry. It's horrible what happened here," I said.

"It is." Geralt paused, as he continued staring at the ground. "You know why I like you?"

That was an odd question. "No. Why?"

"I like you because you don't care. You put up with me too, like Seth did."

"Can I ask why you do the whole charade though? Why not just say you're not confident instead of pretending to be something your not?"

"I don't know anymore. I think I do it as a defense mechanism."

"Defense against what?" I asked.

"Against fear. Against disappointment—disappointing myself, my father. I used to read legends of heroes when I was a child. I still do. I love the unknown worlds, getting lost in the adventure. I always dreamt of being one of those heroes, so did my father. But I'm not. I'm not built for it."

"So you pretend instead?" I asked.

"My father always wanted a son, so when he had me and saw that I was more interested in reading about heroes than being one myself, he was furious. He threw away my books and forced me into training at an early age. But despite all of the training I've been through, I didn't take to it. I'm not coordinated or muscular. He sent me here when he finally gave up on trying to force me into the masculine role he had set out for me. I'm not a hero. I'm not a fighter. It's not my passion."

"What is your passion then?" I asked.

"I'm a storyteller. I can't do those things in real life. I don't even want to. I want to tell tales of the people who do. People like you. I act like a hero because it's the closest I can get to doing what I actually love while still fulfilling a role that my father sees as somewhat honorable. It's a chance to relive some of those books that I love so much.

"It doubles as a sort of buffer too. I don't fit in with these people. They're all so strong and powerful, and they can tell from a mile away that I am not. So if I act like loon, they stay away from me and save me the embarrassment."

"Wow," I said. "I'm sorry you have had to do that. It sounds like your dad needs to loosen up."

"Maybe," said Geralt. "But that's why I wanted to help *you*, because you looked past my facade. I came into the colony screaming about dragons, and you ignored how strange I am. You just listened. You let me be different and still treated me like a person."

I gave him a slight smile. "Well, I'm glad I could be a friend in that place."

"You're more than just a friend, Kaia. You're a hero. You're a leader. You're all of the things that I could never be. Someone I would be honored to tell stories of."

"I don't know about all of that," I said. "I'm just a lone Treek. I can't even lead my own people." I glanced back at where I had just come from.

"You can't convince everyone. That's beyond anyone. What makes you a great leader is that you stick to your principles despite the odds. You fight with all you've got. You're an example to the rest of us—a finder of the lost.

People rally around you because you are who we want to be."

I wasn't sure what to say. It was a lot to take in. I had no idea I meant so much to him, and that I might mean as much to others. I looked out around the rubble at the various groups searching. There was a group of Saurians blasting rubble free. Elves used wind storms to blow away large piles of dust. People I knew and people I didn't, all working for a common goal. They were all hurt in their own right. All of them had lost people close to them. All of them were looking for safety, for peace.

"So whatever you do, and for whatever reason, just know that you did something here." said Geralt. "Even if that monster destroys us all, we'll die knowing that we are capable of more. We're capable of putting our differences aside and caring for people that we have every right to hate. We are better than the wars that have hurt us all."

"Thanks," I said, unsure of what else I could say. "That really means a lot."

"Of course," he said, still lacking the usual flair to his voice.

"So is this the new you then? Thoughtful and caring?"

"I suppose not," he said, standing to a triumphant pose with one leg leaning on a higher rock. "I have appearances to maintain." He ended the statement with a cheeky grin. "Now, I'm off to slay some dragons!" I couldn't help but laugh as he turned back to the rest of the cavern.

I stayed where I was atop the rubble. I looked back down at the ground after he had left and saw something where Geralt had been standing. A thin chain laid there, pinned in a spot that must have been revealed as rocks shifted beneath Geralt's feet.

I dug through the rubble, uncovering more and more of it with each stone. When I finally had it free I held it up to inspect it. It was a necklace with a round medallion on it. The medallion was an old metal, with dark shadows in the crevices of it. It was stylized to look like a dragon that was laying down. It curled its body around 8 gemstones of various colors. I studied the gems. Yellow, green, blue, purple, white, red... They were the colors of the different types of magic. I turned it over and found a stylized etching on the back that read 'SM'.

"What could that stand for?" I said to myself.

My thoughts were interrupted by a commotion in the distance. I looked up to see a group of people had clustered together in a small crowd. They were talking, and some looked ready to fight. But they weren't about to fight each other. Instead, they all looked up. I followed their gaze and found two Avians gliding down into the cavern.

They swooped down on wide wings. The one in front had brown and black mottled feathers with blades tucked into a strap that ran diagonally across his chest. He looked like a skilled warrior. The other was bluish-grey with a spindly neck and long pointed beak.

What were they doing? And where did they come from? They couldn't have been among the abducted colonists. They wouldn't have had time to climb up there and back by now. Even with the ability to fly.

Voices raised as people began to worry about the incoming threat. I saw Tigala and Lolan, standing near the front of one of the defensive formations. I shoved the medallion I held in my bag and ran to them. I couldn't let them get hurt.

The Avians touched down in the middle of the cavern at about the same time as I reached my friends. The Avians stood in the middle in silence.

"Glad you're back," said Tigala when I reached her side.

"Yeah," I said. "Me too."

The grey crane Avian raised his wings. "We mean you no harm. We came to help," he said, though the muscled dark Avian that stood in front of him suggested otherwise.

After a few moments of silence, I asked "Why?"

"Because I know what just crawled out of this cave." He had more information? I took a step forward. Tigala grabbed my arm to stop me.

"Come with me," I whispered to her. "We need answers."

She took a deep breath and followed, as did Lolan, and several others.

"What do you know?" I said.

The dark Avian stepped between us and the grey Avian. Then the grey Avian spoke. "My name is Klaus, and this is my companion, Sparr. Before I explain, can you point me to an old Gnome named Zef? I'm having trouble finding him."

16.5 Cypress

The Avian's eyes flickered white, and then back to normal.

"How do you know Zef?" I asked, more angrily than I had intended.

The crane looked at me. "He's an old friend." His eyes flickered white again as he looked at me. Then, after a pause, he said, "I'm so sorry. I didn't know."

My head dropped. "He's buried over there." I pointed a hand at the tree without looking at it.

"You need to start explaining things," said Tigala. She had some anger in her voice too.

Klaus raised his winged hands in a show of peace. "Sparr," he said. "It's okay. Stand down." Sparr, the brown Avian, relaxed and stepped back next to Klaus.

"I am here to help," said Klaus, "but I need to know you aren't going to kill me for saying some of the things I'm about to say." He looked back at me again. "You were close to Zef?" he asked.

"Yes," I said. "Why do you have to keep bringing him up?"

"Right. I'm sorry. Truly, I am. He was a good person," said Klaus. He looked around at the crowd that had gathered around him. "You see, we were part of an organization. We studied things that some might consider taboo, and we believe things that many would consider very dangerous."

"Like what?" asked Rodrigo. He was standing on the opposite end of the group from me. He was scraped up but otherwise looked okay.

Klaus let out a nervous chuckle. "We believe that all of the races used to live together, to begin with."

"What?" I asked.

"Look, just hear me out, okay?" he raised his wings again. "You have all heard of the book *The Dangers of Magic*, correct?"

Several people nodded their heads.

"Well, that book isn't entirely true. There are secrets hidden in it. The original copies for each race had mistakes in the text. The mistakes were all different, but they all occurred in the same location of each copy. There are more that we haven't deciphered yet. The ones that we did gave us the coordinates for right here, where the doom drake slept."

"Doom drake?" said Lolan.

"Yes," said Klaus. "That monster that crawled out of here, it is the dragon that Shayde Mortem tried to control. That's what we're calling it, for lack of a better term."

"From the book?" asked Rodrigo.

"Yes, the very same," said Klaus. "It is the reason for this island. It is the reason this island was underwater until recently. That monster was put to sleep a long time ago because Shayde had corrupted it so much that the races couldn't defeat it. The best they could do was put it into a very long sleep, and bury it under the ocean."

"How?" I asked. "I've never heard of sleep magic."

"Not sleep magic," said Klaus. "Mind magic mainly. But given how strong and corrupted the creature was, they needed each type of magic to cage it in. Several people sacrificed their lives to put that monster into an eternal slumber in the center of this island."

"And now it's awake," I said, half to myself.

Klaus breathed out. "Yes. You've all read the book right? That monster was imbued with magic from infancy. Magic is part of its being now. It can use any form of magic and it is may be impossible to kill. It's a problem we can't ignore either. The magic corrupted it, consuming the drake's mind and filling it with rage. If we let it go, it's going to be a very big problem. Bigger than the war, bigger than our differences. That creature could destroy us all."

He let the words hang in the air, and so did the rest of us. There was silence as we considered the thought.

"I don't get it," said Lolan. "Why are you telling us this? Why do you care?"

"Because the races lived in harmony once before. I believe it is what we need to do again. Zef believed the same. And if there is going to be any kind of future, I need help stopping the monster from starting its rampage."

I looked at Tigala, at Lolan. I was pretty certain I knew what their answers would be to the implied question. Would we help? They would. Would I? I had walked away from the Treeks, but how did I know this wouldn't just end in more loss? How did I know that we would even be able to stop it? They barely managed before. How were we, a bunch of rejects, supposed to do the same? I looked around the group to see who was still there. Rodrigo watched with his forehead creased. Geralt was looking noble as ever, holding up a Saurian with an injured leg. These people would help. One way or another, they had come around to this cause.

Then I saw Marv. He was a bit behind the group, still stooped over an unconscious Abigail. I remembered the hardships Abigail had gone through, the loss of her mother, the current injuries. I couldn't let that kind of thing happen. I couldn't spend my whole life mourning the loss of my own parents and then do nothing while it happened to thousands of other children. Treek or no, I was not *that* kind of heartless.

"I'll help," I said.

"Me too," said Tigala, taking a step forward to stand next to me.

"Let's do this," said Lolan.

"I assume you have some sort of plan?" asked Rodrigo. He would help too, but he had to be skeptical. It was his nature.

"Uh, yes. The beginnings of one," said Klaus.

"I will help you slay the dragon," said Geralt. "You'll have to beat me to taking the kill for myself though." He looked at me and gave a smile. I had to admit, Geralt was starting to grow on me.

"I do have one stipulation," I said. "Before we do this, we're going to need more information. What else do you know?"

Klaus was finally able to breathe. Touching down in the midst of a group of unknowns was nerve-wracking. Having to talk to a large group of people didn't seem to be one of his fortes either. It looked like he preferred books and study.

"What do you want to know?" Klaus asked.

"Everything. Start as far back as you can. If we're going up against this thing, we need to know what we're getting into and why."

"Right," said Klaus. "Well, The Dangers of Magic is a relatively true story, although it was written in a way to dissuade races from using magic that wasn't assigned to them."

"Assigned? We were born with our magic," said the Tigala.

"Ah, yes. You were, but that's just because it's what your parents and ancestors practiced. We have reason to believe that roughly 500 years ago, races used whichever magic they liked. There was no distinction between races and magic. A Beastfolk could be strong in Nature and Storm magic, while a Treek might be especially good at shapeshifting. The world was a very different place then. We lived alongside each other. Sure, there was war. There were confrontations, and there was evil, but nothing like there is today."

It made so much sense. So that's why there was a Beastfolk at the center of the nature magic veins.

"But that all changed when Shayde came into the picture. He was a Human, an orphan. He never knew his parents or what became of them. Before he could talk, he was taken in by a magic-focused military, the Meceles Accord. They created soldiers so skilled with their magic that they were near impossible to defeat. But they were not a kind group. He was treated as a slave, with harsh punishments for failing to meet the goals set out for him in training. He spent his entire upbringing being controlled by others.

"But being among such powerful mages for so long wore off on him. Or maybe he was especially gifted in his own right. It's hard to say. Regardless, he learned quickly and outpaced his peers. He kept his resentment hidden, all the while suspecting that the Meceles Accord were responsible

37

for the death of his parents. When he was ready, he attacked them from within.

"He took down figureheads of the organization in secret. Lower soldiers caught on to the attack and came after him. He was too weak to take all of them, but before he made his escape, he found an ornate egg hidden in one of the leader's rooms. He grabbed it and teleported out of danger. Shayde later discovered that it was a dragon egg. Still wanting revenge, he began to work with the egg. He imbued it with all of the magic he knew, with the intent of controlling it and increasing his power. But it failed. When the creature hatched, it was far stronger than even Shayde. He couldn't control it and he was its first victim."

"And it went on a rampage?" I asked.

"Yes. It destroyed many cities and left a trail of destruction. Whole swaths of land were leveled. They tried to stop it, but it was too powerful, too versatile. Everything they tried was countered in one way or another by the creature. So they devised a plan to trap it on this island. To do that, they positioned powerful magic users across the island. They simultaneously cast a spell so strong that it could knock the creature out indefinitely, but it also consumed the casters in the process."

"Around the island," I said, "Zef said something about powerful magic. Does that meant those people who sacrificed themselves created the magical veins?"

"I don't know what veins you're referring to, but yes, I assume they would leave behind aftermath along those lines."

"And all of the structures," said Rodrigo. "Those are from the villages where people lived in harmony? Why don't they exist in other places?"

"Well, yes," said Klaus. "The ones still on Daegal were here from the people who used to live here. After they stopped the monster, they sunk the island without taking the time to wipe the land clean of them.

"And when the monster was defeated and the island sunk, the different leaders around the world gathered together. They looked at the destruction caused by mixing magics. They decided that free reign of magic was not safe for the world. Together, they decided that segregation was for the better. I don't agree with the choice myself, but they made the choice in an attempt to protect us, from that monster, and from future possibilities of things like that happening again."

"How do you make the whole world forget their magic?" asked Tigala.

"Mind magic," said Klaus. "The leaders agreed it was necessary and combined their power to rewrite history. They knew things that we still don't know to this day about magic. They chose to eliminate certain types like mind and death magic, maybe others, and they had each race choose a desired type of magic.

"It was a massive effort to do it, and although they were thorough, some things did slip through the cracks. The structures on this island and the books that I used to discover this information are among them. There must have been holdouts that knew the plan and didn't agree with it. They planted seeds of what was going on for people like me to find."

"Did Zef know all of this stuff? Why didn't he tell us," I asked.

"Zef knew some of it. Much of it was made more clear once the island showed up. I was able to use my magic with some of the artifacts found to discern what was going on. But

I didn't have the chance to relay many of my findings to Zef."

Klaus looked about the crowd. We looked overwhelmed, as we should be. It was a lot of information. And hearing that the world already went through a mass brainwashing was mind-boggling enough.

"So, how did the island come back then?" asked a hooded Elf.

"The doom drake's slumber wasn't permanent," said Klaus. "The spell wasn't infallible. The drake desires destruction, almost as much as Shayde desired revenge. And with the increasing conflict around the world, I believe it was enough for the creature to sense it. It was enough magical warfare to rouse the magic within the drake, enough to break the spell that held it beneath the ocean."

"That Human that woke it up, how is he connected to all of this?" asked a female Saurian with her arm in a makeshift sling.

"I don't know. But I was hoping to come here to stop him before this happened. Clearly, I was too late. I am skilled in looking at peoples' pasts though. If you have anything of his, I can see what I can find."

The group was silent. Did we have anything? I had the map. Maybe that would work. I reached into my bag to pull it out but felt something small and round—the pendant. I pulled it out. "I don't know if this was his, but it's worth a shot." I handed it to Klaus, and his eyes went white.

16.6 Interlude - Klaus

Klaus's vision swirled with images. Images of a man in a dark cloak, a boy cowering in the corner of the room, an infant, a man holding hands with an older woman. They didn't make sense. They never did. It was only through Klaus's highly trained and specialized magic that he was able to see all the way back and pick out the memories that were most relevant. It took focus, concentration, and an eye for things of importance. But it also took a deep understanding of how his magic worked—the things it would deem most important and why.

Klaus let the images flood into his mind. They were quick —flashes of a moment in a person's life. But they were all important in one way or another.

He focused his mind on the task at hand. He needed motivations, details, and most importantly, weaknesses. He needed to know what they were up against. It wasn't just the monster, but this Human too.

The first image that came to mind was the image of the boy. He focused on it and it pulled in front of him like a Gnomish illusion might, except this was all inside of his own head, only visible to himself.

The image came closer until he was looking through the boy's eyes. They were blurred and raw. The boy sat hugging his legs in the corner of the room. His body jerked spontaneously, and then again. He was crying.

"Malcolm," said a voice from somewhere deeper in the room. "Malcolm, come here." The voice croaked like a frog. It was old and frail.

The boy stood and more of the room became visible. He lifted an arm to wipe his face on his sleeve and then walked past a lit fire to the small cot in the corner of the room. On it lay a woman. Her skin was pale and her expression weak. On her throat was a green glowing mark, like an ink stain that spread down her neck. She coughed and then breathed out a few words. "Malcom, you're a very special boy. You know that, right?"

"Mom," said the boy. "I'm scared."

The woman smiled back at the boy. "There is nothing to be afraid of. I'll be better before you know it and we can get back to normal life." Her eyes made Klaus believe that she didn't believe the words herself. "But I want you to know that you're a very special boy. Special in ways you don't even know."

Malcolm looked at the floor and the memory faded out.

Unsure of how that was relevant, Klaus searched for the next memory that would help them discover more about this boy. An image came into view of the same boy standing in a field. Before him stood a single cross in the grass. The boy stared at it with no tears in his eyes, but a look of anger instead. He breathed heavy, with his chest rising and falling visibly even from the distance that Klaus viewed the scene. Klaus let the memory take over and shifted into Malcolm's view. The boy turned and walked back to a small house on a hill. He slammed the door open and stormed into the bedroom where his mother previously laid. He sat down on the floor, still breathing heavily. After a moment, he let out a guttural scream. With the scream came fire magic, blasting from his hands. It shot straight up and caught a curtain on fire.

When he stopped screaming, he was shocked. Malcolm spotted the burning curtain and ran to it. He frantically tried to pat it out, but the flame had already spread higher than he could reach.

His head darted back and forth looking for something. He settled on a small bucket of water with a pair of wet pants hanging over its edge. He threw the pants aside and grabbed the bucket, struggling to carry it to the window. He sloshed the water at the flames, but they only served to douse the lowest parts of the growing fire.

The image faded out.

In the next, the soot-covered boy stood shivering outside of what used to be his home. It was now reduced to piles of ash with a few upright blackened timbers. Rain poured and dripped down the boy's head. He stepped forward into the rubble and kicked at the burnt wood.

He walked through the rooms. There was very little left of the world he knew. He found the frame of the bed where his mother laid previously. It was a couple of timbers and a small remnant of the quilt that covered it. He kicked the frame. His foot crashed through the charred wood and one of the upright planks toppled to the ground. He growled and proceeded to kick it several more times until the frame was shattered. He gave it one more kick for good measure, but this time his foot hit something hard.

43

He groaned, grabbing at his foot, and looked for the object that he kicked. Whatever it had been, it was still solid and intact despite the fire. He dug through the rubble and found a metal box pushed out of the rubble. Malcolm bent down and dusted the remaining ash from it. It had a metal handle on top and a grey body. He reached down and picked up the box, turning it over in his hands. He blew on it and a cloud of dust billowed out from it. It was a lockbox, with a small lock on the front latch. He tried the lock, but it wouldn't release. He grunted and then looked around. His eyes settled on the stone that once formed part of the fireplace. He lifted the metal box far above his head and slammed it down on the stone. The lock held on. He slammed it again and again until he heard something break free. The lock dangled from the clasp. Malcolm tore it off and opened the box. Inside he found a medallion of a dragon laying down with gems scattered in its reach. Beneath that was a small book bearing the same design on its cover. He paged through it and found words that looked foreign, or ancient. Klaus gasped as he realized what the boy was looking at.

The memory faded and gave way to another.

Flames burst into the alley. They were massive and hot, charring stone walls that looked to be too far from the flames to suffer any effects. Flames and water magic were exchanged back and forth. A Saurian in a hood tried to defend himself. He was clearly skilled with water magic, but the Human was far better. The flames evaporated the water before it could reach the Human.

The Saurian's expression shifted to fear, and he tried to run. But it was already too late. The Human chased him down, using a blast of fire to launch himself into the air. With another blast, he softened his landing in front of the running Saurian. The lizard's eyes widened as he made eye contact with the Human, and then he turned back to run the way he had just come from. Malcolm sent a blast of fire into the ground beneath the Saurian. The Saurian screamed and fell to the ground with the sizzle of skin and scales against the cobblestone alley.

Malcolm walked forward and the flames lit his face. He looked down at the suffering Saurian, smiled, and then the brightness of fire washed out the memory.

A new memory came forward.

"There may be some things we do that would be frowned upon by most Humans and even other races," said Malcolm. He was older now—maybe in his 20s. He had the shadow of facial hair. His hair was longer and he wore a tortured look on his face, yet he smiled through it. "But I can assure you, everything we do is in the name of protecting and bettering the Human race."

"I understand that," said another Human. She was in her late teens and had tattoos coming up her neck, reaching toward her head. "And I want to join. I want to help in any way I can."

"And you are willing to keep this information a secret?" asked Malcolm. "Once you are part of this group, there is no backing out."

The girl didn't hesitate. "Yes. I am ready."

"Good," said Malcolm. "Welcome. You are now a member of the Shades." He turned around and grabbed folded dark cloth off of a shelf and handed it to the girl. She opened it up and slipped on a cloak identical to Malcolm's.

"Where do we begin?" the girl asked. She looked eager.

"There is much for you to learn, but we are currently in the middle of an operation. We'll have to teach you along the way and as time permits." Malcolm walked away from the girl, expecting her to follow him down the long hallway. It was a stone building, lit by sconces. Malcolm pushed open a door and entered a room with several other people wearing dark robes. They were all positioned around the room working on various tasks. One stood in front of a small pile of dirt, waving his hands and causing a green light to shine from it. Another stood over a plant, chopping it into tiny pieces. Deeper in the room was a fire burning, with one of the Shades holding a pot over it. And then another approached an animal that was hard to make out in the darker part of the room. There was the sound of chains and growling. The Human approaching the animal had something in hand, a type of powder.

Malcolm ignored the various activities in the room and walked to the center where plants were being chopped on a table.

"What's our progress?" he asked.

The Human approaching the animal in the corner looked back. "We may have it," he said. "We have a prototype that has killed a rat, a rabbit, and a snake. We're testing on this coyote next."

"Good," said Malcolm. He turned to the girl, the new recruit. "This is our current project."

"And what is it?" the girl asked, sounding a bit unsure.

"The Treek plague," he said, looking pleased with himself.

"Why would you want to create a plague. Wouldn't that affect everyone? Including Humans?" asked the girl.

"Yes, it will. But we're focusing on water-based plants since Humans are less settled around the water."

"And what about the ones that *are* settled around the water?" the girl asked.

"It is an unfortunate sacrifice, but it needs to be done. They will not be forgotten."

The girl looked down with a conflicted look on her face. "And why do we need to create a Treek plague?"

"Because we need a war. We need to create chaos to get what we want, what my ancestors wanted. With this plague, the Treeks will be to blame. Militaries will mobilize against them. The best part is that we don't even have to deploy it. We figure out how to do it and then we pass the knowledge on to them. They'll use it and it will be their downfall."

"Why the Treeks?"

"Because I hate them," said Malcolm, looking directly at the girl. "And their magic is perfect for creating worldwide damage. We weaken our enemies, buying us time to build our strength and wipe them out entirely."

"And how do we build our strength?" asked the girl.

"You have read The Dangers of Magic?" asked Malcolm.

The girl nodded.

"Most of the book is a lie. I have the actual history in this book." He held the book that he had found in the ashes of his home as a child. "But the true part of The Dangers of Magic is the part about Shayde Mortem's dragon. The dragon still lives. And this is how we wake it up and use it to destroy our enemies."

17 Hazel

17.1 Hazel

I believe," said Klaus as he finished relaying the visions, "that the book that he found may have belonged to Shayde Mortem. If the carving on the back of this medallion is any clue, he might be a direct descendant."

"What was in the book?" yelled someone.

"I don't know," said Klaus. "I may be able to find out with more time."

Someone else cut off the end of Klaus's statement. "He knew all along. He was trying to bring things to this."

"If that book has Shayde's notes about magic, Malcolm could be unstoppable," said another. "He might be able to tame the doom drake!"

"There's no hope of defeating it," said another.

The voices drowned out as I turned away from the group. It all just became incessant background noise as the thought spun in my head. The Treeks didn't create the plague. They may have deployed it, but they were led to that end. All along, it was Malcolm who wanted revenge for his sick mother. All of my people were slaughtered because one person had a terrible upbringing.

I wanted to scream. I breathed heavy and looked around the cavern—the remains of the monster's resting place. It was all a setup. I had lost my people, lost my childhood, and lost my parents because of him.

A hand touched my shoulder. I shoved it away.

"Kaia," Tigala said. "I'm sorry."

"Do you even understand what this means?" I said. My voice was raw with emotion. "All of this time I thought my people had done something horrible. I hated that they were killed, but a small part of me knew that we deserved it for what we had done. But we were set up. We may have never come to that conclusion if it weren't for *him*. My people were slaughtered, my entire race, my mother, my father, because *his* mother died."

"Kaia," Tigala said. Her voice was hesitant, cautious.

I couldn't handle it. I screamed and fell to my knees. I didn't know what to do or how to feel. I sat there for what felt like an eternity. How was I supposed to move forward from this? From the realization that all of this death and pain was the result of one Human's issues.

I heard footsteps come closer to me. No one tried to comfort me this time though.

"Kaia," she said. "I can't claim to know how you feel, but I'm with you. Lolan's with you." Still, I didn't know what to say. I was afraid if I said anything, it would be hostile, angry.

"Let us help."

"How can you help? My people are dead. There is no magic that can bring them back."

"There might not be," said Lolan. "But we can make sure the cycle ends now."

It was a nice sentiment, but how were we supposed to stop him. How were we supposed to stop that monster? What power did we have in this situation? "How? He's too powerful. That drake is too powerful. Malcolm already won."

"Nobody has won as long as we stand against him," said another voice. It was Geralt. He spoke with less vigor than usual, but still with the same optimism. I looked up to meet his eyes. He was in a brave pose. His dirty face showed a sad expression despite his tone. I thought of Seth and Wallace.

"I don't know," I said. "I want it to stop. I want it so bad. But he's beaten us in every confrontation. We have even fewer people to oppose him now than we did any of the previous times."

There was a silence. I'm sure they were all thinking the same things. The crowd that had been asking questions about the story Klaus had told us was now silent. I didn't look in their direction, but I got the feeling everyone was looking at me. Did they pity me for losing my whole race as the result of one person's hatred? Or were they tired of me always preaching cooperation? Were they second-guessing helping me? It didn't matter. None of it mattered anymore. We lost.

"That's true." I heard Rodrigo's voice. "But, you convinced us all to help your cause. None of us expected to be working with other races." He was probably among the least likely on that front. "But you convinced us still. You brought us together. Maybe it is our turn to bring others together."

I glanced in the direction of Rodrigo. The group of colonists, warriors, and Klaus were behind him, listening intently to the conversation. They looked at me with concern on their faces. Some even looked sad. I saw the Elven woman who stood hugging her son to her chest. A tear ran down her cheek.

"What do you mean?" I asked Rodrigo.

"You're right. We can't stop Malcolm. We can't stop the doom drake. We hardly fought off the fire-breathing dragon he sent after the colony. You lost your people, your connections, due to Malcolm's hatred. Let us try and make it up to you by using our connections. Maybe with several armies we can stop him, and that monster, once and for all."

"You really think you can convince your people to help?" I said, my voice low. "We're here not just because my people were slaughtered. Sure, Malcolm set this all into motion, but war was brewing on its own. The Treeks did a horrible thing, whether he taught them how or not. People were looking for an excuse to fight, and Malcolm's plague was just the excuse they needed."

"You're very right," said Rodrigo. "It is so easy for us to see our differences. But maybe Malcolm's greatest mistake was giving us a reason to unite. I'm not saying it is going to work. All I'm saying is it is our best shot."

I looked around at the group. No one rejected his words. They stood and listened. Some even nodded along with Rodrigo. Maybe he was right.

I found Porthos who smiled back at me. Marv gave a nod. Tallesia also looked me in the eye with quiet confidence. My eyes shifted to Lolan who stood closer to the group than me. He gave a nod as well. Tigala reached a hand down to me and said, "We've got more to do. And we're going to need our Treek representative."

I hesitated, then took her hand and pulled myself back to my feet. I stood in front of the group, unsure in my own skin. But they looked back, and they were with me. They supported me in a way no one ever had before.

It was dark now, and the stars shined down on us through the broken ceiling of the cavern. A light in my peripheral caught my eye. It was green, shining off of the cavern wall. I looked and found what must have been Kadero, using a vine to traverse the broken staircase out of the cavern. They were sneaking out.

"Okay," I said. "I'm in. But we don't have much time, do we?"

An Avian with dark feathers spoke up after a moment. He was one of the Avians from our colony. "The monster is still on Daegal at the moment. It looks like Malcolm is giving chase on his dragon."

"How are we going to convince people to help us and get them back here before that thing starts tearing through cities?" I asked.

I saw Porthos lean over to Sillius and whisper something in his ear. Sillius swatted him away shaking his head. I didn't want to force them to say something, but we needed some kind of solution if we were going to prevent as much damage as possible.

Porthos leaned back and whispered to Sillius one more time. Sillius sighed. "If we can get to the Gnome capital, we might have a solution."

I looked around to the others hoping for ideas. It was a start, but I still wasn't sure how we were supposed to get to Losterious. That would take several weeks on boat. We didn't have that kind of time, even with the potential help of Saurians and Elves on the seas.

"The teleporter gate," said Lolan. He looked at me with his eyebrows raised, and then turned his head to Sillius. "We found a teleporter. Could you use it?"

Sillius and Porthos exchanged a look. "If it's actually a teleporter, then yes. That's exactly the kind of thing we need. How do you know that's what it is?"

"Zef told us it was," said Lolan, his eyes dropping to the floor.

"Well," said Sillius. "Take us there. We'll see if we can convince the Gnomes first. From there, we should be able to move people around more rapidly."

ᧁ

We walked in a small group, leaving the others behind to help with the wounded and work on further planning. It was me, Lolan, Tigala, Geralt, Porthos, and Sillius.

Up ahead I could hear the sound of rushing water before I could see it. The foliage hid the swimming hole that was fed by the waterfall. It was where we took a day to relax—where I learned what had happened to Tigala's family. It was also where we were attacked by the water monster. So many emotions were tied into a spot as simple as a river through the woods.

"Here it is," said Lolan.

We carefully stepped across the river, hopping on rocks, and found the broken stone behind the waterfall. We shimmied along the slick rocks into the small room where we found the teleporter gate.

"How did you find this thing again?" asked Porthos.

"Tigala got thrown through the waterfall by a water monster," I said.

"Like a monster that lives in the water?"

"Kind of. A monster made of water," I said.

Porthos glanced at the waterfall behind us. "Right. Well, let's hope it doesn't come back." He turned back to focus on the archway.

"Come on," said Sillius to us with a straight face. "If there is any hope of this working, we're going to need to tie you up." He pulled a rope out of his bag, unraveling it toward us.

"What? Why?" I asked.

55

"So the Gnomes don't see you as a threat," said Sillius.

"We can't just state our case?" I asked.

"I'm not getting tied up," said Tigala.

"Where we're headed, it's not neutral territory. This should lead us into the most protected parts of Losterious. If we show up with some Treeks, a Beastfolk, an Elf, and a Human, their first instinct is going to be attacking you. Even if you show up with Gnomes, they'll want to neutralize the threat."

"It's really that protected?" I asked.

"Have you ever heard of the Gnome teleportation hub?" asked Sillius.

I looked at the others. They shook their heads.

"Exactly. We don't even want people knowing it exists, let alone teleporting into it. I'm not sure they're going to accept *me* without some kind of punishment. If you want to go to Losterious, if you want their help, you need to arrive not looking like a threat."

"Okay," I said. "I'll do whatever we have to do."

I looked at Tigala. Her eyes darted around as if looking for a way out.

"It's okay. If things really go south, you can transform and break out of the rope anyway." I said.

"It still doesn't mean I want to be tied up."

"I know. But we've got this. It gives us a better chance of success."

She grunted but didn't disagree.

"I have no doubt we'll convince them," said Geralt. It was kind of nice to have the endless optimism around, though I wasn't sure he'd be much help in the event of a confrontation.

"Do you have anything you can tell us about the Gnomes that might help us convince them?" I asked, looking at Sillius as he tied us up. Porthos was now busy pouring purple-blue energy into the gate.

"Look. I'm not sure how on board I am with this whole thing. I agree that the monster needs to be stopped before it starts its rampage. But other than working together for the current threat, I'm not sure mixing races is going to help." said Sillius.

"Okay," I said. "So you don't want to give up information because your not sure whether or not we're going to turn back into enemies after all of this?"

"Right. King Slepenstein is a Gnome that appreciates clever thinking. He'll be more likely to help if you can outwit him in some way. But that's the most I'm going to give you. I don't want the Gnomes to think I've joined your cause or anything."

I glanced at Lolan and gave him a look. I was starting to feel less comfortable that the person saying these things was also the person tying us up. That same person was about to lead us into enemy territory.

"Okay," I said. "Well, thanks. We'll take what we can get."

"Are you ready?" asked Porthos.

A faint purple-blue whirl was beginning to spin in the center of the archway. After Sillius had sufficiently tied us up, he stepped up to the opposite side of the portal and added his magic to the mix. The swirl of magic became a shifting wall, like it was a pool we were about to jump into.

Sillius grabbed the end of the rope that bound us and tugged us after him as he stepped through the portal.

57

17.2 Hazel

There was a rush of magic as I stepped through the portal. It felt like stepping through a wall of water, but it looked more like I was inside one of those magical veins that I had run into so many times on Daegal. The river of violet energy rushed against us. Then, with a sudden halt to the motion, the magic disappeared and I stumbled forward in a room I didn't know.

I tried to gain my bearings by looking around, but the motion sickness hit me all at once. I bent forward and puked, the world still seemingly spinning around me. I heard yells and forced myself to look up.

There were Gnomes charging us with staffs that held purple crystals on the tips of them.

"How did they get in here?" one of them yelled as they closed in on us.

"Take them out!" said another.

One charged me with the staff held forward. I tried to push myself to my feet but the dizziness was still working against me. I looked up in time to see the Gnome shove the crystal into my side. It hit like one of those lightning wolves, but in a different kind of way.

My vision blurred and turned to back to a swirl like when I was being teleported. Except this time I could only see bright lights and stars. I tried again to stand, but I had no concept of where the ground was. I placed one foot underneath me and fell backwards, smacking my head against the ground. I tried to push myself back up, but it was no use. Instead, I just laid there as I listened to the confrontation.

There were more incoherent yells, and the sound of scuffling feet. There were flashes, and I couldn't tell if they were flashes in the room or residual effects from the illusion staff that had zapped me. Then, a voice drowned out the others.

"They're safe," said Sillius. "We have them tied up. And they came here to help."

"Other races aren't supposed to be here!" yelled a voice I didn't know.

"I know that," said Sillius. "But I think that King Slepenstein will agree that the rule needed to be broken in this case. If you'd just let us speak—"

"The king is dead," said the unknown voice. "Who are you? Prove you're a Gnome or we'll be forced to take you out as well." The voice raised as tensions did as well.

"Woah. Woah!" said Sillius. There was silence for a moment.

Then the unknown voice said, "He's okay. But how did you not know about the King? Where have you been?"

"Daegal," said Sillius. "It's the reason we're here. There is a very big problem. Who is in charge now if the king is dead?"

"General Bygny has been chosen to take his place for the time being."

59

"Bygny," repeated Sillius. "Bygny is Zef's daughter." He spoke the words more to himself—a way of cluing us in. I wasn't sure if I should count us lucky or not knowing that she was the one we would have to talk to.

"Then bring us to her," said Sillius. "We'll plead our case and she can decide what to do with us." There was another pause. The guards must have been contemplating what to do.

The stars and lights still danced around my head, but the room was starting to come into view. It was a colorful building, but that was about the extent of what I could see.

"Amara is very busy taking over the king's duties. She doesn't have time to see just anyone." said the guard. "You brought us prisoners. Thank you. We'll take it from here." Another pause. "Lead these two out of the palace."

There was the sound of shuffling feet. My vision was starting to come back to me. I looked around and saw Sillius and Porthos being escorted out of the room.

"General Amara needs to hear this. For the sake of all Gnomes," said Sillius. The guards continued to escort them toward the tall doorway.

"We have information about her father," I said. The guard's heads snapped toward me. One pointed a crystal staff at me again, but didn't yet hit me with it.

"No one said you could talk." said the Gnome with the staff.

"He's dead," I said. "We were there when it happened." I knew the statement wouldn't look good. They were probably assuming that I killed him. If only they knew what actually happened. Even if they thought I did it though, it might get us an audience.

The two guards standing over me glanced at each other and then back at me.

"If one of Amara's loved ones died, she would want to know," said the guard standing over me without the staff. "She'd want to talk to them."

The Gnome with the staff sighed. "Fine. Get them up." He turned his gaze back to me. "You are our prisoners. You do not speak unless spoken to. Don't make me explain what happens if you can't listen."

I only responded with a nod. These people were hostile. I expected it, but it hurt to let them push us around like this. I was so tired of the hatred at every turn. I still missed Zef, and wished he was here to help us convince his people. Every one of them reminded me of him in one way or another. It was like you're friend dying and then spending all of your time with his twin. Every time I saw a Gnome, my heart leapt hoping it was him. But it wasn't. And instead, we were stuck here as prisoners—enemies.

I looked over at Tigala. She growled at the guards as they pointed a crystal staff at her. Lolan was standing, but also surrounded by guards. Geralt was getting pushed toward Lolan. He stared up at the ceiling and walls of the room in admiration.

One of the guards pushed my back, causing me to stumble forward. "Move." I listened, and the four of us stepped off of the platform that held the teleporter we had entered through. It was a large ornate gateway made of white stone with ten more like it standing offset behind it. The Gnomes pulled us by the ropes that bound us until we had caught up to Sillius and Porthos. Sillius's forehead was creased with frustration, while Porthos gave us a smile.

I had no clue how this was going to go, and based on the reception, I doubted it would go well.

The Gnomes began to march through the giant white doorway that marked the entrance to the room. Why they needed the door that big was beyond me, especially for small folk. They led us out into the hallway which was decorated with colorful tiles placed in swirling patterns along the ceiling. The walls were a pale purple.

I looked around, trying to find landmarks, or something that I could remember for later—an escape route, if it came to that. The problem was, it seemed that the same patterns on the ceiling kept repeating over and over again. I looked back down the hall, and it looked like we hadn't moved any further down it, despite being in motion the whole time. I turned to look back at the door we had come through and didn't see it anywhere. We hadn't been walking long. It should have been there.

I looked at the others. They seemed to be having similar confusion at the static hallway. I looked at the Gnomes next. They stood in formation around us, leading us forward, even though the hall never progressed. None of them seemed to be using magic, but was this one of their tricks? I noticed Sillius and Porthos's expressions hadn't changed much from when I saw them in the teleporter room. They looked around like nothing was out of the ordinary.

After a few moments of walking down the endless hallway, we were led toward a wall. The Gnomes walked straight at it. There was no opening that I could see—no hidden doors. The Gnomes didn't care. They walked straight into the wall and it swallowed them up. The ropes that led us still pulled us forward. I continued to follow it, but hesitated before hitting the wall. There was a tug on the rope, pulling me. I stumbled forward, and instead of hitting something solid, my vision shifted as I passed to the other side of the illusion.

I could see the Gnomes again in front of me. They didn't even care to give me a glance as I realized the illusion that I had just escaped from. The others in my group looked equally disturbed by the experience, all except for Porthos and Sillius. Were they able to see through the illusion? Or were they so used to it that it didn't phase them?

I couldn't know. I looked around the room we were now in. It was massive. Again, I wasn't sure what the obsession was with huge rooms for the Gnomes. Maybe it was because they were so small. Did they need their buildings to be intimidating to make up for the fact that they weren't very intimidating themselves?

The room had similar tiled patterns circling around the room. It had a round ceiling with echoes of the swirl patter in the corners of railings, floor tiles, trim, and even furniture. Gold and silver accented the colorful ceiling and curtains, and a large curved double staircase took up the center of the room. It was white with silver spiraling handrails.

"Queen Bygny. We have people that—" started one of the guards.

"I'm not your queen," said someone beyond the staircases on the upper floor of the room. "And I have enough to do."

There was a sound of more conversation from the woman, but it must have been to someone else with the words barely audible from so far away.

"I don't feel comfortable calling you 'general' when you're taking the King's place," said the Guard.

"Do it anyway," said the woman up top. "I was put in charge, wasn't I?"

"Yes," said the guard.

"What do you want?"

"A group teleported into our warp room. One of them was a Treek. They say they have information for you about your father."

There was silence in response, and then the clack of boots on the bright marble floor. A female Gnome appeared at the top of the double staircase, looking over the silver railing at us. She had brown hair that was wound in tight curls. A scar marked her neck and continued into the collar of her metalic purple armor. She had freckles, and Zef's eyes.

"Well, good for them," she said. "I could care less about my father." She shooed us away. "Lock them up. We'll deal with them later. How did they get into our warp room?"

"These two Gnomes brought them," said the guard, motioning to Sillius and Porthos.

"And why would you bring enemies into our nation's best-kept secret?" said Amara as she glared at the two.

"There is a monster, loose on Daegal," said Sillius. "We need your help. And they are the ones leading the charge against it."

"I don't see why I should care about any of this," said Amara. "We are fighting enough battles as it is. If Daegal has a monster, we'll pull our forces out until other races defeat the monster." She began to walk back up the stairs. "Lock them all up."

The guards turned to begin ushering us away, but I couldn't let our chance slip away this easily. "He's dead," I called out.

The Gnomes that had been leading me turned on me with a staff ready to shock me again. "I told you not to speak—"

"He is?" said Amara, stopping in her tracks. "How did you do it?"

"I didn't," I said. I wasn't sure how to approach this. I thought Zef's daughter would love him. Having been separated from my own for so long, I couldn't imagine caring so little about whether he lived or died. "He wanted us to tell you that he loves you."

Amara's face had looked casual, but after hearing that it twisted with anger. "Who sent you here?" she snarled.

"It's true," said Sillius. "He died trying to save people. He died working with this group to find the missing colonists. If you'd just hear us out."

She looked at him and then back at me. "No. That seemed targeted. Who sent you here and what do they want?"

"We came on our own," I said. "We need your help."

"Hah," she laughed. "A Treek, of all people, wants help from me? Help from the Gnomes? Do you know why I don't have a mother? It's because your people were so power hungry that they killed even the innocent. I lost her when I was a child." She spoke the last words with a fury that I knew all too well.

"Amara. I'm sorry we brought her here," said Sillius, referring to me, the Treek. That hurt, especially because we were now effectively on the same side. All of us were about to be thrown behind bars and he was apologizing for me being in the room. "But there are bigger problems. We found the colonists. They were held captive as slaves to help uncover a giant monster. That monster is not just going to stay on Daegal. It's only a matter of time before it attacks the Gnomes, along with the rest of the world."

Amara glared at me the whole time Sillius spoke. I was beginning to think maybe Sillius was right. Maybe I shouldn't have come. Maybe it would have been better if I stayed back. What would she do with me now that I willingly came into her custody?

"If you'll let me, I can show you the monster," said Sillius.

"What is your name?" she asked looking down at Sillius.

"Sillius Addleblat," he said. "I am the Gnome representative on Daegal."

"Well, Sillius," said Amara. "We have never heard of such a monster. I'm more inclined to think that the Treek, or this group, or maybe even my father has messed with your mind."

"Please, if you'll just let me show you," said Sillius. He held out his hands in a defensive position, trying to ease the tension. I tried my best to avoid eye contact with Amara in the meantime.

"Fine. Show me," said Amara.

Sillius began to spin the magic in his hands. A shimmer of purple poured out of them, forming a translucent wall in front of him. The purple faded and was replaced by an image of the cavern as the monster crawled out of it. I could see the shadow of Malcolm riding the monster to the surface. The monster clawed it's way up from the rubble and stepped out into the daylight. It roared, making a sound similar to the dragon, but this was much more unnatural, like its vocal chords we broken.

"This monster is loose on Daegal." said Sillius. "From what we know, it craves destruction. It's only a matter of time until it finds it's way off of the island and starts destroying whole cities. The figure riding it is the same one that abducted our colonists. He plans to use the same magic that he used to capture the colonists to control the monster. Regardless of who is in control, if this situation is left alone, it is only going to get worse, not just for the Gnomes, but for the whole world."

"It's not attacking us now," said Amara. "And we're far enough away from that island that I don't think we have a reason for concern." She stared down at us. I looked away, escaping her gaze. "So thanks for letting me know, but we'll deal with it when it actually becomes a problem," She looked at Sillius. "I expect you'll have the colonists back here shortly?"

Sillius looked at us and then back at Amara, looking a little defeated. Maybe he was, but he was giving up too easily. "Yes, of course," he said.

We needed this. Without the Gnomes, there was no chance of us stopping that monster. The first time anyone tried to fight it, they had the strength of all forms of magic. And even with it, they barely stopped it. I wanted to say more, but I couldn't think of a single thing I could say that might convince her.

"Good," she said. She turned to her guards. "The Gnomes can go free since we will be able to clean up this mess without our secret getting out, but if you tell anyone else about our warp room, it will be the end of you." She glared at Sillius and Porthos, making sure she was understood.

Then she motioned toward me. "As for them, do as I said. Lock them up and we'll deal with them later."

67

17.3 Hazel

I didn't know what to say or do. Was there anything that would change her mind? Or were we destined to fail from the start? What was the situation between her and Zef? Here I thought that bringing news of her father would gain us the chance to at least be heard, but it might have even *hurt* our chances.

I looked at the others. Tigala raised her eyebrows, silently asking me if we should attack. I shook my head. We were definitely outnumbered here, and attacking would only damage our message of unity. Getting locked up until they decided on how to dispose of us wasn't exactly a great alternative though.

The Gnome guards led us out of the room by the ropes that bound us. We traveled down the illusory hallway one more time until we came to another door that I couldn't see. Inside were empty jail cells.

I was really tired of all of the cells. Between the colony and the various holding quarters that Malcolm used to keep his slaves in, it was more than enough for my entire lifetime. But I didn't have a choice. The guards shoved us into the cell and locked the metal behind us.

Even for a jail cell, it was a fairly nice room. The walls and ceiling were white with a subtle purple swirl running down it. We all were in the same cell despite there being several empty rooms. I didn't mind though.

"Well that went well," said Lolan.

"Yeah," I said, still not feeling as chipper as usual. "I thought there was a chance at least. Who hates their dad that much?"

"I don't," said Geralt. "But I do understand."

I thought back to the conversation I had with him. A father as repressive as that would explain things, but Zef couldn't have been like that. Right?

"What could Zef have done?" I asked. "I had only ever known him to be supportive and caring. How did Amara have an experience that was so much the opposite?" I looked over at Tigala to see if she had any information.

"I don't know," she said. "We didn't talk much, unfortunately." It made sense. I got the feeling that Zef's playful attitude grated on her more than the rest of us.

"What about you?" I said, looking at Lolan.

"He told me a little bit about it," said Lolan. "He said he made mistakes raising her. He was still extremely proud of her, but upset with himself for emphasizing things that he shouldn't have."

"What kind of things?" I asked.

"He didn't say, but I got the feeling that it had to do with the war. He mentioned it when we were swimming at the waterfall. He said that he wished he knew what he was doing."

"You didn't get any more than that?" I asked.

"No," Lolan said, shaking his head. "That's when the water creature tried to drown us. It cut our conversation short."

It still hurt to think about him. I missed him. It was hard to believe that he was actually gone.

"Did he tell any of you about the whole thing he had going on with Klaus?" I asked.

"Nope," said Lolan. "Not me. I was wondering the same."

Tigala didn't offer any more than a shake of her head.

"He didn't tell me either. I wonder why he kept it secret. I feel like we all were at a point where we trusted each other pretty well."

"Maybe it's because he didn't have time with you throwing yourself into danger over and over again," said Tigala.

She had a point. It was a very busy month or so since we arrived in Daegal. There wasn't much downtime.

"I miss him," I said without much direction to the comment. "Zef would have been welcome company right now, stuck in a jail cell. He *was* the last time we were in this situation."

"Yeah," said Lolan. "I miss him too. He kind of felt like the father of the group. Like he always knew more than he let on."

I nodded. "He was also just a good friend. After spending so much of my life hiding or being hated, it really hurt to lose someone who actually treated me like a person."

"I know what you mean," said Lolan. "I still don't fully get it, but he knew before any of us that we would be friends. He was the one who put this together."

Lolan was right, and it felt good to say these things out loud. Zef's only 'funeral' consisted of the few words I said after growing a tree over his body.

"I didn't know him well, but he was a noble fellow," said Geralt. He spoke quieter than he usually did, reading the tone of the room. "We were all lucky to have known him."

We all breathed an agreement.

"Are you okay?" asked Tigala.

I hadn't realized but I was staring at the ground in front of me.

"Yeah," I said. I thought through my words. "I wasn't sure about all of this. Especially after Zef died, I wasn't sure I could keep doing this. I just wanted to be free of the constant struggle. I wanted to leave with the Treeks."

I glanced at the others, trying to read their expressions. Had they known I was considering it? What did they think of me?

"But this, talking about Zef, it reminds me why we're doing this. This isn't just about ending the war or keeping people from having to suffer the same trauma as all of us. It's also about us. It's about the family we formed on that island. Whatever happens with this, whether we defeat that monster or fail, I'll know I made the right choice. We can lose the battle, we can lose the war, but at least we found each other. You guys are worth the struggle."

I heard a noise outside of our cell and looked. There was nothing there. Maybe I was hearing things in the silence after sharing something so emotional.

I looked up at the others. They smiled back at me. "You're worth the struggle too, I guess," said Tigala. "But sometimes it is *definitely* a struggle."

I chuckled at that.

"I'm glad you chose to stick with us," said Lolan. "We need our Treek leader after all. And if you weren't here, who would I get into trouble with?"

"I volunteer," said Geralt.

My laughter erupted.

"Sounds good," said Lolan through his own laughter. "We'll make sure to include you in future escapades."

"Excellent!" said Geralt with a finger pointed to the air.

We laughed and talked for a bit longer about nothing in particular. It was strange to have a world-ending monster on the loose while we sat in a room and talked like the old friends we were. There wasn't much we could do for the moment though. It was all up to the others.

After the mood had settled down, I asked "So, what do we do now?" I stared at the cell bars as I spoke.

Tigala's voice was grim. "They'll execute us."

Lolan looked surprised at the revelation. "There's nothing we can do? Wouldn't we be more useful as hostages or something?"

"I don't think they care," said Tigala. "She's a warrior. You can see it in the way she holds herself. She's not going to play around with a mixed group of rejects. She'll want us out of her fur. Hair. However you say it."

I wasn't sure what to think of that. I knew it was a possibility. We even talked about it on the way to the gate. But I thought we had a decent chance. Finding out that it was Zef's daughter gave me even more hope. Maybe it was naivety, but I still had a gut feeling that she might come around. I was probably just being too hopeful.

Again, I heard a noise outside of the cell. I stood and turned to look at it, as did the others. Then a Gnome stepped into view.

"Porthos!" said Lolan.

"Hello," he said quietly. He raised a finger to his mouth to shush us. "That didn't go so well, did it?"

"Nope. Did you know she hated Zef so much?" I asked.

"No clue. I had only heard of her before that, and I barely knew Zef," said Porthos. "Sorry, I would have warned you if I had known."

"It is what it is," I said. "Do you have any good news for us?"

"Yup," he said smiling. "I'm getting you out of here," he said.

"How?" I asked.

With the smile still on his face, he sliced the air and opened a portal. He reached a hand through it and I felt a tug on my arm. I looked down to see Porthos's arm sticking out of a second portal right next to me. "Come on," he said.

I looked down at his arm reaching through the portal on the inside of the cell. "Oh," I said.

"We don't have much time," he said.

I looked at the others. They looked back trying to figure out what was going on in my head.

"I…I think we need to stay," I said.

"Why?" said Porthos. "I don't know what she plans to do, but I don't think you're going to like it."

"But if we break out," said Lolan, "there is no chance that the Gnomes will help everyone mobilize against the doom drake." He finished the sentence looking at me—making sure we were on the same page. We were.

"If this doesn't work, it won't matter anyway," I said. "We need the Gnomes' help if we're going to stand a chance against that thing."

"She could kill you," said Porthos. "King Slepenstein used to throw enemies into vats of acid." That did not sound like a good way to go.

"You guys can go if you want," I said looking at the others, "but I think I need to stay."

"Then we'll stay with you," said Geralt.

"Yeah, you'll need us if she decides to execute us," said Tigala.

I heard footsteps coming our way. From the sound of it, there were multiple people headed our way. I looked at Porthos.

Porthos looked at us with worry on his face. "I'd better be going then," he said. He gave a quick nod before disappearing into the hallway where everything looked the same.

I wasn't sure yet who it might be, but I had a hunch. I turned back to the others and looked them in the eyes. "Are you sure you're up for this? There's no guarantee it's going to work."

"I'm with you. Yeah," said Tigala. "This sounds to me like another one of your reckless plans. If it comes to it, I'm going to fight back."

"I figured," I said. "But don't do it unless there is no other option."

"Yeah," she said.

"It's hard to trust someone whose actions don't match their words," said Lolan. "I think this might be the only way to convince her. So yeah, I'm in."

It was good to hear that at least one other person thought it might work.

I looked to Geralt. He straightened his posture as if surprised to be asked a question. "You're the only one who trusted me when I had unbelievable information. It's time I repay that favor."

Just then, several guards rounded the corner into the cell area. They all had paralyzing crystal staffs, colorful robes, and pointed hats. One of them opened the door to the cell and the others came in and ushered us forward with stun staffs pointed at us. We obeyed and walked where they led us.

We entered the unchanging hallway again and walked down it for a time. They led us around a corner, and through the illusion. When the magic fell away we were in a large white room. There was a wooden platform at one end around some kind of cylinder. Its top was flush with the wooden planks of the platform. It had to be the acid.

At the other end of the room was Amara, and two other Gnomes, one on each side of her. They stood on another platform. Amara looked down at us and quickly averted her eyes, looking straight ahead instead.

The guards led us forward to the platform. They pushed us up against the wood and tied our ropes off in a quick knot. They did it for everyone but me. *Not good.*

"Take the Treek first," said one of the Gnomes sitting next to Amara. The guards surrounded me once the others were securely fastened to the wood.

One shoved me with what I assumed was the blunt end of the staff. I tripped and fell. I would have slammed my nose against the ground without having my hands to catch me, but I rolled at the last second, letting my shoulder take the brunt of the impact. The Gnomes laughed at me as I laid there.

"Get up," said one of the guards, smacking me across the ribs with the stick. The others laughed more at the attack, and my inability to catch my breath.

I chanced a look at the others. Tigala was tense, ready to step in. I gave her a look to tell her to stay put.

Even if she did act, we were outnumbered. There was a chance we could make it out, but it was a very small one. And I still had a sliver of hope that Amara would change her mind. She couldn't be so heartless as to execute her father's friends, could she? The guards urging me forward started to give me doubts.

I pushed myself to my feet, my ribs aching from the strike. The Gnomes ushered me up the stairs to the top of the platform. Once I was up there, I could see the inside of the cylinder. It was a bubbling yellow liquid with hints of a metallic silver throughout it.

They're going to throw me in there? I thought. It was one thing to be told about it, but to see the liquid in front of me was terrifying. The idea of melting in some mystery liquid? That was horrifying.

The Gnomes pushed me forward to the edge, jeering at me.

I gulped. Maybe she wasn't going to come around. Maybe this was really the end. I looked back at Tigala and started to give a nod with wide eyes.

She was anxious to act. Tigala began transforming instantly.

17.4 Interlude: Amara

I expect you'll have the colonists back here shortly?" said Amara.

"Yes, of course," said Sillius, the balding Gnome with the mustache. He looked at her like he was unsure of her judgment. She tried to suppress the anger that brought. It was hard enough taking over the leadership of an entire race. She didn't need the constant second-guessing of all the people that didn't think she deserved the position. Nonetheless, Amara did her best not to show that it irked her.

"Good," she said. She turned to her guards. "The Gnomes can go free since we will be able to clean up this mess without our secret getting out." Amara turned to Sillius and the other Gnomes. "But if you tell anyone else about our warp room, it will be the end of you." It was a lighter punishment than she wanted to give since the warp room was so crucial to the success of the Gnomes. But it would have to do. They needed their colonists back and these Gnomes at least knew where they were.

"As for them, do as I said. Lock them up and we'll deal with them later." Amara kept a stern face as she spoke. Sillius and the guards turned and left with the prisoners in tow. The Treek gave one final look to Amara, and it only made her angrier. They disappeared into the illusionary halls of the palace.

Amara let out a breath and slammed her fist on the railing once she knew she was alone. There was so much pressure on her, so much responsibility. It was boiling over and making her weak. She ignored the dampness of her eyes and turned back to her quarters.

Amara sat down at her desk. She picked up a stack of letters that had been curated for her: a letter from a lieutenant asking for reinforcements, another from a local official asking for aid in the town of Galepsy, and so on. She picked one up to read it, but the words wouldn't stick in her mind.

She growled and threw the paper down. She slammed a fist on her desk and then swiped it clean with an outstretched arm. The stand-in leader collapsed into her hands on the desk. *Why am I so ineffective right now? Why am I failing our people?* She thought. *It's just stress,* she told herself.

She stood up from her desk and paced the room. After a moment, she stopped beside her bed, her eyes settling on a wooden box tucked underneath. Amara bent down and looked at the item. It was old. She had kept it since her childhood. It was frivolous for someone in the military to keep such a large sentimental item. She wasn't sure why she had failed to get rid of it. She bent down over the box and opened it.

Inside were papers. There were a few drawings, of a male Gnome with a long beard holding hands with a female with blonde hair. Between the two was a small girl with a large smile.

Amara crumpled the paper and threw it at the ground, snorting at the image. She looked at the other items in the box. There was a stretch of purple fabric, fabric that she had picked out when her mother made a new coat for Zef. This one was extra material with a heart stitched into it. She could remember being so excited when her mom stitched that heart so long ago. It hurt just to look at.

"Why did you have to die?" she asked to the empty room. "You had to die and leave me with him." she shook her head.

She pulled the cloth up to her face and sniffed it. It smelled musty, but still had a faint smell of hibiscus tea—or maybe that was just Amara's imagination. Either way, it made her miss her mother more.

Amara sighed and sat on the floor, leaning her back against the bed. She didn't understand why she was so upset. She hated Zef. Once upon a time she had even told him that she wished he had died instead of her mother. And now he *was* dead.

Amara looked back down at the box. Underneath the papers and fabric, under the stuffed animal owl that was worn to the point that the threads were pulling loose, there was a small tree branch.

Amara squinted at the object, and then pulled it out from beneath the clutter. She held it up in front of her. It was so small now, so much smaller than she remembered it. She looked down at the decorative rapier that hung from her belt and then back at the stick she held in her hand.

Her eyes watered again, but this time Amara didn't try to force back the tears. She stared at the stick remembering her training sessions with Zef—her dad. He had taught her so much. And then he betrayed her.

"Why did you do it, dad?" she asked the empty room.

There was a knock at the door, and Amara instantly tried to compose herself. She shoved the stick back into the box and pushed it under the bed.

79

"What is it?" she said, using her forearm to wipe the tears from her face. She stood and straightened her close.

"General, you are needed in the war room. We need guidance on the invasion." It was a voice she knew to be Frackle, one of her advisors.

"Yes, of course," said Amara. "I'll be there in a moment." There was a pause. "Is everything alright ma'am?" asked Frackle.

Can he hear that I'm upset, Amara thought. She cleared her throat and tried to sound more confident. "Yes. Just give me a moment. I'll meet you there."

"Sure thing," said Frackle, followed by the fading sound of footsteps.

Amara looked in the mirror, making sure that she looked like she hadn't been even remotely upset. When she was satisfied, she left the room and headed for the war room.

She walked down the illusory hallway. With small bursts of magic, she could see through the enchantment, but she had walked these halls enough even before she assumed the throne that she didn't need to check where she was.

She traveled down the hallway at a brisk pace, hoping not to keep anyone waiting. She passed the mess hall and the barracks. When she was passing the jail cells, she hesitated for a moment.

It wouldn't hurt to make sure the prisoners aren't trying to pull anything, she thought, and she took the turn toward the cells.

Aside from the newest prisoners, the cells were empty. All of their prisoners had either been dealt with or had been used as ransom, as a result of the King's passing. The only prisoners they had were the ones who willingly gave themselves up earlier that day. It still didn't make sense to her why a Treek, a Beastfolk, an Elf, and a Human would want to deliver news of a Gnome's passing to his child. *Did they just want to watch me squirm? Or do they actually care about him?* It was a stupid thought.

Amara crept to the corner outside of their cell as they talked amongst themselves. Maybe they would say something incriminating, or maybe they would give up valuable information about enemies of the Gnomes. There was good reason to be checking up on them like this.

"I miss him," said the Treek girl.

She can't possibly be talking about my dad. Why would a Treek miss a Gnome? Why wouldn't she be happy about it, even if she didn't do the deed herself?

"Zef would have been welcome company right now, stuck in a jail cell," said the Treek. "He *was* the last time we were in this situation."

"Yeah," said the Elf. "I miss him too. He kind of felt like the father of the group. Like he always knew more than he let on."

They were talking about Amara's dad. But why? Why did these people think that working together would be productive in any sense? The differences are too great. Different cultures, different customs, and most importantly, they had all hurt each other. Every race had badly hurt every other race. That's not the kind of hurt you can just get over. It burns within you for your entire life until you pass it on to your children. Right?

Amara continued to listen as the group reminisced about her dad. It sounded genuine. They sounded like they actually cared for him. And their memories brought back memories of her own.

Why do I care? Amara asked herself. *He hurt me. He left me when he was all I had left. He doesn't deserve my tears.*

Yet, despite herself, Amara was crying again. She was mad at herself for it, but she couldn't stop it either. *What is my problem?*

Something tapped her shoulder and Amara jumped at the sudden disturbance. She turned to see Frackle looking back at her.

He had a look of shock as soon as he realized she was crying. "Oh, I——" Amara put a finger to her mouth and the advisor stopped talking. She waved him forward and then followed him away from jail cells and to the war room.

⟋⟍

Amara was back in the throne room, eating a quick meal before getting back to work when she heard footsteps approach once again.

"I'm short on time today," Amara said, anticipating the request that was bound to come from whoever approached. She was surprised to see Sillius enter the room instead of one of her advisors.

"Sorry, I was just coming to ask for orders," said Sillius.

"Orders?"

"Yes. We found our people on Daegal, and they should be on their way back shortly through the teleporters. But Daegal was my latest mission, maintaining that colony and the truce there. Now that I'm back..." he trailed off.

"Right," said Amara. "Well, we're planning an invasion on Briqor. If you're up to getting back into the thick of it, we could use any extra bodies there."

"Yes ma'am," he said. Sillius turned to leave the room but he hesitated at the same time as Amara spoke.

"Sillius."

He stopped and turned back to look at Amara. "Yes?"

"Um. Did you know my father? Zef?" She spoke slowly, unsure of each word.

"Yes. I did," said Sillius. He looked down at the ground and then back at her. "I got the impression he cared about you a lot."

Amara scoffed at the statement. "I wonder why he chose to abandon me for that Treek girl and her friends then."

Sillius looked to the side as if he had more to say.

"What is it? Why are you acting like that?" asked Amara.

He scratched his bald head. "I'm still not sure how I feel about this myself. He and that group, they did something on Daegal. They worked together, and they were arguably the most effective group there. They uncovered some things that the rest of us were too afraid to confront."

"Yes. My dad had some weird obsession with other races over his own. But why are you telling me this?"

"Well, that group seems to have really bonded, in a large part due to your father. When he originally said it, I thought he was disgracing you. But I'm starting to think he said it because he cares a lot about both of you. You both have so much power, so much potential that you don't see in yourselves."

"You're not making any sense. What did he say?" asked Amara, trying to parse the statement.

Sillius scratched his head again. "He told me a few weeks back that he cared a lot about the Treek girl, Kaia. He told me that she reminded him of you."

83

17.5 Hazel

I stood staring down at the vat of acid below me. The guards with a staff at my back, urging me slowly forward. It was too late. I turned to Tigala and gave the slightest of nods, and she started her transformation.

"Wait," came a voice behind me.

The guards stopped me, holding me just inches from the vat below. I saw Tigala pause her transformation for a moment. I breathed heavily as I stared down at my fate.

Those were the longest seconds of my life. I wasn't sure if Amara was trying to find her words or if it just felt like a long time because I was staring into that bubbling liquid knowing it would be the end of me.

"Turn her around," said Amara.

The guards prodded me to turn until I faced the general. She stood, next to two confused Gnomes in the viewing area. Her face was red, and she was breathing heavily.

"Why did you care?" she asked.

"What do you mean?" I asked, afraid of saying the wrong thing at such a crucial moment.

"About my dad. Why?" she said. She looked at me with a raw expression that I was having a very hard time reading. I couldn't help but feel like my response would determine a lot here, or maybe nothing at all. I didn't know what she was looking for, and even if I did, would giving her the 'right' answer make her angrier? No. My only option was to be genuine.

"He was my friend," I said. "I had no one, and I went to Daegal to find my people. When I first arrived, he was willing to treat me like a person instead of an enemy. He made us laugh, shared knowledge that was far beyond me. He brought us all together." I looked down at the others. Tigala was still in her Beastfolk form. *Good.*

"I eventually found my people, but when I did, I realized that I already had what I was looking for. I wanted a family, and Zef, your father, gave that to me."

Amara stared at me with the same unreadable expression. *Is she just toying with me? Why does she want to know this now?* My mind stirred as I waited for her response. Had I said too much? Or not enough?

Amara finally broke her stare and looked at the ground. "And he said he loved me?" I looked at Tigala and Lolan, and then back at her. "Yeah. I got the sense he cared about you a ton." Tears poured down her face as she dropped to her knees. She covered her face as she sobbed. The two Gnomes next to her exchanged a look of confusion. I got the feeling they were more of coworkers than close friends.

I stood there between the guards who mirrored the looks of the other Gnomes. They weren't sure what was going on either.

After a few moments, Amara finally spoke again. "Let her go," she said.

"In the vat?" said one of the guards, confused.

"No. Let her free. Untie them."

"General. Are you sure you—" started one of the guards.

85

"I gave an order," shouted Amara. I still wasn't sure what to think. Why would she change her mind so suddenly? I got the feeling it was more than what I had said.

The guards untied my ropes and pushed me forward with a shove that didn't match Amara's tone.

I stood on the platform facing her as she regained her composure.

"I don't know why, but I believe you."

I gave a sigh of relief. It worked. I couldn't believe it, but it worked. We survived! We had a chance to win this war!

"I know it sounds impossible," I said, "that we have all become friends—that we could put aside our differences, but it's not. We're here because we need help, but we're here to help the Gnomes too. That monster has threatened to destroy the world before. And it will this time if we let our differences keep us apart."

"Right," said Amara. "What do you propose we do then?"

"We need everyone's help, but the Gnomes have the most mobility out of all of us. We want to send the colonists back to their people to convince them to help too. Then, if you'll allow it, teleporting would help us keep up with the monster."

Amara wiped the tears away, composing herself as she considered the request. "That's a huge request considering the other races don't even know about our teleporters. We'd be making ourselves vulnerable and we don't even know that the other races will help. How can we be sure that this will not set our people up for attack?" I didn't have an answer. It was a gamble either way.

I opened my mouth to respond but someone else beat me to it.

"The colonists trust her," said Sillius as he walked in with Porthos. "Their group has done more to find the colonists than anyone else, and I believe that if she is able to talk to them, they will respect her wishes."

Amara turned to Sillius. "That still doesn't mean that the other races will help."

Porthos nodded. "You're right. But if there is one thing I know about Kaia, it's that she has a way of understanding others. She's genuine. And people see that in her. I have no doubts she and the others will be able to convince the other races by following her example. After all, she did convince you." Porthos gave Amara a smirk.

Amara seemed to consider it, lowering her eyes. When she looked back at me she said, "Very well. We will open up the teleporters to the people that Kaia designates." She looked back at me. "But if we have problems, it is on *you*. I'm trusting you to keep our people safe."

That was a lot of weight on my shoulders, but it was what we needed. There was no other way to get people to their respective capitals otherwise. We needed to mobilize as soon as possible. This was our chance. "I won't let you down," I said.

∽

I looked down at the colonists. They had collected at Birdsbane, settling into the various ruined houses just until we could figure out how to move forward.

"We need as many of you as possible to talk to your leaders. We need everyone's help in this fight, and we're not going to get it without convincing those in charge. If you want to volunteer for this, please come talk to us. We have a way to transport you quickly and get our armies mobilized."

87

It was weird to be making military preparations, like I was a war leader or something. In fact, war was what I was trying to stop. I wanted us to stop fighting each other so we could accomplish so much more. But to get there, we had to fight first, and we had to do it together.

Amara stood behind me. "This is Amara, the current leader of the Gnomes. She has agreed to help us move around. But your actions are on me, so I'll be making sure we are only sending people who are serious about the cause."

The colonists looked back at me. Many nodded along. Others looked overwhelmed with anxiety about the current situation. Others just look tired. I got that. We had all been through a lot.

"Thanks for all of your help," I said. "The rest of you who don't feel like they can aid in convincing leaders are welcome to continue our recovery efforts. Let's help anyone who may still be stuck in the rubble and those that were injured in the rise of the doom drake."

I gave a final nod to the group and turned back to Amara. "Does that sound good?" I asked.

"Yes. Let's hope they will follow you like Porthos and Sillius said," Amara said.

She still seemed defensive, unsure. It made sense. It's not easy to rewrite your cultural biases. I would know. She was allowed to take her time.

"Good," I said. "If you do have any problems, let me know and we can take care of it."

"I will."

I wasn't sure what else to say. It was still weird to look at her. I could see Zef's features in her. If I ever got to see her smile, I was pretty certain it would match Zef's exactly. And it hurt on a level to see the similarities of the friend I had just lost. Although, maybe she was feeling the same way spending time with Zef's friends.

"Can I ask why you changed your mind?" I asked.

"I'm not sure myself," she said. "I still am mad at my dad for leaving me and betraying his people. I'm angry that he chose other races over his own motherless daughter."

"He left you?"

"It's a long story. I might have had something to do with it too."

"I'm sorry," I said.

"It's fine." She paused as she thought. "I think what changed my mind was hearing about your friendship. I grew up being told that other races were evil. I'm still not sure I believe any different. When my dad left me, it was because he couldn't support me being in the Gnome military. He wanted us to learn to cooperate, just like you do. I didn't think it was possible until I heard you and the others talking about Zef in your cells."

"You heard that?" I asked. I had no idea anyone was around except for when Porthos showed up.

She nodded. "We're Gnomes," she said. "We have ways of being discrete." She gave a half-smile, and even in that, I saw a hint of Zef in her.

"Well, if it makes you feel any better, he convinced me too. I didn't think it was possible, even when I first came to Daegal. But Zef was the one who pushed me out of my comfort zone. He was the one that orchestrated our group coming together. And all I'm doing is carrying on his legacy. I'm not even sure of it all of the time. It's a process, unlearning the hatred, learning love and understanding instead."

Amara didn't respond. She opened her mouth like she was going to say something, and then nodded instead.

"I'm not sure how Gnomes handle funerals, but if you want to pay your respects, he is buried under the tree over there. I hope you don't mind. I grew it as a tribute to him. I didn't know I was going to meet you so soon—"

"It's okay," she said. She stared in the direction I pointed and a smile finally came to her face—Zef's smile. "I think it's fitting."

17.6 Hazel

It was dark out. I could hear people shuffling around, making arrangements, retelling the story of the doom drake's awakening. I couldn't bring myself to join them though. There was too much going on. Zef was gone, and I nearly lost my own life again the previous day. There was so much to do. So many people were relying on me—expecting me to carry them forward and rally others. It was up to me to make sure that none of the people using the Gnomes' teleporters were going to take advantage of the knowledge. I didn't know if I could handle it all. And I still couldn't decide if it was a lost cause to begin with.

"—doing okay?" asked Tigala.

"Huh," I said.

"Are you doing okay?" She looked at me with concern on her face. She stood in the living room of the ruined Gnomish house that we had claimed in Birdsbane. It was the same house that Zef had brought us to. Lolan was behind her, closer to the door. He was sitting down, leaning against the wall.

"Yeah," I said. "I'll be okay." I looked back down at the mossy floor. "It's just a lot. Maybe we can pull this off if we get everyone fully invested, but that's a big 'if'."

"Yeah," she said. "I don't know if we can do it. But we don't really have another option."

"We haven't had a second to rest either," said Lolan. "Ever since that dragon attacked the colony, we've been going at it, full tilt."

"Yeah," I said. It made me think about them. Were they feeling the same as me? Were they struggling with the same things or did they have other burdens? "How's Brendell doing?" I asked Lolan.

"He's stable," said Lolan. "I think he might lose at least one of his hands. I hit him pretty hard."

"Sorry to hear that," I said. "Are you scared?"

"Yeah," he said. "He spent most of his life tormenting me. I don't know what he's going to think when he finds out that I saved him. It may bruise his ego and make him dig in his heels further."

"You've got us though," I said, barely feeling like I meant it. "We're here for you when he does wake up."

"I know. I'll be fine. I know I'll be alright because I have you two now." He gave me a confident smile.

"What about you Tigala?" I asked. I had almost forgotten what brought her here in the first place. "Did your pack survive the collapse?"

"Only one of them," she said. "Katan made it out."

"That's great," I said feeling some hope with the news. "Where is he?"

"He was injured. Lobo is the one that pulled him from the rubble. I tried reaching out once already, but it looks like Lobo has been whispering in his ear. He didn't want to see me just yet."

Lobo. That guy is only trouble for us.

"Sounds about right," I said. "Do you think we need to worry about Lobo? Is he going to try and sabotage this whole thing?"

"I don't know. I don't think he's that stupid, but his stupidity has surprised me before."

I could agree with that. I didn't even want to think about him, but it was important.

"Where are they staying at the moment?" I asked.

"They're camped at the outskirts of town," said Tigala. "They holed up in an old leatherworker's shop."

"Good to know," I said. "We'll have to keep an eye on them." I just couldn't help planning and preparing. Even when I wanted to relax and decompress, I went right back to problem-solving.

I returned my gaze to the floor. I needed to stop.

"Why don't you come out to the campfire?" said Lolan. I met his eyes and saw the concern in his face as well.

"I'm not sure I can handle it right now," I said. "I think I need a break. Maybe some sleep will help."

"Maybe," said Lolan. "But I think talking to others might help more. We don't have to talk about preparations or anything like that. Just a bunch of different races sharing a friendly campfire. I hear the Saurians made some fancy wine."

"I really don't think—" I started.

"Just give it a try," said Lolan. "We'll be with you and you can come back and rest whenever you want." I looked over to Tigala.

"You *could* use a break," Tigala said. "Come on." She reached out a hand. I groaned and grabbed her arm to pull me to my feet.

"Just for a few minutes," I said.

We walked out the door over to what was once the marketplace at the center of town. There was a bonfire surrounded by a group of people sitting on improvised chairs made of boxes, wooden beams, and large stones. There were smaller groups that talked among themselves. Many of the races stayed with their own, but there were a couple of sub-groups with mixed races.

As we walked up the conversations around the fire hushed and then stopped altogether. They all looked at me, the same look of concern on their faces. I knew this was a bad idea. Why was everyone looking at me like that? Was it *that* clear, how hard this was on me? Did they think I wasn't up to it? Was I making them question their choice to work with other races?

I looked up at Tigala with a furrowed brow.

"Come on," she said. "Just give it a try."

Tigala and Lolan led the way to an open spot around the fire. It was nestled in between a group of Elves and the Saurians. Both groups looked our way as we sat. I sat quietly and looked at the fire.

It danced and curled, licking the night sky. It was hot, even from a distance. Was this our fate? Were we to go up in flames just like the remains of these ruined houses?

Lolan walked up with a few stone cups and handed one to Tigala and one to me. I took a sip. It was good—slightly sweet, not too strong. It was unlike anything I had ever drank before. Did the Saurians have a way to use their magic to make wine? I couldn't think of a way, but I also had no clue how to make wine in the first place.

I heard laughter off to my left. I looked and saw one of the mixed-race groups.

"We would make these wings out of the leather stretched across the lightest wood we could find," said an Elf. "Then, one person would call the storm while the rest of us jumped off the cliff. It was a blast." He laughed as he retold the story.

"That's amazing," said a Dwarf. "I've always wanted to fly. The closest earth magic comes to that is launching yourself in the air with a good rock push. But then you have to be skilled enough to catch yourself without breaking both of your legs."

"A flying Dwarf?" said a Gnome. "I'd pay to see that." He let out a heavy laugh.

"Hey, I can be agile." said the Dwarf. "My sister was a dancer."

"A dancing Dwarf?" said the Gnome. "Okay, two things I'd pay to see."

The group erupted into laughter, even the Dwarf. They weren't just cooperating. They weren't tolerating each other. They were enjoying each other's company. It was the first time I had really seen it outside of my own group. How did that happen? I looked up at Lolan nudging my head toward the group. He didn't say anything and smiled instead.

"They're getting along," I said. "They're having fun."

"I know. It's pretty amazing huh?" he said.

"How?" I asked.

He didn't get a chance to respond.

An Avian approached me. She was bright red with black feathers around her eyes like a cardinal, though it did look like a layer of dust and dirt had dulled her colors. "You're Kaia, right?" she said.

I looked up at her confused. I was pretty sure I would remember a cardinal Avian. "Yes," I said.

95

"Hi, um, my name is Taryn," she said. "How do you do it?"

"Excuse me?" I said. "Do what?"

"How are you able to always stay one step ahead? How do you keep your composure in the face of danger? You always manage to know what to do next. You know what's best for us before anyone else does." She sounded giddy. It was like I was some well-known hero or something. But I wasn't. I was a Treek. I was a person without a people.

"I don't know what you mean. I don't think I am. I feel like I'm always ten steps behind."

"No way," she said. "You found us before that doom drake crawled out of the ground. You found the Dwarves and saved them. You took the fire out of a dragon! Didn't you?"

"Uh, yeah. I guess I did those things. But that's—" I said.

"Then you're a hero. You saved us. You gave me another life. You brought me back to my sister. She looked over her shoulder at a yellow-colored Avian in one of the mixed-race groups. "I don't know how I could ever repay you."

"Repay me?" I said. "No, I don't need to be repaid. I did it for myself too. I wanted to save my people too."

"Well, at the very least, thank you for saving me and giving me back my sister. You shouldn't be so hard on yourself. You created this. You made all of this possible." She spread her wings, motioning at the collection of races around the single campfire.

"You're welcome," I said. But I couldn't take all of the credit. I was nothing on my own. "You're wrong though. I didn't do any of this. None of this would have happened without my friends. Tigala and Lolan are as much to thank for this as me, if not more. Zef too. They pushed me to keep going every step of the way. They made this possible, and every other person that believed in us. Every person that died trying to help us get here. They all deserve thanks. We are not the result of one person's actions. We are a people, and it is up to all of us to continue to tell others what we've learned. It's up to us to teach others to give up their hatred."

The Avian looked at me now with a curious look. She stood there for a moment studying me. "Wow, you're even more amazing than I expected." She smiled big through her orange beak. "Other people may have helped, but that doesn't change the fact that you've been leading the charge every step of the way. I'll let you get back to enjoying the fire, but I wanted you to know that we appreciate you."

I nodded. "Thanks. It's hard for me to understand it, but hearing that does help." The Avian smiled one more time and then returned to the group with her sister.

"That was weird," I said.

"It's true though," said Lolan. "We have already made a difference. You have made a difference. If it weren't for all of our expeditions, none of this would have been possible. Maybe you blame yourself for the collapse when we found the Dwarves, but this one would have happened either way. We were lucky we got there when we did. If we didn't push as hard as we did, all of these people might have been dead. We saved these people, and that's thanks in a big part to you."

"But why me?" I said. "You were there too. So was Tigala. Heck, Geralt was there."

"Hey, I resent that," said Geralt. I looked over to find a grin on his face. He sat among some of the Beastfolk at the fire.

"Sorry, I didn't mean—" I said.

"It's okay. I am not the strongest fighter," he said. "But I am valiant!"

"Haha, very true," I said. I turned back to Lolan and Tigala. "But still, what about Zef. He died to free them. Why do I get all of the credit?"

"Because you have already lost everything," said Tigala. "You have more reasons than any of us to hate. You lost people close to you, sure. So has everyone else. But not a single one of us has lost their whole race. You have every reason to want to tear us all to pieces, but instead, you put your life on the line for others over and over again. That Avian was right. You're a hero." I didn't know what to say to that. Then a voice rang out.

"Here's to Kaia," said Geralt raising a cup high above his head. "Wherever tomorrow leads, we owe our lives to her selflessness."

The crowd cheered in agreement.

18 Oak

18.1 Interlude: Victor

Victor focused on the hurt he had within him—the people who had hurt him and the ones he loved. He focused on the pain, the damage, and the hatred he had for the ones who took his brother, his sister. And it felt good.

He threw his arms down at the floor. A blast of fire shot from each, hitting the floor and launching him into the air. He twisted his arms around and landed. Flames poured out in a circular blast around his landing, sending his opponent backstepping to stay clear of the fire. The flames danced and licked the air.

"Well done, Victor," said Master Tavish. "I have never seen anyone perform the firestep with such power at your age. You're proving to be a very powerful fire mage."

Victor stood straight and then bowed his head at Master Tavish. "Thank you, Master." The boy he had attacked was still patting his clothes to put out the flames.

"Now, let's give it another try, but this time, Victor, you will be defending the firestep," said Master Tavish.

"Yes sir," said Victor. He stood in a ready position, with his arms forward, and hands poised. He kept one leg forward while bouncing on the back. His opponent, Kevin, was another boy about his age, but he was a bit jumpy. Kevin didn't seem like he wanted to be there. He didn't commit himself to his training, and everything fire-related seemed to scare the kid. It didn't make sense why he wouldn't give his all to defend his people. *Maybe if there were more people like me, we wouldn't have to continue fighting,* thought Victor.

Kevin finally got into a ready position himself. He spread his arms and stomped his front foot before throwing his hands down as Victor did, but his actions lacked power and confidence. Maybe Kevin had nothing to fuel his magic, or maybe he just didn't know how to channel that anger yet. Either way, it was pathetic.

Small spouts of fire shot from the boy's hands and he jumped forward in a way that made Victor think the flames didn't actually propel him at all. Kevin landed and a small flame licked forward from each foot before he lost his balance and fell over.

Victor couldn't leave it there though. He needed to show that he could defend as well as attack. Victor bent forward while swinging a foot behind him. He used the momentum to lift himself off of the ground in a front flip, scooping up the small flame produced by Kevin. He multiplied its power, wrapping himself in flames as he spun. Then, with a fist to the ground, he landed with another firestep, slamming down. The fire poured out again and crawled across the floor in a circle around him. Kevin leapt to his feet, dancing to get the flames off of his clothes.

"Kevin, you need to work on yours," said Master Tavish. "Remember, you need to focus your anger. Don't you have anything that makes you angry?"

"Yeah, I guess," said Kevin. "Sometimes my brother hides my things." Master Tavish gave an annoyed look. "You can't think of anything more than that. We need real anger to fuel our magic, especially when we're learning."

"I'll try," said Kevin. It was pathetic that he even pretended to be a future fire mage. He didn't deserve the title with his lack of commitment. Time spent trying to convince him to try was time that could have been used to teach new techniques or combat training.

Kevin focused on his hands with his forehead creased. He seemed to be focusing much harder than before. He was quiet as he stared at his outstretched arm. It was pointed at Victor, but Victor wasn't scared in the slightest. Kevin could hardly cook dinner with his magic, let alone hurt someone like Victor.

Then, Kevin's face seemed to change. Concentration changed to what looked like genuine anger. Had he found something to truly provoke his magic?

All of a sudden, there was an explosion that tore through the roof, lighting Kevin in a flame that rivaled any that Victor had seen before. Kevin screamed with fury. But unlike a controlled flame of fire magic, the fire ate at his skin. His clothes burned in seconds and his fleshed turned black and bubbled. When the flames left him, all that remained was a charred husk.

But the fire didn't fizzle out when Kevin stopped moving. Instead, the pillar of fire continued through the roof of the building, tearing the hole in the roof in a straight line behind Kevin. It claimed several more students as it tore the building in half.

"What is—" said Master Tavish. She was too confused to finish her question.

The fire finally stopped. Victor stared at the wreckage. The charred bodies of his classmates, the burning hole in the roof of the building. How did Kevin manage such a powerful spell, and why did it kill him? He looked at Master Tavish. "Was that Kevin?"

To answer his question, the earth shook for a moment. Dust poured from the holes in the ruined building. The earth shook again, almost knocking Victor off of his feet. Then, he heard a thunderous unnatural roar.

His eyes went wide as he looked at Master Tavish. "Get out of here," she said. "I'll handle this."

"No way," said Victor. "I can help."

Master Tavish didn't take the time to respond. She ran through the front door and looked to the sky to find the source of the destruction. Victor followed.

There, at the center of Brighton was a monster so tall that it dwarfed the tallest buildings of the town. It was covered in black scales with shimmering purple fins the size of hills hanging from its back. It stretched its head to the sky and screamed once again.

"What is that?" asked Victor.

"I don't know," said Master Tavish. "But whatever it is, it is much stronger than us. If you choose to help, you may end up like your classmates."

"I won't," said Victor. "That thing doesn't know what it's in for." Master Tavish nodded and darted off in the direction of the giant. Victor wasted no time, following her.

The town was already in shambles. Buildings were bent, with bricks smashed to dust. Victor could see neighboring streets where his view should have been blocked by the walls of buildings.

The monster's path was clear. The path of destruction extended in a line from the academy pointing straight at the creature.

In the distance, Victor could see blasts of flame showing that other fire mages were already trying to stop the onslaught. The giant looked unaffected. But there was something else in the sky near the monster's head. Floating in the sky was a lizard the size of the academy itself—a dragon. A pink glow streamed from the dragon to the giant monster.

The monster lumbered on without slowing at all. It threw a claw down as it screamed and walls and roofs were thrown across the city.

Victor caught sight of Master Tavish looking back at him as they ran. *Was she making sure I was up for this?* thought Victor. He didn't care. He was going to fight. It was what he had been training for, to save his people.

They reached the base of the monster, the tail dragged through the road in front of them, digging a trench through cobblestones and dirt. Master Tavish ran under it, heading toward the monster's feet. Victor didn't want to just cripple the monster though. He was powerful. He was a faster learner than most. He wanted to destroy that monster and show everyone what he was capable of.

The tail swung and Victor jumped to land on it. He used a blast of fire to adjust his balance as he landed on the moving appendage. Victor climbed up the tail just before it hit a neighboring building. It smashed the stone wall and Victor barely held on to a ridge of scales. He gained his footing again and continued up the monster's back. It was easier the further he got from the tail, but it was still a moving scaly surface.

Victor reached the first of its purple fins and grabbed the individual bones that supported it. The fin stretched out far above him, blocking out the sun and hiding him in shadow. Still, he continued.

Victor poked his head up past the top of the fin to see a fire blast coming straight for him. It was no doubt an attack from a Human that didn't know Victor was up there. Victor ducked behind the fin as the fireball slammed into the creature. He could feel the impact and then the heat as the wave washed over the creature. But the monster was unphased. The flames rippled along its skin like fire on stone.

It's immune to fire magic? Thought Victor. He looked up at the creature's head, and fear began to sneak into his mind.

He took a deep breath, gritted his teeth, and thought, *No. Everyone has a weakness.*

Victor continued his climb. He stood on the lowest fin and had to jump to reach the second. With one hand blasting beneath him to give him a higher jump, the other hand grabbed on. He held on tight, pulling his body up to where he had a better grip on the bony fin.

As he climbed he looked down at the city. Several blocks in the center of the city were ruined, but the path of destruction didn't continue to the edge of the city. *Did the monster jump into the center of the city?* Thought Victor. *How can anything be that strong?*

More blasts of fire slammed into the creature. Several more hit in the same spot—a concerted effort. The monster reacted to those. It screamed and lifted one of its legs high into the air. It slammed the foot down and a tidal wave of water materialized from the impact.

Victor watched as the water ripped through more buildings, sweeping up fire mages and civilians in one fell swoop.

Water magic? I thought it used fire magic on the academy.

Victor watched in confusion. But he couldn't give up. If there was a way to stop this thing it would have to be through its head. Victor screamed at the creature and continued his climb.

He reached the top of the next fin when the rain started. Quicker than any storm he had seen roll in, this one turned a sunny day into an instant downpour. The scales were slippery under Victor's hands, but he kept climbing, using the occasional fire blast to adjust his hands when they would slip.

He was almost there, almost at the point where he could make a devastating blow to the creature. As he looked up to see the lightning-framed head of the monster, he realized that there was someone already up near the creature's head. Riding on the dragon that was following the monster was a figure in a red cloak and hood. The pink glow that Victor had seen earlier was pouring out of the figure's hands.

Victor reached the lower neck, only progressing by pushing himself up on the bone spikes that lined the creature's spine. When he got close enough to be heard, he yelled over the wind and rain to the figure. "What are you doing? We need to kill it!"

The figure looked at Victor as if confused. The pink magic flickered at the distraction. "We can't destroy it," said the man. "It's too useful a tool. We need to control it."

"What are you talking about? It's destroying Brighton!"

"It's a small price to pay to have this monster on our side. Imagine what we could accomplish with it!" said the figure.

Victor looked at the man confused. He wasn't making sense. There is no way to control a creature, especially of that size. The man must be insane. Victor didn't have time for the lunatic. He climbed to the top of the creature's head and leaned over one of the monster's eyes. The boy's head and chest hung over what had to have been at least a hundred-foot drop. But before Victor could act, the monster's eyes went white. A moment later, the monster swung its head side to side. Before Victor was thrown from the creature's head, he focused on all of the people who looked down on him— the people who never thought he'd be good enough—and let the fire blast out of him. It engulfed the creature's eye and brow. Victor watched the burns form on its skin as he fell.

"Help!" he yelled, turning his attention to the man riding the dragon. The man looked down at Victor and then back at the monster, doubling his efforts with the pink magic.

Victor fell. The wind rushed around him and the monster screamed. With the howl, came a rush of terrible wind. Out of nowhere, a tornado formed, grabbing him up in it. Bricks and wood planks swirled around him, as well as other figures. *Bodies?* Thought Victor. He breathed heavily and scraped at the air that spun him in circles. He forced out blasts of fire to try and push him free of the cyclone, but it was too strong. Then, all at once, it dissipated.

Victor struggled to right himself and gain his bearings. He was rocketing toward the ground two or three times as fast as he had been before. The ground grew closer and closer. He closed his eyes anticipating the impact.

The wind was knocked out of him as he changed direction. He struggled to breathe as he opened his eyes. Red flames lit his vision as he looked up at the face of Master Tavish. She held him in her arms and slammed into the ground with an impact that caused her to scream out in pain.

Her grip on Victor loosened as the two skidded to a halt in the ruined city street. Victor lifted his dust-covered face to look at his master. She laid there in the road, bloody and broken, unable or unwilling to prop herself up, she said, "You need to get out of here."

"I need to kill that thing," said Victor, his voice shaky despite his intended tone.

"No," said Master Tavish. "The battle is already lost. Get out of here. Bring word to Castille before the monster gets there too."

"But," Victor said. He didn't know why he stopped. Then he realized. A shadow loomed over them. He looked up and saw the massive foot of the monster, coming right for them.

"Go!" cried Master Tavish.

Victor stood and blasted the bottom of the giant's foot as he hobbled away from it. A flash of flames came from Master Tavish as well, but it ended when the foot slammed into the earth. Stone pillars shot up from the ground in the wake of the footfall, nearly missing Victor as he ran. The monster could use earth magic too. Dust flooded the street. Victor tried to find Master Tavish in the midst of the cloud, but the path behind him was dark.

With a cry of terror, Victor ran.

18.2 Oak

What do we know so far?" I asked. We sat in the center of a large room of what looked like a library. The books that littered the ground were barely recognizable now. After being waterlogged for hundreds of years, it made sense. Several people I had come to trust, and some I still didn't know well sat around the table.

"The Saurians are mobilizing and on their way to the island. They will only have a small army here in a day or so," said Srak.

I nodded and continued looking around the faces in the group.

"The Gnomes are on the island already. They're camped near the east side of town," said Porthos.

"The Elves are working on mobilizing," said Tallesia. "Though we are a more segregated people, controlling several mountain ranges and plains. We are working on spreading the word and getting all of the groups to join together, but it's a slow process."

"Same goes for the Beastfolk," said a gorilla Beastfolk. I recognized him from when we first came back to the colony. "Lobo somehow managed to get a ride through the teleporter room, and I'd imagine he is part of the resistance."

That was not good. I would have to follow up on that to keep him from giving away any details about the Gnomes.

"Do we have any word on the Avians, Dwarves, or Humans?" I asked. I looked around for the different representatives I came to know through the colony. Of the three, Kethral was the only one there.

"The Avians have seen the threat and were fairly easy to convince. They are also on their way. We should start seeing the first of them tomorrow, though I'm not sure how helpful we'll be against a monster like that."

Tibil was absent from the meeting. I had heard that he died holding up a boulder far too large for his magic to lift. It bought time for the colonists with him, enough time for them to escape. Tibil wasn't so lucky though.

Instead, Cairn was there. "I spoke to the Dwarves myself. They know about you and what you've done for them. They are willing to help. They'll be here in a week by the looks of it."

A week? That was too long. This monster could leave the island by then. And at that point, we'd be chasing it through a trail of rubble. Once it left, the destruction would begin.

"Okay," I said.

I sighed, not sure of how to feel about the news. I looked for a Human at the table. Rodrigo was off speaking with the Human leaders. Geralt was at the meeting in his place. "We do not yet have word from the Humans. Last I knew, they were conflicted since the person that made all of this happen was a Human. Rodrigo has his work cut out for him. I plan to speak to my father tomorrow to see if he can aid in the cause."

"Thank you," I said. "And what news do we have of the monster?"

"It's moving slowly at the moment, but it's growing stronger by the day." said a white cockatiel Avian. "We need to attack soon if we're going to stop it." He had been in Kricoo's group. I was pretty sure his name was Arayoo.

"How about the location? Is Malcolm still out there?"

"Yes, Malcolm has been tracking it on his dragon. He goes in a few times a day to try and use mind magic on the creature, but so far it has proved ineffective. If we do face the monster, there is a good chance that we will have to confront Malcolm and his dragon as well."

His dragon that couldn't breathe fire anymore, I thought, feeling a tad proud of myself. "I wouldn't expect any less," I said. "Let's keep trying to convince as many races as we can. I don't think we have long until we are forced to act. We'll need all the help we can get."

The others nodded and we broke from the meeting. Tigala and Lolan joined me as we entered the streets of Birdsbane. There were people on stretchers outside of some kind of ruined church building. Cavel worked alongside the Human apothecary treating patients.

We headed back to the Gnome building we were calling our house. It wasn't a great place to sleep, but I preferred it because it was one more memory of Zef that I could cling to.

I processed the meeting silently as we walked. As good as it was to have so many people joining the cause to take down the monster, I was pretty sure it wasn't going to be enough. That thing was a world-ending threat the first time it came to power. And sure, it was submerged in the ocean for hundreds of years, but we couldn't assume it was any weaker.

"What's wrong?" asked Tigala.

"We still don't have enough," I said.

"People? The races are assembling to attack it. This will be the biggest combined effort in our lifetimes."

"Right, but it's still not enough. You saw that thing. It's going to take more than a few armies."

"So what do we do?" asked Lolan.

"I have an idea, but you're probably not going to like it."

"What is it?" said Tigala with a skeptical tone.

"Remember that forest of wandering trees?" I said.

"Yes," said Tigala. "They forced you to jump off a cliff the last time you ran into them."

"Yeah, they did. But before that, I got the sense that I might be able to convince them with more time."

"How? I heard they wanted you dead for creating them. It sounds like you're the last person that should talk to them."

"I think I'm the only person who can. They see everyone else as enemies, people willing to cut them down for their own gain. Some were angry at me, but others were considering what I had to say. Maybe if I show my face after jumping to my death, they'll be less likely to try and kill me again."

"You have some death wish. Why do all of your plans have to be built around you potentially sacrificing yourself?" asked Tigala. Her tone was angrier now.

"It's not intentional. We need more people though. We can't take that monster on our own, and unfortunately, that means we need to convince people that would normally kill us."

"It doesn't always have to be you," said Tigala.

"It doesn't," I said. "But this one does. They know me. I survived them twice already. I'm the one that created them. I have the best chance of succeeding. Besides, I feel like I need to atone for my people. Even if they didn't come up with the plague, they're the ones who used it."

"You are not your people, Kaia," said Tigala. Her forehead creased in distress. "You've already done more than enough to atone for your people. They did a bad thing, so have all of us. Everything we're doing is to try and move on from the hurt of the past. We need to continue on like none of that happened."

"No," I said. "I don't want to forget. I wish we could, but that's not how it works. No matter what I do, your parents are still going to be dead because of the Treek plague. Lolan. Your parents will still be dead because of Wikith. Brendell will have trauma from the brainwashing for the rest of his life. We can't forget, because forgetting would be allowing it to happen again. What we need to do—what I need to do—is learn from the mistakes of my people. We need to learn from our mistakes, and figure out how to live with each other."

Tigala looked at me but she didn't speak. I looked to Lolan, he had a similar reaction.

"Fine," said Tigala. "But just because we can't forget our mistakes doesn't mean you have to make up for the whole Treek race."

"Yeah, maybe not. But there are so few of us left to do it. And I don't see anyone else stepping up."

"Do not sacrifice yourself for this," Tigala said through clenched teeth. She was angry. I thought about it and remembered the story she told me about her sister, the day she lost that arm. It was because her sister sacrificed herself to take out the Gnomes. No wonder she was so adamant.

It's not that I was planning on sacrificing myself for everyone else. I didn't want to die. I had no clue how this was going to play out. But I had lost my own race. I didn't have my own people. And I couldn't sit around and let this kind of thing keep happening. If dying meant I could save children from being orphans and families from being torn apart, then maybe it was worth it. But that was a heavy thought to have, and not one Tigala would want to hear.

"Okay," I said. "I'll do my best. But I'm going to need help if I'm going to survive this."

"Yeah," said Tigala. "I'm coming."

"I'll do what I can too," said Lolan. "Waiting around here is just making me anxious about Brendell."

"Should we bring anyone else?" I asked.

As if I summoned him, at that moment I heard a voice behind me. "I'd like to join." I turned to see the old Treek from the crater walking toward me with his elk companion.

"Palem? I thought you left with Kadero."

"I did," he said. "But I've been thinking about what you said. I want to survive. I want to protect the Treeks. And honestly being here is a bit terrifying." He winced as he gave a slight smile to Tigala who towered above both of us. "But you're going to need all of the help you can get against that monster. We need each other."

I didn't know what to say. I thought I had lost any connections I had with the Treeks. It was such a relief to see him. Instantly, I felt a weight lifted off of me. As much as I loved Tigala and Lolan, and the other friends we had made, they still weren't *my* people. There were things about me that they would never get, but having another Treek around was what I had been hoping for since I was a kid. It was why I came to Daegal in the first place.

"We're glad to have the help," I said. I looked at the others. "This is Palem. He knew the village I was born in."

"Hi," said Tigala.

"Glad to have you," said Lolan.

"Glad to help," said Palem still looking a bit out of place. "Oh, and this is Bubba." He pointed to the elk that accompanied him, chewing on a small branch.

"Is bubba any good in a fight? Or just for transport?" asked Tigala.

"He's not great against a magic-user, but he can be pretty intimidating when he needs to be," said Palem.

Tigala nodded.

"Where are we going by the way? I think I missed that part," said Palem.

"Oh, right," I said. "We're going to see if the trees that I animated can help us fight.' His eyes widened as he processed the thought.

"Well, that will surely be interesting."

18.3 Oak

"So, what do you think Brendell is going to do as soon as he wakes up?" I asked Lolan as we walked. The forest floor was chewed up and muddy, showing that we must be close to the wandering forest.

"Honestly, he'll probably try and kill me again," said Lolan. He smirked at me, but I got the feeling that he wasn't joking.

"Even once the mind control wears off?"

"Yeah." He sighed. "He hated me because of what I am and because he had to live a secluded life to protect me. I think attacking me was his way of coping."

"That's horrible. I thought he changed though. Didn't you say he saved you?"

"Yeah. He did. And that was the last time I saw him before all of this. He always looked for ways to make me squirm, ways to show that he was stronger than me. Believe it or not, but I used to idolize Wikith Cresall. I saw him as someone who had it all together. He knew who he was. He was unmatched at storm magic. He was someone I could look up to. But then I got the chance to see him perform. Brendell took it one step further, tricking me into exposing my secret in front of Wikith. That's when we both discovered that Wikith hunted down half-breeds." Lolan's expression darkened. "Wikith likely killed my parents. He went to strike me down and Brendell realized what he had done. He stepped in the way and allowed me to escape. That one time, he showed that he cared about me. But that doesn't erase a childhood of attacks and ridicule."

"That's horrible," I said. "I'm sorry."

"It's okay. So yeah, when he wakes up, there is a small chance that he's grateful that I saved him. There's a much greater chance that he wakes up and is mad at me for not letting him fix the problem himself."

"Wow," I said. "Well, if we're not around when he wakes up, have someone come get us." I said.

I looked to Tigala who was walking silently along with us. She nodded.

"Thanks, guys. I appreciate it."

"Of course. I know you'd do the same for me."

He smiled at me, but there was still a trace of worry behind his eyes.

"So, uh, how long have you three been working together?" asked Palem.

"We met here on Daegal," said Tigala. She still looked a little timid around Palem, but she was trying at least to acknowledge him. I wondered if it had to do with her own hurt caused by the Treeks. Maybe she suspected he had been part of the plague.

"How did you find each other?" asked Palem. "Forgive me for prodding, but I like to dig into mutually beneficial relationships. I use it in my magic, but this is kind of along the same lines."

"No, it's okay," I said. "We didn't really mean to work together. We all came here looking for our people and didn't really have search parties to work with. Lolan started the whole thing though."

"Yeah," said Lolan. "I had never seen a Treek before, and I was curious about what Kaia was doing alone in the woods. I followed her, and we were attacked by an ogre. One thing led to another and we ended up being accidentally forced to work with each other."

"We had a fourth member too," I said. "But he didn't make it out of the cavern." My eyes dropped to the ground.

"I'm sorry," said Palem.

I looked at the others. Just talking about it hurt them too. I could tell. Lolan caught me looking and offered me a slight smile.

"It's okay," I said. "I'm just hoping we can carry on his legacy."

"And what was that?" asked Palem.

"Lolan was the one that put this whole thing into motion, but it was Zef that held us together. He knew exactly what he was doing when he made us ask Tigala for help."

I looked at Tigala. I knew I was referencing things that wouldn't quite make sense to Palem at this point, but I didn't care. I was saying it more for us. We hadn't gotten much time to process what was going on. There was never enough time for that kind of thing on this island.

"Zef made us a team—a family. He's the one who made us realize what we were really looking for," I said.

"Agreed," said Lolan.

Tigala grunted an affirmation.

"Well, he sounds like quite the visionary," said Palem. "I wish I could have met him."

"Me too," I said, thinking about how ironic it was to tell a Treek that I wished he met the Gnome that I had met on this island.

The path ahead of us grew muddier by the second. Dirt pulled up in clumps making uneven ground that needed to be climbed hand over hand at times. Palem rode on Bubba, occasionally looking like he might fall off as the elk took leaps to the next bit of stable ground.

Up ahead, I could now see a forest of trees that I didn't recognize. I double-checked the map of Daegal that Malcolm had in his watch room. It tracked the wandering forest in this direction toward the river, close to where we had created them. But what was interesting was that there were supposed to be no trees in this area at all. Yet a forest stood directly in front of us, still, positioned around the river.

"Do you think that's them?" I asked.

"What?" asked Lolan.

"The forest," I said. "Do you think that's the wandering forest?"

"They're not wandering," said Lolan. "Do they go dormant like that?"

"I don't know," I said. "I've never seen them do it, but that doesn't mean they don't. Maybe they're sleeping?"

"So what do we do about them?" asked Tigala. "If that is them and we walk in there, we'd be surrounded."

"Yeah," I said. "I don't know. We could try yelling for Grollok from the outside."

"Yeah. I vote for not entering a forest of trees that want to kill us," said Tigala.

Palem chimed in as if he just realized what we were talking about. "You animated all of those?" he said with wide eyes staring at the patch of trees.

"I think so. I had boosted magic when I did it."

"Heh, I'll say. And you can control them?"

"No," I said. "I can control maybe a couple of the smaller ones at a time, but those ones have minds of their own."

"What do you mean? You can give them commands?"

"No," I said. "They're living, thinking creatures now. I don't know how I did it, but they talk and think for themselves."

Palem gave me a confused look. "I've never heard of that. Your people couldn't create minds."

It *was* weird, but I didn't know anything about creating animated creatures. I didn't know what was normal and what wasn't. But now that he mentioned it, I wasn't sure how *that* part of it happened.

"Maybe mind magic somehow got in there," said Lolan.

"I don't know mind magic," I said.

"Maybe it's something in the land. Maybe it's a result of that monster sleeping in its center or maybe there was a mind magic vein nearby. I don't know." Lolan shrugged.

"That would make more sense," I said. "That's a scary thought though, to think that mind magic can grant minds to things that wouldn't otherwise have them."

"Yeah," said Lolan.

"Are we ready to do this?" Tigala asked. She looked anxious staring up at the towering trees.

I looked at the others who looked back at me with raised eyebrows. No one was ready, but we had to do what we came here for. We needed their help.

"GROLLOCK," I yelled.

There was no response. The trees stayed just as still as they had. I stood there in the silence staring up at the trees.

Were these the wrong ones? Did the magic wear off? Or were they sleeping? Do treants sleep?

"Hello?" I yelled again. "It's me, Kaia. I'm the one who created you." Still nothing. I exchanged looks with the others.

"I don't know what to do," I said. "We can look for Grollock and see if we can provoke him to talk, but that would mean going in there."

"Can you help control them at all?" Tigala asked looking at our newest member.

"I can bend branches and move vines, but against a force that large, I wouldn't do any noticeable damage. If they are in there and want to swarm us, there's is nothing I can do."

Tigala nodded.

"GROLLOCK!" I yelled again. "I came back! You couldn't kill me last time. Here I am."

"Don't ask them to kill you," said Tigala.

"I'm just trying to get them to wake up. I don't know." I said, shrugging.

I reached out with my magic next, focusing on the closest of the large trees. I sent my magic to its lower trunk, trying to move it even in the slightest amount. The green glow formed on it as the others watched. Nothing. I couldn't even budge it.

I looked to Palem. "Can you tell if they are still animated?"

"I can try, but I'm not even sure what that would feel like." He put a hand forward and reached toward one of the smaller plants. The green glow formed as he focused. The sapling swayed with his magic, and then the glow dissipated. "It felt a little easier to use," he said, "but that may just be because we're on this island or because it was previously affected by your magic."

"So we still know nothing," I said. I looked to Tigala. "What do you want to do?"

Tigala furrowed her brow. I knew she wouldn't like the idea of waltzing in there, but I wasn't sure we had much choice at this point.

"I guess we go in. But we stick together," she said, looking at me.

"Okay," I said. I was okay with that given how things went the last time I ran into these trees. I didn't want to have to sacrifice myself again. Tigala didn't want me to either.

"I'll take the lead," said Tigala. She stepped forward into the forest.

The trees loomed over us. Every breeze that swayed a branch made me a little anxious. It was quiet too. There weren't many animals that I could see living in the forest. It *had* to be the wandering forest, but I had no way of knowing why they were no longer wandering.

We walked in silence through the trees. The ground was churned and turned up by stomping root clumps, making our progress slow. I heard a faint noise up ahead. There was a trickle of flowing water. I checked the map again and saw the river that ran through the region. It was the same river that fed into the waterfall above the teleporter, but miles upstream from it.

I looked up at the towering trees. Moss and vines hung from them. Their branches provided a patched shade over the forest floor. At any moment, they could come back to life and attack us. They could wake up and we would already be surrounded.

"What was that?" Tigala said in a hushed voice. I looked at her and saw she was in her tiger form, her ears pointing in a direction ahead of us.

"I didn't hear anything," I said.

"I saw something up there," said Lolan, looking in the same direction as Tigala.

"Should we spread out?" I said.

"No," said Tigala. "We stick together."

"I just meant—"

"Shh" Tigala crept forward with careful steps. She had spotted what she heard. She ducked down below the brush and didn't make a sound as she moved. After a few tense moments, Tigala pounced from the bushes several paces ahead of us.

There was a scream, and then a voice. "Get off of me!" We ran to her, unable to see through the dense trees and brush.

When I was within view, I saw Tigala in her Tiger-form growling at a blue female Saurian with a spear. The Saurian pulled a hand from behind her toward Tigala and a stream of water shot at the tiger. Tigala dove to the side dodging most of the impact. The Saurian followed up with a spin of her spear and a small wave tumbled across the land behind her. It swallowed her and she disappeared beneath the water. A second later she sprung from behind a tree and jumped at Tigala with the spear poised to strike.

"Wait!" I said.

The Saurian paused for a split second as she caught a glimpse of me.

"We don't want to hurt you," I said.

18.4 Oak

I really wished we brought a Saurian with us today to convince her that we weren't dangerous. The Saurian breathed heavily as she realized she was outnumbered. Her eyes darted around, and then she turned and ran.

She swept her arm down as quickly as she had turned and sent a torrent of water at Tigala's feet, tripping her up. The Saurian ran for the river.

"We don't want to hurt you," I said. "We work with other races." It was pointless. How were two Treeks, a Beastfolk, and a half-Elf-Human supposed to look unintimidating to a stranger of a different race? We weren't.

The Saurian continued to run. She was more nimble than some of the others I had seen at the colony. She was quick too.

We ran after her. I hadn't seen her before, meaning she wasn't part of the colony and wasn't one of the abducted colonists. *Is she a native of Daegal? How does that work?*

"My name is Kaia," I yelled. It sounded so stupid, but maybe introducing myself would help. It didn't. The Saurian kept running down the bank toward the river.

When she finally reached it, she stopped and faced us. She still breathed heavily but looked much more confident with the water at her back. Given what she had done in the middle of the woods, I was nervous to see what a properly fueled attack from her would look like.

"Stay back," the Saurian said. "Let me go before I am forced to hurt you."

I raised my hands trying to look unimposing. "We just wanted to talk. We don't usually see unknown people on Deagal." Actually, I guess we had. I probably should have been more nervous that she was a Human disguised as a Saurian, but I got the feeling that Malcolm was wholly focused on the doom drake now.

"We're from the colony." I said. "The one where they had the truce. We're not going to hurt you."

The Saurian looked at us, with downturned brows. She was skeptical, and she had every right to be. "What do you want to know?" she asked.

"What are you doing out here? How did you get here?" I asked.

"That's not important," she said. "I'm here. Now let me go and we can all walk away from this."

"Okay," I said, trying to think. I wasn't sure what exactly I had expected her to say, but I was hoping for more. "Do you want help?"

"No," she said. "I'm fine on my own."

"I felt the same way when I first came to Daegal," I said. I looked at Lolan. "This island taught me pretty quickly that it's not safe to go alone."

"I'll manage." She still stood poised to attack, while the four of us stood higher up the bank looking down at her.

"Okay," I said again. "But you should know, this forest might be extremely dangerous. The trees might be alive."

"Is that a threat?" she asked.

"No! No," I said, surprised at the response. "This is a magical forest. Last time we saw them they were—"

"I don't care," she said. "Just let me leave."

I looked at the others hoping they might be able to say something to change the tone of the conversation. They looked just as lost as me.

"Yeah, okay," I said. "If you do want to find more people, even more Saurians, we're in the town near the towering mountains toward the center of the island."

The Saurian stared at me for a moment and then turned to cross the river.

We stayed put and watched her leave. I wasn't happy with how that interaction went, especially when I finally felt like we were making progress in getting people to work together. Whatever was going on with her, she hadn't been around the colony and probably hadn't seen the drake, given her tone. I hated seeing anyone go out into Daegal alone, especially now. She didn't know what dangers were waiting for her here.

"I wonder what she's up to," said Lolan.

"I wish we knew. She was so hostile," I said.

"Can you blame her?" asked Palem. "She was attacked by a tiger and then chased by an Elf and two Treeks. I wouldn't be happy either."

It did make sense, and if anyone could relate out of the four of us, it was Palem, our newest recruit.

I looked up at the trees again. "Well, should we continue our search?" I asked.

Just then I heard a noise that was all too familiar: the sound of roots pulling from the earth. It was followed by a scream in the direction the Saurian had just left us.

"I think I found them," said Tigala.

The Saurian was now out of view, but we could see the canopy shake up ahead.

"Come on!" I said.

We ran forward through the brush, toward the moving tree. I kept my eyes on each tree we passed curious if they too would wake up and join the chaos.

When the Saurian came into view she was in the bark-covered hand of one of the trees. It was standing back up, clutching her. I looked up to the tree. It was the one with the broken top. He had been one of the ones convincing others to kill me the last time I saw them. *Great.*

"Stop!" I yelled up at the tree. Lolan, Tigala, and Palem stood at the ready behind me.

The tree looked down at me.

"Yeah, you remember me?" I yelled.

"YYEEEWW," said the tree in its ancient creaks and groans.

"Yeah," I said. "I'm the one you tried to kill, twice now." In the distance, I heard the sound of more roots pulling from the earth and saw the distant sway of branches.

"HOOOWWW DDIIIID YEWWW?" the tree asked, not forming a whole question.

"I'm stronger than you," I lied. "I created you, and I can't be hurt by you." I saw Tigala eyeing me. *Was that too much?* I had to try something different. The last time almost got me killed.

"Put her down," I yelled, "gently!"

The tree stared at me for a moment, and then slowly lowered the Saurian to the ground. He hesitated and then loosened his grip. The Saurian jumped from the branch-like hand and kept both the tree and our group in her field of view.

More noises of trees uprooting and groaning filled the forest as they awoke.

"WWHYYY AARRRREE—"

"No," I said, cutting him off. I had to assert my power to pull this off, at least that's what I thought. "What were you doing? Why were you and the others still for so long."

The bark on the tree's face shifted slightly, making it look confused. "RRREEESSTTT," it finally said.

"You were all resting here?" I asked. "Why here?" I didn't ask because I needed to know. I was just curious. I wanted to know how these tree people worked. I wanted to know more about something that I had a hand in creating.

The tree continued to look confused as more trees began waking up. The Saurian seemed to realize that she was probably safer close to us than if she went off on her own at this point. She took a few small steps toward us.

"TTHHHIIIRSSSSTYYYY," said the tree. It turned its head to face the river.

Huh, so they need to drink water. That makes sense.

Some of the trees that had woken were now making their way to us. One, in particular, I recognized. Grollock approached with his glowing green face.

"YYYEEEWWW LLLIIVVEE," said Grollock.

"Yes, I do. And I need your help," I said, trying to still display that confidence.

"HHHAAAAHHH," said the broken tree, laughing at the request.

"I need your help because I know you want your kind to survive," I said. "There is a monster that is looking to destroy the world, trees included. And I think you don't actually want to hurt me. We're stronger together."

Grollok looked at the other trees around him. What was he thinking? Did they think? They must, but it was still so weird.

"HOOWWW DOOO WEE NOOOO SHHEEEEE MAAADDE USSSSS?" said the broken tree.

"SHEEE HASS PLLAANNTTT MAAGGIICC" said Grollok.

"SOOO DOO WEEE," said the tree.

"Why does it matter?" I asked. "That monster is going to kill you. It's going to kill all of us." I saw the Saurian trying to sneak out while the attention was on me. She hid behind the leg of one of the taller trees and poked her head out looking for an opening to sneak to the next bit of cover.

The Saurian sprinted to the next trunk. I didn't say anything. If she could get out of this unscathed, good for her.

"SSHOOOOWW UUSSSS," said the broken tree.

Show them? What did he mean? I reached out with my magic and grew a vine. It stretched up and snaked around mimicking the movements of my arms to make it exceptionally clear that it was following my commands.

"MMMMAAAKKEEE USSSS," said the tree, clarifying.

Oh, I thought. I wasn't sure I could do that again, not without the nature magic veins. I reached out to the vine again and expanded it, growing extra limbs to look like arms and legs.

The Saurian made another dash between cover. But this time, something went wrong. I chanced a look when I heard the splash of water. She was facing off against one of the smaller shrubs that likely just woke up. It stood back up, dripping wet, and lunged at the Saurian. She probably could have handled it on her own, but all eyes were on the Saurian now. One of the trees grabbed her again before she could hurt the sapling.

"SSHHHEEE FFFIIIIGHHHTTSS USSSS," said the tree holding the Saurian.

"She's defending herself. Let her go. She doesn't know what you are," I yelled at the trees.

"YEEWWWW CAMMMEE TOOO KILLL UUUSSSSSS," said the broken tree. "YEEEWWW CAAMMMEEE WWWIITTH MMMOORRRRR."

More what? People? I shook my head. Just when I thought I might have convinced them.

"Look, I'll prove I made you. I'll make more. But when I do, you let her down unharmed." I said staring up at them.

"SSHOOWWW USSSS," said Grollok this time. I got the impression that was him agreeing to the deal, but it was hard to read these creatures. Or should I call them people?

I focused on the vine once again. I poured my magic into it, strengthening it but keeping it flexible for what it was about to do. I turned the tip of it toward the ground. It scraped at the moist earth and pulled its root clump free. The vine coiled around the moist dirt and held it in the center of its body. More vines stretched out strengthening its limbs and forming what looked kind of like a head. When it was ready, I made it run forward and then bow to the trees.

"There you go," I said. "I made you, and I need your help. But more importantly, *you* need your help."

"NOOOTTTT USSSSS," said the broken tree.

I looked at the tree and then at my vine monster and then back at the tree. *Not us?* I thought. *What was that supposed to mean?* I looked up at them. They were sentient beings. Did he really want me to create another living, thinking creature like them?

"I can't do that part of it again," I said. "That was only possible because of the veins of nature magic."

"SSHHHEEE LLLIIIIEDDD," said the broken tree. Grollok looked down on me in silence. He agreed.

"I didn't lie. I created you, and I think I could do it again with the right situation."

"LLLIIIESSS," the broken tree said.

The tree that held the Saurian started to move its hand. I wasn't sure what it was about to do but I didn't want to find out.

"Stop!" I yelled. I looked around frantically for some way of tricking them, some way of convincing them that I was the one who created them. If only Zef were still here, he'd be able to create an illusion. But he wasn't.

In the split second it bought me, I looked up at Grollok again to try and read his 'expression'. I stared into the green glow and couldn't make out any kind of emotion from him. But then it hit me. *The green glow!* I thought. *That used to be the green veins!*

"I can do it," I said. "Don't hurt her." I looked at the tree holding the Saurian. It remained still for the moment. "Grollok, I need you to come closer though."

The tree looked down at me, and after a moment, it lifted one of its giant tree trunk legs. It stepped down directly in front of my vine monster.

"Okay, one moment. Nobody hurt anyone." I said, hoping they would listen.

I glanced at Tigala. She looked back with a look of concern, but she didn't stop me. She knew this was our only way out of this mess.

I focused on the vine creature I had made. The magic that controlled it glowed green, brightest in the root ball at its core. Then I focused on the glow coming from Grollok. The biggest mass of it was centered on the treant's chest. I dug into it, much like I had so long ago. Slowly, I began pulling from it, dipping my toe into the well of magic and falling in to my waist, so to speak. The magic rippled out and flowed down toward the vine creature.

It was impossible to direct perfectly, impossible to regulate the flow of magic. The green glow reached the vine creature and flooded our vision.

18.5 Oak

The magic slammed into the vine creature and it instantly began to grow. It grew taller and denser, faster than anything I could have done on my own. I was already canceling the magic in anticipation of things going horribly wrong, but it still wasn't enough. It was three times my height in seconds. After a few more, it was half the height of Grollok.

The trees around us reacted. Many stepped back and away from the explosion of magic. Grollok stood his ground.

The vine creature began whipping around violently. One limb ripped through the canopy striking a tree in the distance. It still wasn't big enough to do any major damage to the tree, but it was still growing. Another vine slammed down on the ground between me and Lolan. It left a rut big enough to bury someone in.

We backed up too. I kept trying to push the magic away from the vine monster, but it was too strong.

The vine creature grew and now stood the height of Grollok himself.

Grollok, for his part, looked like he was also having trouble with the magic being sapped from him. He was clutching at his chest. But when he saw the vine monster reach his own height, he threw his arms forward and slammed the vine creature in the chest.

The vine monster stumbled backward, away from Grollok and toward us.

"Look out!" yelled Lolan. We all dove for cover. One stray foot headed my way, but I wasn't quick enough to outrun it. Right before it touched down, I felt a tug on my arm and was pulled onto the back of Bubba. Palem steered the elk out of danger.

"Thank you," I said, catching my breath.

He didn't have time to answer. Another foot was coming our way. This time Bubba charged toward the foot at Palem's command. The foot sailed over us, barely clearing the elk's antlers.

It crashed into the ground behind us.

"Hold him down. I can't control it anymore!" I yelled, hoping Grollok got the message.

"BBBIIINNND HIIIM," bellowed the treant.

Other trees stepped forward and tackled the vine creature. It continued to fight, flailing and scratching at the earth, but it was far outnumbered. Trees piled onto it, holding down limbs and keeping it from doing any more damage.

When the dust had finally settled, I looked to make sure everyone was still okay. Lolan was on Tigala's back, who was in tiger form. As for the Saurian, she was still being held by the treant who had caught her.

I looked up at Grollok. "We had a deal, let the Saurian go." Grollok looked a little less stable than usual. He still held one hand to his chest as he looked at me and then at the captive.

"FRREEEE HHHEEER," he said.

The treant stooped low to the ground and placed its branched hand on the ground. The Saurian looked at me with wide eyes before stepping onto the stable earth. She took a moment to get her footing and then darted off into the forest.

And here I thought maybe she'd talk to us after all of this. Wishful thinking.

"I made you. And I have the power to make more of you," I said, staring up at the broken treant. "I need you to listen to me. There is a monster, far bigger even than all of you. It wants destruction, and it will come for all of us. So stop fighting me and my friends. Let's work together to save our people."

Grollok looked at the broken tree and then another. *This might actually work.*

"WWWUUTT DDOOO WEEE NEEEDDD TOOOO DOOO?" asked Grollok.

I looked at the others and then back at the trees. "Come with us. We'll be attacking the monster shortly. You can come with us and help."

Grollok stared at me for a moment. His chest rose and then fell. "WWWEEE WIILLL HHHELLPPP," said Grollok.

I smiled. "Follow us."

We had been walking for a couple of hours when we decided to take a break. We found a nice spot among the hills and small plants to rest in the shade of one of the towering pillar-like mountains. The treants and twig creatures seemed to enjoy the break as well. They chose to stand still and soak up the sun.

"That went well," I said as I grew some small berry bushes for us. I wondered if the others were getting sick of my berries.

"Yeah," said Tigala. "We got lucky."

"Where do you think that Saurian came from?" asked Lolan.

"I was wondering the same thing," I said. "None of you have seen her before, right?"

"Nope," said Lolan.

Tigala shook her head and Palem started on his own nature magic creation.

"Do you think it was another Havik situation?" I asked. "Maybe it was someone using illusion magic to look like a Saurian.

"Maybe," said Lolan. "But at least in Havik's situation, he was a lot more hostile. If that was Havik, Malcolm, or one of his subordinates, she wouldn't have been so hesitant to attack. She didn't want a fight."

"True." I finished growing a handful of berries and distributed them to the group, I even gave a few to Bubba who gobbled them up.

Palem was nearing the completion of his creation as well. It was a cucumber vine, with loads of the fruit hanging off of it.

I heard something near the cliffs. I looked over and saw the same blue Saurian we had saved from the trees.

She took slow steps toward us, eyeing the towering trees as she did.

"It's okay," I said. "They're resting, and I told them to leave you alone anyway."

"Why?" asked the Saurian.

"It's like I said. We weren't trying to hurt you. We want to work together. We were just curious how you got to Daegal. We thought we knew everyone on the island at this point."

"How did you know how to do that?" she said. Her eyes moved to something behind me. I turned and found the vine monster in the distance, still struggling to break free of the two treants that restrained it.

"Oh, I'm not entirely sure," I said. "I was put in a tough situation a little bit ago and the only tool I had was a massive vein of nature magic. I used it and it went haywire. It's how I created all of them."

"Did you mean to?" she asked. She sure was interested in the magic, but unwilling to give answers of her own. Maybe it would help ease the tension she had with us though.

"No," I said. "This time I did, but I wasn't sure it was going to work either. And I'd prefer not to create more of them. They're kind of dangerous."

"Yeah," said the Saurian. "Thank you, for saving me."

"You're welcome," I said. "I'm Kaia. And that's Tigala, Lolan, and Palem." I pointed to each of them in turn.

"This is Bubba," added Palem.

The Saurian looked us over. "Kesq," she said finally. "I'm here because I'm running from someone. Someone wants to use what I know as a weapon, but it's too powerful."

"Well, not to sound just like that someone, but we need something powerful to stop this monster that just woke up," I said.

"Yeah," said Kesq. "I saw it."

"You did?" I asked. "Where?"

"It was further up the stream where we met, close to where the stream met the ocean. I watched it stalk closer and closer to me with a dragon trailing it. And then, all of a sudden, it disappeared in a mist of violet energy."

"It teleported?" I asked no one in particular. I looked at Tigala.

"We need to tell the others," said Tigala.

"Yeah," I said. I stood up and began walking toward the trees.

"You're going to stop it?" asked Kesq.

"We're going to try," I said. "That thing wants to kill everyone in its path. It tried destroying the world once before, and it's going to try again."

Kesq took a deep breath. "I'll help," she said.

I turned to make eye contact with her. "Thank you. We can use all the help we can get." I looked back to the trees, "Grollok! We need to move." The trees that were still 'awake' and holding the vine monster stomped their feet down. It was enough to stir the trees around it and send a shockwave all the way to me. The other treants and plants began to stir themselves awake. Once I found Grollok with his glowing features I said, "The monster teleported somewhere. We need to find it before it does major damage." Grollok looked down at us and then bellowed out the word: "MOOOVVVVE!" The rest of the trees sprung to motion.

"Grollok," I yelled up again, barely audible over the tearing of dirt from ancient roots. "I think we're going to need a ride too. We don't have a lot of time."

Grollok stepped forward and lowered a hand in front of us. I was the first to step onto the bark-covered appendage. The rest followed, with Kesq being the last to join, hesitant to step onto the hand of a monster that was previously trying to kill her.

Grollok lifted us up and began his march back to Birdsbane to join the rest of the survivors. He lifted us to what would be considered his chest, close to the green glowing markings. And then he walked with us held in front of him.

It was wild being lifted up so quickly, being at the top of the canopy. It was even wilder that we were moving with something at this height, and that something was a tree that I brought to life. I looked down at the ground and felt queasy. This was not a height I wanted to fall from.

I looked at the others, trying to distract myself from the height. Kesq, most of all looked out of place. She sat on the tree's palm with eyes wide, as if she was afraid the floor beneath her would give out at any moment.

"So, any chance you're going to tell us what you know that could have been used as a weapon? I promise we won't hold you hostage for it, no matter how useful it might be." That didn't come out exactly as I had hoped.

She gave me an odd look which only barely masked the fear from the height and dangerous tree monster that carried us. Then she said, "you already know it, to an extent at least." She lifted her chin at the glowing center of Grollok. "That glow, it's known as a beacon—an extremely powerful source of magic. Tapping into them is dangerous, but grants amazing power with the respective type of magic."

"Woah," I said. "I didn't know they had a name. I thought it was just a strange occurrence on Daegal."

"It is," she said. "There are a lot of them here. I can sense them. The knowledge I have is how to use them; how to tap into that power, even of a different type of magic, and use it to make you stronger."

"What's the downside?" asked Tigala. She never liked toying with magic, especially different kinds.

"Well, it's hard to control if you don't know what you're doing, but it sounds like you might have already experienced that."

"Yeah," I said. I glanced at Tigala again. "So you could teach me to harness the power of those better?" I asked. That could change the whole dynamic of the battle that we were preparing for. If we could use those veins, the beacons, then maybe we'd have a chance at taking down the doom drake.

"I could," she said. "But I'm not sure I want to yet. I want to make sure you are what you say you are. It's not the kind of knowledge that just anyone should have."

"Fair enough," I said. But I really wanted to know. That might be what we needed.

She didn't seem to want to say more than that at the moment, and I didn't want to pry and make it look like I was going back on my promise of not holding her hostage for the knowledge. I'm sure she wasn't happy about having to keep the information from people who would abuse it.

Instead, we kept quiet as the treants continued on toward our current base of operations. It wasn't long at all before we could see the wyverns flying among the spire mountains, and then the ruined town of Birdsbane. But when we saw the town, I noticed there was someone running from the town toward us. They were small, like an ant coming to attack us.

"Hang on Grollok," I said. "There's someone coming." I pointed and the others looked. "Let me talk to them. They might think you are enemies."

Grollok didn't respond but slowly lowered his hand instead. We touched down and I climbed off of the tree to find Rodrigo at the head of the approaching group.

He looked at me, and then the tree that lowered us down. I'm sure he was considering the history we had over me creating this forest of wandering monsters. Still, he spared no time to tell us, "The doom drake. It attacked!"

"What? Already? Where?" I asked, unable to contain all of the questions I had.

"Brighton," he said. "The city is gone."

19 Sequoia

19.1 Sequoia

"What do we know," I asked, looking around at the leaders who had gathered around us at the edge of Birdsbane. Behind me, the trees stood like towers, shading us from the sun.

"It showed up in Brighton," said Rodrigo. "It attacked without warning and destroyed the city. We don't have much information from the town, but it sounds like there were very few survivors."

Very few survivors, I thought. *A few months ago and that could have been me.* The city where I had spent most of my time over the past 7 years was now wiped from the map. It was the town where I met Chipry. And now it was gone. I was beginning to think that we were never going to have enough people to take the monster down.

"What do you mean 'without warning'," asked Tigala.

"It just appeared," said Rodrigo. "Last we knew it was on Daegal. Then it showed up in Brighton. Our source didn't see it arrive, but he said he definitely didn't hear it coming. There were no earthshaking steps, and there was no destruction leading up to where he started the attack. It wasn't there one moment, and then it was."

"So it can teleport," I said. *Great. As if taking down a stationary enemy that was capable of destroying the world wasn't enough.*

"That's what we assume," said Rodrigo.

"Do we have anything else?"

"We have seen the remains of Brighton with our magic," said Arayoo. "Based on the wreckage, we are fairly positive that it is using multiple types of magic. There were patches of broken earth, flooded areas. There was a forest of thorns tearing through buildings. There is likely no limit to the kinds of magic it has."

I stared back at them, unsure of what to say. I knew that I needed to be focused. I needed to give hope to those who had none. I needed to inspire them and convince them that we could win this fight, but to be honest, I didn't believe it myself. How were we supposed to stop a world-ending monster that knows all of our magic better than us? How could we stop something so massive with only the *slight* support of *some* of the races?

My eyes lowered as I tried to think through our options. I needed time. I needed time to gather more people. I needed help.

"Is there anything else?" I asked, afraid of the answer.

"Yes," said Arayoo. I winced at the word. "The doom drake is on the move. It seems that its next target is Briqor."

I took a deep breath and looked back up at the group. "What do you propose we do?" I asked. I looked around, and my eyes settled on the Dwarf present. It was Cairn, the Dwarf who lost her husband in the collapse at the earth magic veins. She looked tired. She must have just gotten back from trying to convince Dwarven leadership to join the fight.

"We have to go," said Cairn. "I think we have all of the help we're going to get at this point. And the longer we let that thing rampage, the fewer potential people we have to help."

I nodded. "I agree." I scanned the faces in the group. They all watched me, wide-eyed. "Let's move. We get everyone that we have on the battlefield against the drake." I took a deep breath and looked at Tigala to my right, and Lolan to my left. I looked at Palem on Bubba, Rodrigo, and Tallesia whose head was still bandaged from the cave in. "Whatever happens out there, it's been an honor working with all of you. I'm proud to call you my friends."

They looked back at me with apprehension. Rodrigo was the one to break the silence. "It has been an honor following you." He looked at the rest of the crowd and said, "Now let's go show that thing what we're made of!"

There was a cheer in response.

"Follow me," I said. "Anyone that can fight, we leave via the portal at the center of town. I'll talk to Amara about redirecting our incoming armies to the battlefield."

The group dispersed with a new sense of urgency. I started to walk toward the town when I realized I still had an army of trees behind me. I turned back and looked up at Grollok.

"We'll figure out how to transport you there as well. For the moment, stay put and rest up. I think the Gnomes should be able to figure something out."

Grollok nodded his head and then went still. The trees slipped into their resting state and I turned toward the town.

⁊

We stood in an open field outside of Briqor, watching the horizon intently. It was only a matter of time until the doom drake crested over the hill. I was so nervous. Was this a suicide mission? Maybe. But we had no other choice. We had to stop it. We had to stop more people from getting hurt. We had to stop it from tearing more families apart and creating orphans. We had to make the world a better place than the one we were given.

Our army was huge. It looked bigger than I expected it to. The Avians were there in formation. They brought a couple hundred soldiers. Many carried spears, but they had units of archers, as well as others that carried leather sacks with rocks in them.

The Dwarves were there in the greatest quantity. Their forces might have been closer to 500 or so, with more joining the group by the moment from the city we protected behind us. They wore ornate armor. There were even a few that wore stone suits like the one Marv had found in Crag. Was that a common thing? Or were they pulling out all of the stops for this fight?

The Elves were there in a strict formation. They wore their yellow and gray robes with tall decorated helmets. Above them, the wind whipped about, a storm prepared for the monster. Some held staffs with wings attached to them by their side as they awaited the monster.

The Beastfolk still hadn't shown up. Maybe we hadn't had enough time to convince them. Or maybe they refused. I hadn't had a lot of time to look into each race's issues over the past few days. We were on a time limit and it was starting to show.

The Saurians were in a very loose group, with no clear leaders. Most carried crude bone weapons, even the ones that I knew to be magic users.

As for the Gnomes, there was only a handful of them. It might have been about 50, with about 10 of them in mechanical suits that I had seen being used to excavate the doom drake in the first place. I was hoping there were more that I couldn't see due to their illusions, but I couldn't tell. Maybe Amara wasn't as committed to this as I had thought. Maybe she was only willing to help so long as it didn't mean sacrificing her people. Whatever the case, it was something that could cost us.

The Humans were the last race present, aside from me and Palem. They also stood in a strict formation like the Elves, but their stances were more readied, less casual. They were a see of red cloaks, staring at the horizon. They even brought two catapults with them that held balls of what looked like hay.

As for the wandering forest, I guess the Gnomes were having trouble moving creatures that big. They were nowhere to be seen.

Our army wasn't enormous. Still, it was amazing to see. Never in my life had this many people of different races come together for a common goal. And to think, it was all because of the work we did on Daegal. I looked at Tigala and Lolan. It was the result of our group working together and showing that it could be done. Now the test was to see how large of a scale it would work on.

"Are you ready?" I asked looking at Tigala and Lolan.

"Can you really be ready for this kind of thing?" asked Lolan.

"I don't think so," I said.

"I don't like this," said Tigala.

"Me neither," I said. "But this is our way forward. If we want to have any kind of life, it can't be with that monster rampaging through the world taking down city after city."

"It's not that," said Tigala. She breathed out and shook her head. "I'm tired of losing people. I've lost so many, one after another. I don't want this to be just more loss."

"I know what you mean," I said. I didn't want it to be more loss either. I didn't think I could handle losing either of them. It nearly killed me to lose Zef. And that was after losing my whole race. We couldn't let this thing wipe us out and just cause more loss. "I don't know what to say. It's not like I can make any promises that we'll make it out of this."

"We will," said Lolan.

"Huh?" I asked.

"We'll make it out," he said. He looked at me and smiled halfheartedly. "There's no other option in my mind. We need to make it out of this because if we don't, there's no more world anyway."

That was a morbid way to look at it.

"Yeah, I guess," I said.

"But really," he said, "for the rest of my life, I'm never going to forget you two. If either of you dies, I won't let your story die with you. This is too important. Stopping this monster is only part of it. What we really did here is show the world that we are all the same. We may be different races. We may have different magic. But we're all people. We all want to be loved and to be safe. We just need to figure out how to look past our differences to see each other as people."

He was right. This wasn't about just stopping the monster. This was about showing others that it could be done. It was about us working together—doing what no one thought was possible.

I looked over at him. "Well said. I'll do the same for you two as well. And for Zef." Tigala didn't say it, but I could tell by the look on her face that she agreed. This was our chance to prove what we had found on Daegal, family among other races. And as scary as it was to wait for the monster to crest the horizon, I knew I'd be okay if this was where it ended.

"But let's not give up just yet," said Tigala. "We've still got a giant to topple." She grinned as she said it, ready for the challenge.

I nodded back at her. "Right."

Something shook the ground. It was subtle, but definitely something. My composure faltered slightly as I looked toward the horizon. Murmurs echoed through the army as they wondered if this was it.

In a moment, a dark figure peaked over the top of the hill. Its massive head glowed with pink magic—the metallic black scales reflecting some of the light. Curved grey horns framed its eyes which glared at us with a pale green glow. It lurked forward. More footfalls shook the ground, each one harder than the last.

The tall purple fins appeared as it continued, swaying back and forth with each step. In the distance, I could also make out the silhouette of Malcolm, riding his dragon. He still was trying to control the monster. Had he made any progress? What was the end goal here? How long did he expect it to take? Would he gain control eventually? It didn't matter anyway. One problem at a time.

This was my first real look at it when there wasn't dust covering the area. It was massive and horrifying with its lethargic movements.

So you're the one that wants to take my family from me? I thought. I stared at the monster, and for a moment, I thought it looked directly at me. *We're not giving up that easy,* I thought.

The monster continued glaring in my direction. Then, it raised its head, took a deep breath, and released a howl so loud that it was hard to keep my footing.

He was ready too.

19.2 Sequoia

"This is our shot," I yelled. "If we don't stop it here, we might not ever stop it. Give it everything you've got."

The army didn't respond, they just watched in silence as the colossus lumbered forward, seemingly growing taller by the second as it climbed the far side of the hill.

"You know what to do," I said. "Look for weak points, and exploit them. Work together. We're more effective if we can use our magic in tandem."

I looked at the army. Many of them looked scared. I was too. I couldn't imagine us defeating such a powerful monster, but what other option did we have? Our ancestors stopped it once before, we could only hope that we could manage the same.

Was there anything else I could do to prepare—to give us some kind of advantage? I tried to think of the tricks I had learned with my magic. I thought of the plant monsters and treants—the versatility my magic had. Then I remembered Palem and Kadero, using carried dirt to help in situations where they had none. I reached down and picked up two handfuls, shoving them in my bag, and in the pockets of my skirt. I couldn't imagine needing it in a battle that took place on a grassy hill, but it couldn't hurt to have it.

"It's time to fight!" yelled Rodrigo to his army of Humans. "Let's stop this monster. For Brighton!" The Humans cheered, and Rodrigo began to charge forward. The Humans followed, creating a chain reaction as the other races joined the charge

We joined too. My heart and mind raced as we ran toward a monster big enough to crush any one of our armies with a single footfall.

"You have any good ideas?" I asked Tigala and Lolan as we ran. "Any thoughts on weak points or ways we can hurt it?"

"No," said Tigala. "I'm just hoping we can overwhelm it." I turned back to the creature and looked for anything that would help in the coming fight. Along its chest was a swirl of shifting colors. It had to be a result of the magic that it was infused with, like Grollock. Maybe that could help? Or maybe that would count as a beacon? I looked for Kesq and couldn't find her. Maybe I would see her out there. More likely I'd have to experiment with it first.

The first of the Humans reached the colossus and began firing large blasts of magic at it. Some fired on their own, but many formed groups of five to ten Humans and collectively formed massive fireballs to launch at the drake.

It screamed in response and slammed down a foot. A bronze glow rippling out from the foot produced a series of stone pillars that shot from the ground, tearing through the thickest section of the Human formation. Several Humans were launched into the air.

The Avians were close behind. A few flew to the air, catching Humans that had been launched. Flashes of purple magic preceded several Gnomes appearing in the air, grabbing falling Humans, and then disappearing again.

Good. We were working together, so far at least. That was what we needed if we were going to make it out of this.

There were more races attacking the doom drake now. Saurians were shooting torrents of water at and under the monster's feet. Other Saurians ran forward and froze portions of the water into ice. They weren't trying to lock the foot in place though. Instead, they were making thick icy patches beneath it, limiting the monster's traction. The foot began to slip and the Saurians continued their assault.

The monster, for its part, was focusing on storm magic. The sky darkened with black swirling clouds, and lightning jumped from cloud to cloud. Rain began to pour down without relent.

I looked to the Elves who had now reached the creature as well. They focused mainly on creating a thick fog, that they directed above the battlefield, toward the drake's face. They struggled to send it high enough to block the creature's vision due to the monster's own storm.

The drake screamed and used a claw to swipe through a portion of the army. Bodies flew through the air, and three furrows in the ground were all that was left behind. This wasn't good. We were barely hurting the thing.

I looked to Tigala and Lolan who both seemed to be figuring out where and how they could help. I gave them a nod, and they returned it. Then I ran for the monster's legs where the Saurians were.

It was chaos. There were so many types of magic firing off that it was hard to know what was magic and what wasn't. The ground was pulled up, and people yelled orders or screamed for help.

I ran through a group of Avains that held spears. They were charging the beast as well, several with white glowing eyes.

A group of Dwarves was shifting stones, altering the battlefield to make it hard for the monster to stand on level ground. I ran through the maze of earth spikes, continuing toward one foot.

The doom drake screamed again. I looked up to see it looking back down in my general direction. It breathed deep and then red flames blasted from its mouth.

The flames barreled toward me. I looked around for something to take cover under. I settled for an angled earthen spike that the Dwarves had made. I felt the heat, but it was reduced, more so than I even expected from the makeshift shelter I had found. I peaked around the spike at the sky and saw the flames being redirected. They rippled outward in a dome shape well above my head. I looked around and saw Rodrigo with a group of other Humans using red magic to control the torrent.

The flames faded out and I was back to running. The monster swung its claw behind me. I only heard the screams of the warriors it struck.

I looked back wondering if there was anything I could do to help. I found a Gnome still strapped into a crumpled machination. He was screaming and clawing at his legs.

I rushed to his side. "What is it?"

"It's melting! My legs!" he screamed.

"Hang on, I'm coming," I yelled. I climbed onto the machine and began prying at the straps that held him in place. Once they were free, I saw the real problem amidst his screams of pain. His leg was pinned in the metal, the section glowing red with heat.

I grew a root as fast as I could, thinking back to Riak and how he was able to dig much better with roots than vines. I snaked it into the metal and used it to pry the two pieces apart. When the Gnome had the slightest opening, he pulled himself free with his hands, leaving his legs limp behind him. He toppled onto the battlefield and panted for breath. I looked at his legs. They were black and gooey from the burning metal. I couldn't tell if I was looking at skin or fabric.

"Help!" I yelled. "We need a teleporter!"

I looked around for anyone that could fix this and as I did, I heard the word 'teleporter' echo around me. I looked down to see the Gnome creating an illusionary cone of purple magic. He was amplifying my request.

In a moment, Porthos appeared in front of us in a swirl of violet energy. He looked down at the Gnome and then back at me with worry on his face. "I'll get him out of here," he said. "Stay safe."

"You too," I said, but he was already teleporting away.

I looked around at the battlefield. It was still chaos, but the groups were starting to mix more than when we had arrived. Humans seemed to be positioned throughout to protect against fire attacks. Saurians were now hitting the drake from all angles. Dwarves were creating obstacles and cover all over the battlefield.

We were surviving, so far at least. We were finding ways to help each other. I looked up at the monster. It was still as big as when we first saw it. I looked for wounds or weak points. There were pockmarks of red flesh showing across its body now. They were scratches relative to the size of the creature itself, but at least it was progress.

I was close to the monster's foot now. The Saurians were still trying to trip it. However, it was so large that they were having trouble affecting it. I wasn't sure that I could help, but I needed to try. With enough plants, maybe we could pin it. And if we could pin it, maybe we could actually topple this giant.

The foot stepped forward, breaking free of the Saurian's restraints in a spray of ice shards. But the step helped, putting me closer to it. I ran to where it was due to touch down and began growing plants on the spot. I focused again on roots, hoping that the tougher exterior would be enough to hold the monster's foot.

The foot landed with another earth-shattering impact. Bronze light spread from it in a series of cracks spiraling outward. The Dwarves yelled, preparing for the incoming attack.

The earth erupted. Stone exploded out, launching people into the air. Others were swallowed up into holes in the ground. I saw the split that was headed for me and did my best to grab onto the root I had been growing. The widening crevice loosened the root from the soil, and it began to collapse into the pit. I used my magic to make the root throw me in the direction of nearby ground that had been untouched. I landed, skidding against the dirt and rock, scraping my arms. It was the least of my worries in a fight of this size.

I pulled myself to my feet and searched for my root that had sunk into the hole. It was still intact, and only part-way underground. I looked back at the drake's foot as I heard the sound of moving earth again. An aftershock was headed my way, along the same path as the crack that had already been formed. It was closing the cracks that had just opened up.

I focused on the root and slammed the top of it onto the solid ground outside of the crevice. It pulled itself out just in time for the ground to close up.

The monster's foot was now stationary. Now was my chance, if I was going to have one. I wrapped the root around it, focusing all of my magic into it. It grew stronger and stretched to cover the entire clawed black foot. I dug it back into the ground on the opposite side and made it fork into the earth to anchor it. Then I grew more.

The second one went faster than the first. It felt different, like when I had used magic in tandem with Riak.

"Thought I'd help," said Palem. I looked and found him standing next to me with Bubba at the ready. His hands glowed green with magic.

I gave him a slight smile and doubled my efforts on the root.

Saurians arrived at the monster's foot, and they too began washing out the earth beneath it and freezing the water in its place. They created spikes of ice anchoring it to the ground.

Then more earth shot up around the foot, but this wasn't meant to harm us. Dwarves had circled around it, with Cairn being one of them. They worked in tandem, covering the foot with stone.

Palem and I had finished our third root now and it was properly anchored. This was working. We might be able to get the doom drake prone. Then we could hurt its more vulnerable parts. Now we just needed something to lure it to step forward.

I looked up at it. It was sending down another torrent of fire that was being blocked by the Humans. It looked angry as it screamed at us.

"Hit it harder!" I yelled. "Get him to take another step!" A female Human with short hair looked at me and nodded. She yelled an order to nearby Humans that I couldn't make out. They collectively formed a massive fireball. Before they launched it at the monster, they backed up, allowing it to grow larger with each step. It was something the monster probably wouldn't want to get hit with.

The monster screamed again and tried to take another step forward to swipe at the Humans. The drake tried to pull up its foot causing rock and ice to pop around it. Most of it stayed put, holding the foot where it was. Palem and I focused on strengthening the existing roots as the foot pulled. It was strong, but our anchors were holding. The monster's weight shifted forward. He was off balance, but just as I thought we had him, our restraints broke in a spray of stone and ice.

My heart dropped, but then I realized we had done enough. The monster had already leaned too far forward and its foot was held back long enough that it wouldn't be able to catch itself. The doom drake fell forward. People screamed as they hurried to get clear of the falling colossus. Flashes of violet marked the Gnomes teleporting in and out to save people from the impact. Avians with white glowing eyes led others to locations they deemed safe from the fall.

"Get ready!" I yelled. "We need to pin it down as soon as it hits!" The monster fell like a falling tree—no, like a falling mountain. It was slow and fast at the same time. It finally touched down. The earth shook hard enough to knock me off of my feet. Dust billowed out from the drake and for a brief moment, everything was still.

We couldn't waste any time. If we wanted to stop it, we needed to take advantage of anything we could, and that included the monster being prone.

I sprinted into the cloud of dust and blindly formed vines and roots. I could only tell where they were by the faint green glow through the dust. I told them to search and I could feel where they met resistance and where they didn't. I could feel the basic form of the monster, though I had no sense of texture to be sure they were reaching over the heavy scales of the beast. Nonetheless, I had a pretty good idea of where it was, and sent my vines over it, winding and twisting to form a web of knots wherever possible.

I saw more spots glowing green that weren't from me, and was able to make out the faint silhouette of Palem riding Bubba not too far from me. His vines connected to mine.

"Come on!" I yelled, hoping others would join soon. "Pin it down." Other cries rang across the battlefield. It was so much noise, between explosions, shifting rock, screams of pain, and commands from the various battlefield commanders. I continued to focus on my plants.

More people joined the effort. Rocks tore from the earth and rested on the monster's limbs. More ice formed around its edges, working its way slowly over the bulkier part of its colossal back. There was even a Beastfolk, shaping some kind of metal to extend the same way Mila had managed to stretch her limbs. The metal reached across the monster. One more anchor point. One more chance that we might actually be able to keep this thing down.

Is this really going to work?

The monster was still for the time being. Did we hurt it? Was it resting? Then, there was a huff of breath from somewhere around the monster's head. I looked and saw the dark silhouette of the creature's head and neck, lifting from the ground. I guess no one had pinned that part yet? It raised well above our heads and stayed still for a moment. The ambient light around it seemed to get brighter. Then it screamed again.

It twitched its body, trying to break free of the restraints. Some rocks broke and some of my vines snapped, but it was stuck.

Then the drake decided it had had enough. Its front arm flexed with muscle, and there was a loud series of pops and cracks as the monster pulled its top half free.

It screamed again, angry that its lower half was still pinned. Then, with a burst of violet smoke, the monster disappeared entirely. *Where did it go?* I thought, afraid of what the answer might be.

It seemed others were thinking the same thing. Someone yelled, "Up there!" I looked in the general direction that a nearby Avian pointed. Up above us was a dark shadow looming over us, and it was coming down fast. I ran to escape the impact of its body once more. It slammed into the earth and this time a tidal wave formed from its feet and continued outward.

People were sucked up into the water and slammed against the ground, debris, and other people.

Why did it even let us trip it if it can just teleport out of restraints? I thought. *Was it playing with us? Was it enjoying the slow destruction of a small army that had the audacity to challenge it?*

I ran toward the wave. The water rushed forward, but I saw what I was aiming for. I scaled one of my vines that had been holding the creature down, and the water slammed into it. It swayed at first, threatening to pull free of the ground. I focused, strengthening the roots, begging it to hold. But the water was quicker and stronger. It pulled out and plunged me into the backside of the tidal wave. The water swirled and slammed me against the ground, rocks, and anything else. It hurt. When I finally gained my bearings enough to pull my head above the water, I opened my eyes.

The looming monster was no longer there. It had disappeared entirely. Was it using a different kind of magic now? Did it disappear with illusion magic?

I continued looking for it and didn't see it anywhere. Then, behind me, I heard a distant explosion of masonry. I looked over my shoulder and found that the doom drake was already in Briqor. It teleported in. The city erupted with destruction, and it was too far away for any of us to help.

19.3 Sequoia

The doom drake tore through the city. Debris exploded into the sky with each strike. And we were miles away.

I looked around for others. Many were reeling from the previous attacks and the fall of the monster. The dust still hadn't fully settled and the monster was already well into destroying Briqor.

Was there any way for me to get there? Maybe I could help evacuate? They did announce that it wasn't safe there, but we had hoped we could slow the monster down. They were supposed to have more time to evacuate. There was no way that everyone was out by now.

I didn't care how far it was. I had to try. I had to do whatever I could to get there and protect the people who were caught unaware. I began running. There had to be a way.

The monster continued its rampage in the distance. It was hitting harder now, destroying buildings much faster than it had made attacks on us. Had we not affected it at all? Why would it not kill us quickly and get it over with? I knew it was bent on destruction, so why not destroy? Maybe it was saving its energy for the town. But that didn't really make sense. It didn't seem like it slowed at all. Maybe it was testing us, seeing if we were an actual opponent. Maybe it got bored with attacking us.

I couldn't be sure about any of it, but that was the best I could think of. Still, it was hard to believe that we were that ineffective against it.

There was a shadow above me, and I looked up to see a dragon flying in the direction of the monster. Malcolm. Even the distant sight of him made me angry.

I was a distance from the carnage behind me now and I was already winded. It had been a long day, and I was already running a lot to try and take down the monster the first time.

I heard something just behind me. Footsteps hit the ground not too far away. I looked back and saw Porthos, a violet portal still blinking out of existence behind him.

"What are you doing?" he huffed.

"We didn't stall it long enough," I said. "There are still people in there."

"You're trying to help them escape," he said as a statement rather than a question.

"I can't let it kill more, especially people that are unable to protect themselves. There are families in there."

"I can teleport you part of the way," said Porthos, "but not that far." It was further than the range I had seen any Gnome teleport without a teleportation gate. I would need an army of Gnomes to get over there quickly, and Gnomes were among the least represented at the battle.

My eyes settled on the shadow again and I looked back up at Malcolm's dragon.

"Can you get me up there?" I asked, still running.

"Why would you want to do something like that?" asked Porthos.

"That's the fastest route over there. I need to get there, and he is no doubt headed to Briqor to try and tame the doom drake again."

Porthos took a deep breath. "You're sure?"

"Yes," I said. "Put me on the tail." I stopped running and Porthos focused on the purple glow in front of him. As it grew, he spread his hands further apart as if stretching open the portal that was being formed.

"Good luck," he said. "Don't get yourself killed."

I couldn't make any promises.

"Wait, Kaia," Tigala called after me. "I can fly you there. Let me transform." She was far enough behind us that she had to yell to be heard.

I looked back at her and then lowered my eyes as I swallowed hard. She stopped her pursuit, knowing she wouldn't reach me in time, and I stepped through the portal.

In an instant, there was a rush of wind around me. I fell through the air and caught the dragon's tail in my chest. I grabbed as soon as I realized what I had hit, and kept myself from slipping free of it.

The dragon roared at my arrival, shaking Malcolm, and another person who sat behind him on the beast.

"Woah, calm down," said Malcolm, agitated.

I watched nervously as they kept their heads facing forward. Then I repositioned myself so that I had a better grip on the dragon. I threw a leg over it and hugged the tail with my whole body, to keep a low profile in their peripheral and to keep myself attached well.

I knew I should have waited for Tigala to fly me to Briqor. It was safer, and I'm sure I broke her trust in me on some level, but I needed to deal with this first. I needed to deal with *him*.

"We need to go back," said the Human I didn't recognize. "We must have gotten something wrong. Despite all of the mind magic you have put into the colossus, it still doesn't show any signs of listening to you. We need to either figure out why or stop it. Brighton is already—"

"I already told you no, Arthur. It will give in eventually. It's just a matter of time," said Malcolm.

"But you don't understand. We're lucky it hasn't turned on us yet. If it does, then all we did was unleash it on the world. I know you have better plans than that, but we need this to work, or we need to stop it."

"It will work. We're not going back." Malcolm's anger was audible. "If you want to, leave whenever you feel like it, but I have a mission, and I am going to see it through. This is how we make the world a better place."

"Only if it works," said Arthur.

"It will," said Malcolm.

Arthur must have counted that as Malcolm ending the conversation. He didn't press further and instead sat awkwardly behind Malcolm, just in front of the dragon's massive wings.

It was hard to believe that this creature had attacked the colony just a couple of weeks ago, and now I was riding it to an even bigger threat.

I looked up at the two Humans again. Malcolm kept his face forward and shoulders stern. How did he think that controlling that monster was making the world a better place? Sure, people fight. Other races have hurt Humans. But everyone has the same story. We all were hurt by others.

Maybe it was just my experience on Daegal talking, but I was beginning to think that race meant very little. It was superficial. Sure, some people looked different than others.

Different races had different cultures and customs. And different races had problems with each other. But as a reason to hurt someone, it was just a line drawn in the sand. It was an excuse to avoid dealing with the fact that we all do things we regret. We all hurt other people. To ignore that fact was to become the people you are trying to destroy.

But at the same time, I hated him. The last time I had seen Malcolm, he had told me that he killed my family. I had wanted to kill him. I wanted him dead for what he did. And now, I hung onto the dragon that he rode with him completely unaware. This was my chance if I was ever going to have one.

Should I? I thought. I readjusted myself and grabbed the knife I had strapped into my belt. I didn't know who Arthur was, but he didn't look like the type to be any good in a fight. I could probably knock him off of the dragon without him having a chance to defend himself. And then, I could take Malcolm out. I could stop him from mind-controlling the monster. I could remove the person that caused so much pain from the world. One less monster to deal with later.

Even if we could take down the monster, we would still have to deal with him. It was only a matter of time. I might as well save us the time and do it now, right? I would be helping our cause. Wouldn't I?

I took a deep breath as I imagined it. The anger still boiled inside of me, imagining him killing my parents. Him being the one that left me an orphan, alone in the woods. He took my childhood. He took my culture from me. He turned me into a thief. And he hurt countless others in the same ways or worse.

Abigail lost her mother. So did Coran, as frustrating as the kid was. He took Cairn's husband. He killed Garlar,

Ferek, Seth, and Wallace. He killed Zef. He tortured countless people, all for the chance to kill more—to eradicate the earth of all other races. If anyone was a monster, it was him.

But could I do it? Could I plunge a dagger into someone? I looked at the blade. It wasn't just any dagger, it was my father's. My father wouldn't have done it. He respected life too much. He only fought that final day because he was forced to. Because he knew that if we went peacefully, I would have died along with them.

My face was hot with rage, yet I couldn't convince myself to do it. Killing Malcolm would solve so many of my problems, right? I would finally get revenge for the people I had lost. I would avenge their deaths. My parents. Zef.

What would he do in this situation? I thought. He would probably make a joke and try to convince Malcolm to join our cause. I shook my head again. Killing Malcolm felt like the easy solution. It felt the way to fix things the quickest. But everything told me that it wasn't what I should do.

I didn't care. It was what needed to be done. This was no longer a game where we get to go camping and searching the woods for missing people. No, this had turned into a war, whether I liked it or not. And you can't be weak in war. You have to strike first before you are struck.

I began crawling forward with the dagger in hand. I glared at the two of them as the wind blew past my face. I was angry, and I let all of that anger flood into me. I needed to do it. I needed to be the good soldier and take advantage of the opportunity provided to me. I needed to kill Malcolm.

I crawled forward slowly, pushing against the wind. Each inch I gained was an inch closer to ending the pain, ending the hurt.

I reached out for the back of Arthur and hesitated before I grabbed. Malcolm spoke at that exact moment.

"The drake attacks in a cycle," he said. "It destroys and then re—" The rest of the words faded from my mind. *Cycle.* It brought back a memory of Zef.

Hatred breeds hatred. Someone has to be the first to break the cycle.

I stopped in my tracks thinking over the phrase, wishing I could find another meaning for it, or a way to ignore it. But I couldn't. Zef was right. If I killed Malcolm now, it wouldn't solve anything. It would only damage me. It might stop some of the pain right now, but it would break more ties. It would only hurt more people in the long run. It would hurt me. I would be a killer. Not by accident this time, but with the literal blood on my hands.

I tried to turn back and get back to my seat on the tail to avoid being seen, but at that very moment, the doom drake roared, and a stray fireball flew our way. Malcolm yelled to the dragon, and it swerved to dodge the hit. The quick change of course knocked me off balance and threw me forward into Arthur's back.

Arthur screamed as he lost his grip on the dragon and slipped off the side. I did everything I could to hold on and try to grab him at the same time, but I wasn't quick enough.

Malcolm turned his head around. "Arthur, are you—" Then he saw me.

"You," he said with an anger that rivaled my own. "How many times do I have to kill you?"

169

19.4 Sequoia

I looked at Malcolm and then over the edge of the dragon that we stood on.

"I didn't mean to," I said.

"Oh, didn't you?" said Malcolm. "This is what we do. Why wouldn't you be just waiting for your chance to kill me?"

"No," I said. "I decided not to." I looked down at the knife still in my hand and tucked it back in at my hip. "I want your help."

He let out an abrupt laugh like he was genuinely surprised that the words came out of my mouth. "You want my help? And what would I possibly help you with?"

"Stopping that monster. It killed Humans. It's going to kill more. Arthur was right. Whatever you're doing isn't working and we need to stop it before it's beyond stopping."

"Ah, so you were listening in too. Clever. It must have been a heck of teleportation spell to get you up here," said Malcolm, ignoring my request. "No. I'll control that monster, and then I'll kill all who stand in the way of the Humans."

"Even if you do, do you really think that's going to solve anything?" I said. "If you kill every single other race, wipe them out, you'll find new lines to divide yourselves on.

Maybe it'll be height or hair color. Something will become the new line in the sand. At what point does it stop if you allow it now?"

"We're Humans," he glared at me now. Had I said something that resonated? "We take care of the Humans while every other race has and will kill us at any chance they get. It is up to us to secure our place in this world. This is how we do it."

"You're wrong. This is how you continue the cycle of grief. You are fueling the inevitable end of life on this planet by keeping that thing alive." As if it wasn't clue enough that the monster he woke up had tried to end the world once before.

Malcolm sighed. "I really hoped you would have something more interesting to say to me before I finally killed you."

My eyes widened. I had run into Malcolm before, not just in the cavern that the monster crawled from. He was with Havik. He was probably the Elf in the cave under the tower. He was the one who tamed the dragon in the first place. He was strong, with multiple forms of magic. He was strong enough to take me out in an instant. I had to stall.

"Wait," I said. "What's the rush with killing me? What if I'm right? What if you can't mind control that thing. I'm not saying it's necessarily going to go down that way, but if you couldn't, wouldn't you want help to stop it?"

"I wouldn't accept help from a Treek most of all. If I fail to control the doom drake, which I won't, then I will take it out with the help of other Humans."

I looked over the edge of the dragon. We were over Briqor now. *Good.* I scanned the ground for something that might make for a softer landing. It was all stone buildings.

"But would you want to sacrifice Human lives to take that monster down? Sure, you can protect yourself against it, but what about the Humans that only wield fire magic? They have no real defenses against the monster's other magic. Why not send in the other races to kill it and then you could clean up the remaining forces."

"Then why do I need you, a single Treek? I could kill you now and still enact your plan."

"Because they believe in me. If you kill me, they won't unite. Keep me alive and they'll rally around me to fight the monster."

"Hmm," said Malcolm, contemplating the point. "That's a very good idea," he said. He relaxed his posture a fraction. Then, without warning, he threw his hands up and shot a blast of fire at me. I barely managed to dodge it in time without toppling off of the dragon.

"But I think I'll take my chances. You're too much of a nuisance to keep alive." He raised his hands again and leveled them at me. I didn't have time. I dove off of the dragon as the heat burned the tips of my hair. I plummeted toward the ground below.

The wind rushed around my face as the tiny town of Briqor grew closer and closer.

This was a stupid thing to do. The kind of thing that Tigala would have yelled at me for. And I'm sure she was already mad at me for teleporting to the dragon in the first place. I looked around for a wyvern, hoping she had somehow caught up with us. No such luck. I wasn't going to hear the end of this one, that is, if I got the chance.

The city grew closer by the second. Ruined streets and buildings would be my welcoming party. I had to think of something, but it was so hard to do with the wind making it impossible to keep my eyes open for more than a second.

Think. Think. Think. What can I do? I could try and reach out for plants in the buildings, but by the time they were in range, it would be too late to grow something to catch me. I couldn't see any parks or grassy areas from where I was, and the only thing that would help in an area like that would be a tree. I might be able to bend the branches to soften my landing. But that was if I had a tree to work with. I didn't.

Something was flapping against my thigh in the wind. I grabbed it. It was the pocket of my skirt, heavy with the dirt I had filled it with!

I wasted no time, pushing my magic into the small clump of dirt as I fell.

I could grow a vine, but that would only be useful if I landed on it in the right way. I could only control the fall so much. So instead, I decided to rely on my ancestors. Apparently, I was good with animating plants because my people were as well. I hoped they would be with me now.

I grew a vine creature like the one I grew to show off for Kadero and Coran. Vines spilled out of the dirt clump wrapping around each other. The ends flailed in the wind, making them annoying to control. I wound them tighter and wrapped the cord of vines around the central dirt clump, still inside of my pocket.

Once I had the dirt secured, I grew more vines out of every side, using the first vines to pull the clump free of my pocket. They wound around and formed limbs for the creature. But I couldn't just settle with a small plant creature. I needed something big. Big enough to take the impact and keep me from going splat.

I pushed harder. Then I thought about what Palem had told me. Nature magic comes easier with hope. I focused on the hope I had for Lolan to have his brother back, free of the brainwashing. I thought of Tigala, the friend she had become and how far we'd come together—the hope that I could see her again and apologize.

The vine monster grew faster, doubling its speed. And it was good because I was getting close to impact. I looked down at the ground and began to panic. *No. Hope,* I thought, trying my best to refocus.

I closed my eyes as I thought of the friends I had made along the way and the hope I had that we would all survive this monster and get to celebrate together.

I could feel the vine creature grow even faster than before. I used as much of my magic as I had available, strengthening it and making it more sturdy.

We spun in the air. The ground would be close, but I kept my eyes closed. I called the vine creature to grab me. It hugged me against its chest and put its back to the wind.

Then we hit.

I woke up with my head pounding. Around me lay a pile of vines so long that I couldn't see the end of them. They laid over buildings and streets like someone had spilled green paint in streaks across the city. My landing place was a darker green and slimy from the plant matter that instantly turned to mash as it hit. But it was enough. I survived!

I pushed myself to my feet and the smaller vines fell off of me, deflated. I couldn't believe I had made that. I created a plant giant, without using the nature magic from Grollock. Just as amazing was the fact that it saved me from the fall by exploding beneath me; a giant nature pillow.

But I didn't have time to focus on the plant giant I had made. I had to help. The town was in danger, and many innocent Dwarves would still be there.

I hobbled toward the monster as quickly as I could manage. I looked up to see Malcolm had made it to the monster's head and was using his pink magic again.

I didn't know how we were supposed to take the monster down, but I feared having to take on Malcolm almost as much. I couldn't think about that now. Now I needed to help. I needed to get anyone I could free of the chaos.

I ran, keeping an eye out for anyone in trouble. A few Dwarves passed me, a family with several young children. The mother clutched one as she ran. They saw me and looked with wide eyes as they ran in the opposite direction of the monster.

I continued, heading for the destruction.

Ahead of me, a crater broke through the road and still burned with fire magic. Several buildings were torn to pieces.

"Help!" I heard someone scream. It was coming from one of the buildings.

I changed course and ran toward the sound.

The building's front wall was still intact, made of a single slab of stone. As I stepped in, I could see the collapsed upper floor bowing toward the next room.

It was a short house, perfect for the Dwarves but limiting for me. With every step, I was watching my head as well as my footing.

The next room was some kind of common room. It had seating areas and a stone table. The side wall was blown out entirely showing the remains of the neighboring building.

And there, between the two houses was a female Dwarf. "Help!" she screamed again, not seeing me.

"What happe—" I started, until I saw what she was yelling about. One of the exterior walls had fallen in a large chunk on another Dwarf. Another female Dwarf laid in the rubble, struggling to get her lower half free from being pinned beneath it.

The Dwarf that was calling for help looked at me with wide eyes. Her blonde hair was frayed and unkempt.

"I'm here to help," I said, raising my hands. I seemed to be doing a lot of that gesture lately.

The blonde Dwarf kept her eyes on me while turning her head to face the Dwarf under the rubble. "Uh. Can…Can you get her out?" she said, hesitating with each word.

"I can try," I said. "You don't know any magic?"

The blonde Dwarf shook her head.

"Okay, but you're going to have to trust me. I'm going to do what I can to get her out." The Dwarf nodded as she continued to stare at me.

I worked on my magic, growing from the dirt in the front yard of the neighboring building that was visible from where we stood. I would normally just grow a vine, but Palem had gotten me thinking about the plant creatures. I was good at it. It was in my blood. And having a creature at my disposal would be helpful for other people as well. So I grew a vine monster. I made this one smaller than the last. It was harder to grow than the one that I grew while falling. Maybe my magic had kicked in at double strength because my life depended on it. Or maybe it was easier to focus my hopes when they were about to be taken away. Either way, I grew this plant monster until it was about the height of Tigala. The blonde Dwarf's expression didn't change the entire time, other than becoming more pronounced.

I told the creature to take a step, uprooting itself and spraying dirt as it walked. It walked over to the rock laying on the pinned Dwarf. It was hard to be precise with the large monster. I wasn't used to it whether it was in my blood or not. I took it slow, commanding the creature to bend slowly, then stick limbs beneath the stone. Then, the creature squatted and lifted the rock slightly. The stone groaned at the pressure. I had the creature lift a little further, and the pinned Dwarf pushed herself back. The blonde ran over and grabbed her friend by the armpits, pulling her backward. When the Dwarf's legs were clear of the slab, I let it fall, sending a wave of dust over us.

The blonde Dwarf looked up at me, "Thank you." She let the words hang.

"Can you two get out of here alright?" I asked.

"We'll manage," she said, holding the injured Dwarf upright with an arm around her shoulder.

They began hobbling toward the edge of town. I walked over to my vine creature and looked it over. It was impressive. Being made of a series of twisted vines, I could see it being extremely useful in a fight. It was so much versatility packed into a neat package that could move around with me.

I had it lower its hands and stepped into them. Then, at my command, the monster lifted me up and I climbed onto its shoulders and sat down. I held the vines on the top of its head as reins, and let the creature carry me out into the street where I could look for the next person in trouble.

But when I arrived back on the road, I looked around for the doom drake and didn't see it anywhere. *Is it laying down or something, doing more damage on all fours?* But the sound of buildings being destroyed had also stopped.

177

I commanded my vine creature to climb the ruined edge of a building, with me still mounted on its shoulders. It took some work, but we finally made it to the roof of the building. I looked out on the horizon and my suspicions were confirmed. The monster was gone. And worse yet, Briqor had been reduced to rubble.

20 Ash

20.1 Ash

What do we do now? It was the question all of us had been thinking. It had only been two days since Briqor was destroyed, and five more towns and cities had been leveled since then. What were we supposed to do? We only had small armies in comparison to an unstoppable world-ending beast. And people weren't willing to trust the other races enough to band together. Even with more ambassadors reaching out each day, it wasn't enough. There was too much hatred. Too much pain and hurt. There were too many things that they were unwilling to overlook, even if it meant that we were all going to go down together.

It was frustrating. I looked out over the rooftops of Birdsbane in the direction of the cavern that the monster had crawled out of. "I'm sorry, Zef," I said under my breath.

It was hard to imagine what he would have done in this situation. Was he wrong? More importantly, was Malcolm right? Were we destined to fail from the start? I shook my head.

Tigala sat on the edge of the rooftop in front of me, staring out at the city pretending she didn't hear me climb up.

"Hey," I said. "Can we talk?"

"Go ahead," she said.

"I'm sorry," I said. "I wasn't trying to hurt you."

She didn't say anything and just continued staring with her back to me.

"I needed to answer something for myself," I said.

"Did you?"

"Yeah," I said, lowering my eyes. "He killed my parents. He took my people away. I had to decide what I wanted to do about it. And I didn't know if I could be honest with myself otherwise."

"And what did you choose?"

"I chose to spare him. As easy as it would have been to kill him then and there, it's not what we're fighting for. I would be just as bad as him if I did it."

Tigala nodded. "Do you know why that hurt so much?" There was emotion in her voice.

"Because you've lost a lot of people?" I guessed.

"Because my sister did the exact same thing to me, and she didn't come back." Tigala looked down over the ledge. "I've spent years thinking about what I would say to her if she did survive. I wanted to scream at her. I wanted to hug her. I wanted to punch and shake her."

She took a deep breath. I wasn't about to interrupt her.

"She sacrificed herself for a greater cause. And now that I'm here, I've realized that her cause was flawed. She died to kill hundreds of Gnomes and win a battle in a war that was never going to be won." Tigala turned, not facing me, but enough for me to see the anger in her face. "And what does she have to show for it now? What do I have to show for it?" She held up her stump of an arm and stared at it.

"You didn't know any better," I said quietly. "It's how we were raised."

"It doesn't change the fact that my sister is gone because she believed in something too strongly."

I swallowed. "Are you saying you don't want to do this anymore? You don't want to fight for this cause?"

"I'm saying it was stupid. It was reckless like all of the previous times you dove head-first into something you didn't understand. I think this is the right thing to do. Maybe I'm wrong, maybe I'm right. But the next time you throw yourself into danger, think about the people who care about you." She twisted around to look at me. "It's great to fight for a cause, but don't let that cause consume you. You won't always be so lucky, and when you aren't, you're going to leave people behind that have already lost a lot."

"I'm sorry," I said. "I didn't know."

"Say it," she said. "Say you'll think of me before you attempt something like that again."

I nodded. "I'll think about you next time."

"Good," she said. "I don't expect you to let the monster win just because I'd be hurt. I just need to know you're thinking about the consequences." She pushed herself to her feet.

"I will," I said.

Tigala stepped off of the ledge and walked toward the ruined section that provided a path back to the street. "We should go to that meeting in the town square."

"Yeah," I said, and I followed her down the rubble. I stayed silent, unsure of whether or not she'd still needed to cool down a bit.

We still hadn't debriefed from the battle at Briqor. There were no teleportation gates near the battlefield since it wasn't a region with many Gnomes. Without gates, teleportation took a lot more time, especially with so many people. So we were brought back to Birdsbane in groups. I stayed to help feed the remaining soldiers that were waiting to be teleported out, while Tigala returned in an earlier group to help with sharing information.

"You okay?" Tigala asked.

"I don't know," I said. "Is anyone okay while that thing keeps rampaging around?"

She shook her head.

"Do you have any ideas?" I asked.

"No. I know we can convince some people to help, but to convince enough to stop the monster? It doesn't sound possible at this point."

"Maybe we can do it another way. What about the veins? If Klaus was right, those would have been the remnants of the people who trapped the monster on Daegal in the first place. Maybe there are clues there. Maybe we can use the veins to stop it."

"That's a lot of maybes," she said. "Besides, you almost killed all of us the last time you used those veins."

"Not entirely true. When I grew the treeling for Grollok, I used the vein that was now at the center of his chest. That's kind of the same thing. And he's on our side now. We have a walking bank of nature magic with us."

"Again, it's a lot of maybes. We don't know enough to keep coming out on top when we're in over our heads." She looked in the same direction that I had been looking. "Zef died because of our lack of knowledge."

"He—" I stopped. Had he? He was helping me escape. If we had known what Malcolm was planning, then yeah, we would have been better prepared. But how were we supposed to know that beforehand?

"Yeah, I guess you're right," I said. "But we can't just wait for the world to end. We can't wait for the doom drake to come for us. There has to be something we can do."

"Maybe there is, but I don't know what it is," said Tigala.

I sighed. It hurt to know what I knew and not be able to do anything about it.

We arrived at the town square of Birdsbane. The city laid in ruins around us. The people spread across it finding makeshift seats and platforms to get a better view. The armies that joined in the attack against the titan were represented in a smaller number, but it still made for a larger showing of people in this courtyard than our previous gatherings.

"Thank you all for coming," said Klaus. He stood on the steps in front of a church addressing the crowd. Others stood with him, Rodrigo, Tallesia, Sparr, and Sillius among them. They were people I knew to be in the core group that was looking for a solution to the doom drake problem. I was part of the group as well, but aside from providing information, I opted to skip the presentation this time.

A woman I didn't recognize stood close to Rodrigo. *Is that who Rodrigo was looking for on Daegal?* I thought.

"As many of you know, we have mounted an attack on the doom drake and it did not go as we had hoped it would. The monster has proved more powerful than we had expected. We have seen it use fire, earth, storm, water, nature, and teleportation magic, but we should assume that it can use any known form of magic."

People exchanged glances. Some whispered to each other.

"Our magic has proven ineffective against the giant, but that does not mean hope is lost. This creature was beaten before, and we can do it again."

I wasn't sure I would have used the word 'beaten' to describe what happened before. It was *delayed* before. That was the best they were able to do.

"One weakness that has been reported is that it seems unable to use two types of magic at the same time. Even when it used storm magic, and a thunderstorm remained through the battle, the Elves reported that the storm slowed each time the monster focused on a different type of magic. We have reason to believe that this may be something we can exploit in future battles."

I hadn't noticed the storm getting weaker when the doom drake used different attacks. Then again, it was hard to keep track of much in the thick of it. It was pure chaos at the feet of that monster.

"Also of note: the doom drake only seems to be attacking at full strength when destroying towns and cities. The army that confronted it reported that the monster failed to land any devastating attacks on our people. It also played along, exchanging blows long enough for our soldiers to knock it down. Then, once it had fallen and we may have been able to attack its vital areas, it teleported to Briqor instead. But we are unsure why it didn't teleport there in the first place and avoid the fight entirely. Maybe it was curious, or maybe it has to wait between teleports.

"Either way, we plan to make another attack on the creature, but before we do, we need to have as many people as possible. The monster is on a rampage. It will destroy us all as long as we don't oppose it. Please, I urge you all to convince as many people as possible to help us stop this threat to the world."

"What's the point?" said someone. "If that thing didn't hold back, none of us would be here. I'm going home to be with my family in the time I have left."

There was a sound of agreement throughout the crowd as others considered the option. They were scared, and they should be. I was scared too.

"Yes, that is an option too," said Klaus. "While fighting together is our only chance, it is still a very slim chance. We may lose even *if* we had everyone working together. So if you believe that spending the time you have left with loved ones is the best choice for you, we won't hold it against you. You may use the teleporter to return home when you are ready."

I looked at Tigala who returned a worried glance. There were more murmurs in the crowd, and then one person pushed through toward the edge of the courtyard. Others followed, shuffling out of the crowd and presumably returning to prepare for their departure. When the crowd had settled, we were left with about two-thirds of the army we had before.

"For those of you who do plan to stay, thank you. Please, convince as many as you can to join the fight. Our next planned attack is in three days."

20.2 Interlude: Brendell

The deep breath hurt. Brendell's chest rose and fell, but it felt distant. It was somewhere else. Somewhere where he wasn't.

Where was he? He wasn't sure. Somewhere locked inside of a dream. Everything was black. There was no movement, nothing to focus on. He was trapped in an endless expanse of darkness. A motionless ocean.

His chest rose and fell again. It grew closer this time. His head, also distant, rolled to the side. The motion was delayed, like the ripple of a far-off stone thrown into the water.

His chest rose and fell again, this time something caught. Something didn't feel right. It was rough. And the incoming air scratched at him. He reacted, coughing. The action shook his body and brought back pain he didn't know he had. His head pounded with the sudden motion. His back was stiff and ached. His throat felt as if it was tearing apart.

Then the real pain hit. His hand hit something hard, and his head rolled back to where it had been resting. He wanted to scream. Maybe he was screaming. He couldn't tell. But whatever he was doing, it brought on more coughs—coughs that shook his body and amplified all of the pain.

The world came back to him faster this time. Like the water was quickly draining from his sea of solitude. Each of his motions still pushed against the water, but less with each passing second. Then, the noise came to him. He could hear something, quiet but growing louder. It was chaotic and shrill. It was his own voice.

He screamed at the pain. He felt something on him, holding him down. Hands. Someone else's. *Where am I?* He thought. *Wikith?*

Just the name brought back the anger. He remembered. He remembered how he had worked with him for a time when under Malcolm's influence. He remembered when Wikith captured him and planned to use him as bait to lure out Lolan. He remembered Lolan, escaping. The fury of storms ripped through Brendell. With his sight not back to him, Brendell screamed louder and felt the current of lightning rip through and around him. The familiar smell of ozone filled the air.

The hands on him were no longer there. *Good.*

His body was coming more and more under his control. He moved an arm, slowly, but it did as he expected, feeling around the platform where he laid. He then tried his eyes. They opened and the sea of darkness was erased with piercing light. It hurt. His head pounded worse than ever before. He squinted, wishing his eyes would adjust.

He waited. The hands were still gone from him, no longer holding him down. He must have killed whoever it was. He hoped it was Wikith, or Malcolm. That's what they get for crossing him.

When his eyes finally began to understand the scene, Brendell could see he was in some sort of building. He sat up slowly, trying not to provoke the lion of a headache roared in his skull. He saw blurs and shapes at first, but they solidified into furniture and people. He didn't recognize them. There was a Human, and a Dwarf. There were others. An injured Saurian laid nearby. And a Hippo Beastfolk knelt next to a person a little further on that was covered in blood. But they all stood still, staring at Brendell.

What is this? Are they killing people?

Brendell forced himself to stand despite the aches and groans of his atrophied muscles. He held out his arms to his sides, summoning more of the lightning that he had already called. The spark began to flicker between his fingers.

"Brendell. Stop," came a voice from behind him. It was muffled, his ears still adjusting, but it was familiar. Brendell turned to see Lolan, in his cloak, ready to fight back.

A mix of emotions flooded into Brendell's mind. There was anger, from growing up with the half-breed. Lolan took away everything he hoped for in life. He couldn't grow up like a normal Elf. He couldn't spend too much time with his peers for fear of them finding out about his freakshow cousin.

Then there was a feeling of camaraderie. Regardless of where they came from, or who they were, they did have a hint of friendship for the sheer reason that they grew up together. They knew things together that no one else did. They had been through a lot, even if they were on opposite sides for most of it.

"It's okay," said Lolan. "You need to sit down. You're still recovering. You need rest." *Recovering?* Thought Brendell. *From what?*

He tried to recall his last memories before waking up in this strange place. He remembered the cave. He remembered working with Wikith to surprise a group. He remembered Lolan was among them. Then, he remembered the flames.

Brendell tried to move the fingers on his hand. It felt like they were okay, despite some stiffness. Then, he dared a look down at his hand. In its place was a bandaged stump. He pulled it up to make sure he wasn't seeing it wrong. He wasn't. His hand was gone.

Brendell fell to his knees and screamed. A localized storm brewed above him, an accidental reaction from his outcry.

"Brendell, I'm sorry. It was all I could do to—"

"Stop!" shouted Brendell. He glared up at Lolan. It was his fault. If it weren't for him, he would still have a hand. It was his fault that he was here, among enemies, and permanently handicapped.

The storm grew larger and lightning began to flicker above as Brendell pushed himself to his feet. Brendell stretched out his intact arm toward his brother. "This is all because of you."

Lolan shrunk back, but the lightning didn't strike him. Brendell held his hand still. There was something within him that stopped him. A nagging feeling told him that it was more complicated than that.

"It's the brainwashing," said someone else. Brendell turned to see a Dwarf. "Malcolm used mind magic on you. It's still lingering in your brain."

"What do you know?" growled Brendell, accusatory.

"A good deal. I have helped many Dwarves that were under the same effect. It will go away with time." Brendell looked around at all of the people staring at him. Why were they here? Why was he here? "Lolan took your hand. You're right about that," said the Dwarf. "But he is also the one who got you free of that cave. If it weren't for him, you would have either been dead from the collapse or still enslaved by Malcolm."

Brendell glared at Lolan, who looked back with his head lowered.

"Where am I?" asked Brendell.

"It's called Birdsbane," said Lolan. "These are the people trying to stop the monster that Malcolm woke up."

"Hah, how do you plan to do that?"

"We're not sure yet."

"And you're all…" Brendell paused, "…cooperating?"

"Yes. There are bigger problems in the world. And through our time on this island, we've found that we can actually accomplish a lot together." Brendell relaxed for the first time since he woke up and let the storm fade. Lolan may be stupid, but he wasn't the type to lie. Still, the realization that he didn't have his hand hurt more than anything.

"Have you fought it yet?" Brendell asked, looking down at his bandaged stump.

"Yes. Once. It didn't go well. It was a lot stronger than we expected."

"Oh yeah? You won't beat that thing. You know this isn't its first try at destroying the world, right?"

"Yes, we've heard some. But we don't know everything about it."

"Has Malcolm taken control yet?" asked Brendell.

"No, we're not sure he will. It sounds like even his own people don't believe in him."

"Who?"

"Arthur."

Brendell scoffed. "Arthur didn't think the monster *existed* either. Malcolm is going to succeed. He's been training for this his whole life."

"What do you mean? Do you know more about what's going on? We could use any information to help us take it down."

"Yeah, I heard things. Being among his elite defense units, he kept me and Wikith close."

"What do you know then? Anything that we can use against the monster?"

"I know that Malcolm is dangerous, maybe more dangerous than that monster. He has a notebook from Shayde Mortem and is a direct descendant. Shayde unlocked things about magic that people never fathomed. He was a visionary, constantly testing and learning how to use magic in new ways. He discovered new types of magic. And all of that research, it's in Malcolm's hands. He's learning it. It takes time, but he is learning.

"Not just that, but he isn't the type to take no for an answer. If he says he's going to do something, he's going to do it. Every step so far, he had planned. He had meticulously sought out the puzzle pieces needed to bring us to this point. If he would have failed at any step along the way, he would have waited longer until he had the skills and people needed to succeed. So, yeah. He'll control that monster. It's only a matter of time."

Brendell looked around the room again. Now that his senses had fully come back to him, he could see his surroundings better. It was a church or some kind of decorative building with vaulted ceilings and colorful windows. The people around him were of all different races. There was a Treek girl and a Beastfolk close to her. There was an old Avian, standing a bit further back with another of his kind. Saurians, Gnomes, Humans, they were all there. And most of them were still staring at him, processing the words that he spoke.

"Where is Wikith?" he asked.

"I don't know," said Lolan. "I left the others to handle him while I distracted you." The statement still sent a surge of anger through Brendell, but he pushed it back. Now was not the time to fight. He couldn't be sure how these people would react, and if they fought back, he would have a hard time escaping with his life.

"And he didn't die in the collapse?" Brendell asked.

"I doubt it," said Lolan. "He killed many of the people I was with that day. I would be surprised if he didn't survive."

Lolan looked down at the ground. There was something eating at him. Did he feel guilty for those deaths? He would. He always was a weakling.

"You said you heard things," said the Treek. "Did you hear anything else? Do you know how long until he gains control of the doom drake?"

"Doom drake?" said Brendell. "What a lame name. Why not call it something like death titan or the colossus?"

The old Avian in the distance made a noise, but Brendell couldn't make it out.

"Do you know when?" asked the Treek again.

Brendell focused on her. She was familiar—someone that Malcolm had hated. A nuisance.

"I can't know for sure, but he had planned to have it under his control within a week." Brendell thought for a moment. He had so little left. He only had a single hand. His family probably forgot about him by now. And here he was in a mixed-race chapel in a city he had never heard of before. If he could direct his anger toward anyone, well, it was easiest to pin it on Lolan. But he was trying. Trying to not hate him, and trying to see the shared experiences as the closest thing to a brotherly relationship that he had ever experienced. So if he couldn't blame Lolan, Wikith was next, with Malcolm taking a close second.

"You said you're trying to stop that monster. Are you going out to attack it again?"

"Yes," said Lolan. " We plan to attack again in three days. But you need to rest. You're still recovering from—"

"I'm coming," said Brendell. "Wikith needs to see how much I've learned from him."

20.3 Ash

"You don't understand," I said. "We have to tell the others about this."

"I don't think *you* understand," said Kesq. "This is very powerful magic. It has the potential to change the world. We can't just go around telling anybody about it. That's why it took me so long to even tell *you* about it."

"But if there was ever a time to change the world, now is it. A murder dragon is running around destroying the world, city by city. We need to change the world and get rid of it."

"But it is dangerous information in the wrong hands," said Kesq. She was looking more and more concerned the more we spoke.

"Come on guys. Don't you agree? We could use this," I said, looking at Tigala and Lolan where we stood outside of the abandoned Gnome house that we had been calling home.

"It does sound risky. We could be creating another monster to deal with after the doom drake is defeated," said Tigala.

"But what does it matter if we never get that far?" asked Lolan. "I think we need to use every trick we've got. And if it is something that we can use against the doom drake, then we can do more damage if more people know about it. We'll deal with the problems later."

"Right," I said.

"I still think it's too dangerous. I've spent half my life protecting this information. I know people who are looking to take advantage of it."

I was frustrated. Why wouldn't we use all of the tools we had to take down the doom drake? So far it was looking like there was no hope. And now the world threw us a bone. Even if people would take advantage of it, there would be just as many people to push back against those people. But she didn't want to hear it.

"What if we only tell it to a select group that we trust. The representatives have mostly shown that they are looking to protect their people. The ones that are still around are trying to find ways to stop the monster and work together. So we can tell them and go from there. Maybe we can tell them ahead of time not to share this information. Then we at least have a little more firepower the next time we attack it if it is near a beacon."

Kesq stood there silently looking back at me. She wasn't happy. I could tell despite my trouble understanding Saurian facial expressions. Then she said, "Fine. But only a few that we can trust to keep the information to themselves."

"Deal."

ॐ

"So we can use these beacons that you mentioned just by focusing on the magic of those that created it?" asked Amara.

"It's not that simple," said Kesq. "It's still a skill that requires practice. It's not intuitive, but the more you try it, the easier it is to use. The problem is, when you first start out, it's more difficult and the results are often explosive.

Once you're able to control it well, you can be a lot more precise with it."

"Explosive is good," said Rodrigo. "Even if we don't know what we're doing, we could still use the messy results against the monster."

"Yes, but there could be a lot of collateral damage as well," said Tallesia. "Our people will be out there. An explosion of fire is good against the doom drake, but not against our soldiers."

"We could try and position ourselves separately from the army," said Cairn. "That way there is less potential for collateral damage."

"Yeah, the problem is that the person using the magic would still be in danger," I said. "I know from experience. When I first tried using a beacon, I would have died if it weren't for my group saving me."

"Also, none of this is relevant if we can't get the doom drake close to a beacon," said Klaus. "Is that correct?"

"Yes," said Kesq. "I have only been able to use a beacon within a five-minute walk of one. So we need to first lure the monster toward us somehow."

"But can't you make more beacons? We can bring one with us," said Sillius.

"I can, but it takes time, and we don't exactly have a lot of time," said Kesq.

There was silence. It was good information, potentially world-changing if we could find a way to use it. But it was never that simple.

We all stood in the dirt-covered living room of our abandoned Gnome house staring at the ground, thinking of a possible use.

"Well, if we can't use it immediately to fight the doom drake, why don't we focus on things we *can* do with it?" said Palem. He was still a little less talkative in big group situations like this. I wasn't sure if he was shy, or if it was because he was a Treek, or if he just likes to listen before he speaks. "We need more people to fight against it, correct? Can we use the beacons to talk to more people at once?"

It was a great idea. Could we spread the word fast enough that we could get more people in time for our next attack on the monster?

"The illusion beacon," said Lolan. "It was on the map, wasn't it?"

"Yeah," I said, pulling the map out of my bag. I unfurled it in front of me, and others gathered around. Not too far beyond the valley of the dead was a drawing of a house. Above it was the word 'illusion'. "Would that work?" I asked, switching my gaze between Sillius and Kesq.

They exchanged a glance. Sillius shrugged while Kesq said, "It's worth a try."

"I can try sending an illusion far away," said Sillius, "but I've never been able to do it very far before."

"That's okay," I said. "We need any advantages we can get. If there is a chance that this works, I think we should try."

"I would be interested in coming as well, for the sake of understanding these beacons you speak of," said Klaus. The feathers on the back of his crane-like head bobbed while he spoke.

"Would you come?" I asked Sillius.

He looked around, not finding another Gnome in the room. "Sure. But I don't want to be out there long. I have preparations to make."

"That's fine. I don't expect it will take a long time. Kesq, can you join us too? It would be helpful to get pointers from you. Hopefully, it will save us from another magical explosion."

The blue Saurian nodded. "I have nowhere else to be. I want to make sure you're using it correctly anyway."

"Good. Anyone else?" I looked around the room. No one else spoke up. So that was our group. "Alright, get whatever you need and meet back here as soon as possible. We'll head out immediately."

Rodrigo hung back while the rest of the group dispersed. He walked over to me, Lolan, and Tigala. "Are you sure you're up for this? What if you get into another situation like the one in the forest?"

"I think we'll be okay. It's just illusion magic, right?" I said.

"Illusion magic can do a lot of damage," said Tigala. "The more powerful Gnomes can mess with your head in ways that traumatize you. If that beacon explodes, we could all go crazy."

"Oh," I said. "Well, that's a scary thought."

"Let's just be as careful as possible," said Lolan. "We have a couple of days to do this, so we'll take our time."

I nodded.

"Good luck," said Rodrigo. "I'd come myself, but I have matters to attend to with the Human leaders. They're hard to convince even if we can reach more of them with the beacons."

"Thanks," I said. "You too."

Rodrigo nodded and walked out, leaving us alone to get ready for the journey.

"Are you okay to leave Brendell?" I asked Lolan while I grabbed a few things for the trip.

He nodded. "I wouldn't miss this. Brendell is resting a lot to make sure he is healed up for the battle. He's still working out how he feels about me anyway. I think he could use the space."

"Okay," I said, getting the last of my things in my bag.

Once we were all packed up, we waited in the street in front of our house for the others to arrive. Kesq was the first. I wasn't sure she had gone anywhere. I couldn't imagine she had a lot of stuff to bring since she was a runaway in the first place. Klaus and Sparr were next to arrive. They didn't carry anything on them besides what was strapped to them and a single book carried by Klaus. Then came Sillius with his usual scowl buried beneath his thick eyebrows and wiry mustache.

"Okay, let's head out then," I said.

"Are we walking the whole way there?" asked Sillius.

"Yeah, I don't know what else we would do," I said.

"I can take wyvern form and carry two of you," said Tigala.

"Wyvern? Like the ones from the cliffs?" asked Kesq, pointing to the towering mountains.

"Yeah, that's where I learned the form," said Tigala.

"Let's fly the wyverns there then," said Kesq.

"What?" said Tigala. "They're wild animals."

"Yes, but they are tamable," said Kesq. "My people have been doing it for as long as our history books goes back. You just need the right motivations. And since you can turn into one, that should help."

"I'm not sure I'm okay with this," said Sillius.

"Didn't you say you had things to do?" I asked. "If we take wyverns there and back, then we can get back quicker."

"Yeah, I guess," said Sillius, still making a face.

"We're willing," said Klaus, referring to himself and his brown-feathered companion, Sparr.

"You're sure about this?" Tigala asked Kesq. "They have poisonous stingers on their tails. They're not something you want to mess with."

"Yes, of course. I learned how to tame animals like them when I was a kid.

"Let's do it then," I said.

☌

We hiked out of Birdsbane and into the towering cliffs where the wyverns circled high above us, like vultures waiting for their meal. It was a hot, sunny day, with clear skies as the backdrop behind the flying lizards.

"So what do we do now?" asked Tigala.

"Can you get us up there? We have to get close to tame them," said Kesq.

"I can get the two of us up there if you want to ride on my back," said Tigala.

"Okay, let's do that then," said Kesq. "But before we go, Kaia, can you grow us a couple of juicy fruits?"

"Uh, yeah," I said. "Like what kind? You want watermelon?"

"No," said Kesq. "Something tropical, like what you'd find in a lizard's environment. Bananas, mangos, papayas. Something like that."

"I can do bananas pretty quickly," I said.

"Sure," she said. "That should work."

I focused on the ground and the water-filled trunk of the banana tree. It wasn't as quick as the vegetables I usually grew for meals, but it did come up quickly. I focused on the hope of this mission to move it even faster, and the tree sprung up in no time. Soon, clusters of bananas were hanging down from the branches and turning from green to yellow. Kesq grabbed a bunch once it was ready and climbed onto the back of the now transformed Tigala.

"We'll need three wyverns including Tigala, correct?" asked Kesq.

I looked around and nodded. There were seven of us, and Tigala was a wyvern herself. So two more would put two people on each wyvern.

"I'll ride one wyvern back, but does anyone want to volunteer to ride the third one back down?" she said.

I thought of volunteering, but my promise to Tigala came to mind. Would this count as one of those moments when I was putting my life in danger?

Before I could finish the thought, Sparr stepped forward. "I will ride the wyvern down," he said. Then he hopped on Tigala's back behind Kesq.

"Good luck," I said.

Tigala nodded her wyvern head, snorted, and then flapped her giant leathery wings. Dust sprayed as she took to the sky.

20.4 Ash

They had been up there for about half an hour when we finally saw wyverns coming down toward us. I was nervous that it wasn't them and wild wyverns were coming down to devour us while our group was split up, but we weren't *that* unlucky today.

Tigala was the first to arrive, a lone wyvern recognizable by the scar across its face and the favored right wing. She was trailed closely behind by two other wyverns of equal size. They landed behind her, one with Sparr on its back, and the other with Kesq. When they saw us, the two of them began to snarl and raise their tails in the air.

"Growl at them," said Kesq.

Tigala turned and growled back, louder than the two of them combined. The two wild wyverns sunk back, lowering their tails.

"You're the alpha," said Kesq, "they'll follow your lead, but sometimes you need to remind them that you're in charge."

Tigala nodded.

"Keep your eyes on them while the rest of us mount. Make sure they don't try anything," said Kesq.

Tigala obeyed, staring at the wyverns with a hard expression and teeth bared.

Klaus joined Sparr, and Lolan and I climbed onto Tigala's back. That left Sillius with Kesq. The grumpy Gnome slinked toward the lizard, giving its head a wide berth, and grabbed Kesq's arm as she pulled him up in front of her.

"Everyone ready?" I said.

There were nods all around, though Sillius was slower to respond, keeping his attention on the wyvern's head and tail instead.

I patted Tigala's shoulder. "Let's go. Head toward the doom drake's nest. The beacon should be beyond that." Tigala didn't waste any time. She flapped her wings and jumped to the air. With a scream, the other wyverns joined, launching from the ground with their riders.

We stayed low at first, winding through the mountainous cliffs well below the frenzy of wild wyverns above us. Once the mountains broke away, Tigala soared higher in the sky, like I had when I rode on Malcolm's dragon. It was beautiful, seeing the land from so high up. I had spent so much time wandering around this island, but this was the first time I got to see so much of it at once. It was like the map in my pocket had come to life.

I could see Birdsbane, not far behind us. The people there were just dots. There was a muddy trail marking everywhere the wandering forest had been, including where it started out. Ahead of us, the valley of the dead shambled like an eerie pale sea. North of it, I found the spot where the Gnomes had landed and had been mostly destroyed by the animated trees.

"This is so cool," said Lolan.

"I was thinking the same thing," I said.

"Look," he said, pointing behind us, "I can see the tower from here." I twisted around, following his finger to a grey dot sticking out of the forest. Beyond it, the trees stood higher than the rest. It was the cliff where I had first met Lolan that day when he saved me from the ogre.

We had come so far together. We had been through so much in such a short amount of time. And seeing it all from so high up made it feel so far away and small. We had risen above the traditions that kept us segregated and hating one another, and for a moment, the anxiety about the doom drake disappeared. I was safe, and I was with the people I cared about the most. Zef was gone, but I knew he died with purpose, and that has to be the best way anyone can die. As for the rest of us, we were still together. We had each other.

Just then, we reached the end of the valley of the dead and would have reached the church where Malcolm had holed up, but that church was no longer there. Instead, there was a giant hole marking the place where the doom drake once slept and then climbed out of the earth. It was enormous —even bigger than I had expected it to be from a bird's eye view. It brought our situation right back into the forefront of my mind. I was still glad to have Lolan and Tigala with me, but it was no longer just because I cared about them. It was because I was scared. Scared of that monster that left a lake-sized crater in the island. I was afraid of what it would do to us, and what it was no doubt doing this very moment. The doom drake was out there ending lives, breaking up loved ones, and there was so little we could do.

I looked up, focusing on the horizon instead. The wind blew my hair all over the place.

"You okay?" asked Lolan.

"I don't know," I said. "I don't know how we're going to do this."

Lolan sighed, "I don't know either," he said. "One step at a time I guess."

"Yeah," I said.

The other wyverns flew next to us, slightly behind Tigala. Maybe they were taking advantage of the windbreak that Tigala provided, like birds sometimes do, or maybe they were waiting for a chance to attack. They seemed to be doing well, not trying to eat their riders yet. So that was good. Would it last though? Were they safe enough to keep around? How long would Kesq's quick-taming hold up?

I glanced at Kesq. She looked back with no expression I could make out. She seemed confident, unafraid of the wyvern she rode. Sillius, on the other hand, hugged the neck of the monster with wide eyes.

"That must be it," said Klaus, pointing ahead of us. His grey and white feathers flicked in the wind and pressed against his body, making him look more skeletal and old.

I looked to where he was pointing and found the landscape riddled with structures. They were small and made out of wood or stones. There was ample room around each one with what looked like fences made out of stacked stones. It must have been a small farm town overrun and falling apart from age and nature. The buildings only formed a small cluster though, and looking at them, none stood out in particular. The purple glow of magic veins was also absent.

"Where?" I asked, yelling over the wind.

"Up the hill," Klaus yelled back.

I looked back at the village and followed a faint path with my eyes. It went out of the town and up a grassy hill. There, I began to see the purple veins. They were faint from the distance, but it was definitely them. The veins stretched down the hill, spreading out the further they traveled down the hill. The central point of the magical veins was directly beneath an old run down mansion that sat at the tallest point of the hill.

That was it then.

Tigala dipped down, and let out a monstrous howl as she did, signaling for the others to do the same.

We circled around the mansion, with the purple veins becoming more and more clear as we descended. The mansion was enormous as far as buildings went. It almost looked like a small castle if it weren't for the wood plank siding, wooden trimmed windows, and iron rails on balconies. It stretched across the hill casting its shadow on the town below.

Tigala circled around one more time and then landed hard on the ground. Lolan and I were launched from her back and sent skidding in the dirt.

"Sorry," she said, with a wet growl to the words.

"It's okay," I said dusting myself off. "We made it."

The other two wyverns touched down much more smoothly than Tigala had, on the grassy hill just in front of the mansion. The veins that stretched around us looked a lot like the ones we had seen in the cave under the tower, just with more purple than blue this time around.

Kesq, Klaus, and Sparr got off of their wyverns without a problem, but the wyverns stood there eyeing us all up. They clearly were not tamed well, but I wouldn't expect them to be with only a half-hour of teaching.

Sillius slid off of the wyvern slowly and then ran away from it as soon as he hit the ground. Once he was further than

207

everyone else from the flying lizards, he sat down in the grass panting.

"Everyone alright?" I said.

"Good here," said Klaus.

Kesq nodded as well.

The wild wyverns were not looking as okay as before though. The one that carried the Avians began snapping its jaws and raising its tail once more. The other followed suit, cornering the Avians and Kesq. The three of them took fighting stances as the wyverns closed in.

Tigala roared at the creatures, but they didn't seem to care.

"What do we do?" I asked as I ran toward the others.

"They're hungry," said Kesq. "The flight must have worn them out. Do you have any more fruit?"

"Yeah, hang on," I said.

I started growing another banana tree as quickly as I could while the wyverns continued to close in. Tigala ran forward, slamming a shoulder into one of the lizards. It jumped on her wrestling her to the ground.

"Does this usually happen?" I asked as the tree reached about the height of my waist.

"Yes," said Kesq. "They're not tame, they were just intimidated. That only lasts as long as they think they are weaker. I think Tigala's landing might have shown them otherwise."

Great.

Tigala and the one wyvern were tangled up, pinning each other to the ground and throwing barbed poisonous tails at each other. Neither was able to land a hit. The other wyvern stared menacingly at the group. It stalked forward and then charged. The group scattered, but in the fray, Klaus tripped on one of the veins. It sent the crane Avian sprawling and his book rolling out of reach. He tried to right himself, but the wyvern was already on him. It grabbed him with its two hind claws and took to the air.

"Klaus!" shouted Sparr, and he took to the air as well, flapping his dark brown wings. He was nowhere near as maneuverable as the wyvern though. He flew up, readied his spear, and charged after the monster.

I didn't know what to do. We couldn't lose Klaus. He was our only real connection to what Zef was up to, and he knew so much. Plus, I wouldn't wish getting devoured by a wyvern on anyone.

"Lolan," I said. Before I finished saying his name he had an arrow nocked.

He followed the wyvern with his bow and let loose. The arrow sailed through the sky, but it looked like it was going to be off its mark. Just before it sailed past, Klaus's eyes went white. Then, he jerked his body, sending the wyvern right into the path of the arrow. It struck the lizard in the shoulder. The wyvern screamed.

I had finally finished growing a few bananas. I peeled one and yelled, "Kesq!" as I threw it to her. She caught the banana and ran over to the wyvern Tigala was facing off against. She held it up, but the monster barely noticed the fruit. Instead, it turned on Kesq and threw a tail strike at her.

Then, Kesq disappeared. Or, rather, a faux ground appeared between the wyvern and Kesq, hiding her in illusion. Sillius stood nearby with his hands raised and a purple glow pouring from them. Tigala took the chance to pounce on the monster and stab it with her tail. The creature screamed and kicked her away. It then took to the sky and

209

bolted after Klaus, who was still in the clutches of the other wyvern.

The lizard carrying Klaus now had several arrows sticking out of it, but it still flew. However, it did slow it down, allowing Sparr to close in. He swooped down and stabbed the creature between the shoulders. It screamed and lost its grip on Klaus who spread his own wings as soon as he was free. Lolan fired one more arrow at the wyverns, and both chose to escape with their lives over fighting us.

The Avians reached us safely and Klaus walked over to pick up the book he had dropped. "That was eventful," he said as he dusted off the tome.

"Are you okay?" I asked.

"We'll be alright," said Klaus, "but it looks like we won't be able to return so easily."

"I guess not," said Kesq. "Sorry. I thought they were dumber than they are."

We all turned to look at the mansion in front of us. "I guess it's time," said Sillius.

"Yeah," I said. And we began our climb toward the mansion.

20.5 Ash

The house sat on top of the hill looming over the town like a dragon watching over its lair. It was old, with planks of wood siding falling off. Not a single window was still intact and the paint was mostly gone. The roof displayed several arched window dormers and more holes than shingles. It would have once been a nice building—a home for some wealthy occupant of Daegal. But it had long since succumbed to the decay of time.

Tigala had transformed back, with the threat of the other wyverns gone. She joined the rest of us in staring at the building. With the pulsing purple glow of the veins showing through all of the house's holes, I was a bit intimidated. Even more so than I was in the cave or the treetop village.

Tigala didn't seem to mind though. She walked forward to the front door and shook the handle.

"It's locked," said Klaus. But almost before he could finish the statement, Tigala was crashing through the rotted door. Klaus jumped back in surprise, grabbing his book like it was more important than his own safety.

Tigala brushed the dust off of her arm and said, "Come on. We've got a giant to topple." The rest of us followed her into a foyer. It was fancy, with bookshelves, a cabinet, and a nice lamp that looked like something the Gnomes would have put together.

Klaus immediately shuffled to the bookshelf, thumbing through books and blowing away dust. Sparr stood behind him, half facing the shelf while keeping an eye on the rest of the room.

The purple veins continued on through the house, but it was hard to tell yet where the center might be. I exchanged a glance with Lolan, and then Tigala. This was unlike any of the previous "beacons" we had found. It was just a regular house. Nothing weird at all.

"Who's there?" yelled Sillius. The short Gnome jumped and backed away from the doorway.

"There's someone here?" I asked.

"He was right there. I saw him. It was a smallfolk. He ran across the room," he said, pointing out the smallfolk's path across the next room with his finger.

I hope this isn't another run-in with Havik. Tigala was already turning tiger. She stalked toward the doorway, as did Kesq with her spear raised. They walked through the doorway slowly. Their footsteps made the floorboards creak. The two lined up facing the wall where the person should be.

Tigala pounced and Kesq charged. Then, after a moment, everything was quiet. Sparr and I went in next to see Tigala and Kesq looking around, confused.

"There's no one here," said Kesq.

"Yeah," said Tigala. "If it was a Gnome, they're not invisible. Maybe they teleported out?" Sparr immediately headed back to the foyer, where Klaus was still searching through books.

"Who would it have been then?" asked Lolan. "Are there more Gnomes on the island? Or was it...?" He looked at me showing that he shared my fear of Havik's return.

"That was my thought," I said. "I don't know how he would have figured out where we are, or why he would come here instead of taming the doom drake. But if he's here, this could be really bad."

"We need to stay in a group," said Tigala. "No splitting up." I looked around and everyone seemed to be in agreement. Whoever was here, it couldn't be for good reasons.

"Lead the way," said Sillius looking at the rest of us.

Tigala wasted no time, walking forward with the stealth of a predator. The group followed into the next room. It was a great room, with benches placed in front of a large fireplace. There were a few more books on a wall in this room, which Klaus noticed right away.

As my eyes scanned the room, a fire lit in the fireplace. I jumped back, wondering how it happened, and looked toward Lolan. He was looking in the opposite direction unaware of the fire. I looked back to the fireplace, and there was nothing there.

"Did anyone else see that?" I asked.

"What was it?" asked Kesq.

"The fireplace just lit for a moment," I said.

I looked at the others who all had equally puzzled looks on their faces.

"Come on," said Tigala. "We need to get this over with before anything happens around the veins." I looked down at them. The purple light pulsed through the veins and glowed on the walls giving the whole house an eerie hue.

We stepped through the hallway, one by one, into what was a kitchen.

"Takar?" said Sparr at the rear of the group. I turned to see him staring into the room we just left.

"Everything okay?" asked Klaus, who had been just in front of him.

"It's her," said Sparr.

"Where?" asked Klaus.

Sparr raised a feathered finger at an empty end of the great room behind us. We all looked through the door unable to see anyone.

"But she's dead," said Sparr.

"Are you sure it was her?" asked Klaus.

"It looked just like her," he said.

"Okay, well, maybe that Gnome is playing tricks on us, or maybe someone else is. We need to keep our eyes peeled."

Or maybe it had something to do with the illusion veins that we're creeping past.

We continued on into the next room. This one was a lavish dining room. The table was set in the center of the table with dishware still set out. Some had been knocked to the vein-covered floor and were shattered, half covered by the purple glowing magic.

"Still no sign of the center of the veins," said Tigala. "Maybe it's upstairs."

"We just have to find the stairs," said Kesq.

We stayed together, huddled in a group as we entered the next room. Old food, now nearly unidentifiable, sat on the stovetop and counter. More dishes were scattered on the floor. Tigala led the group, but upon entering the room she stopped in her tracks.

"Gatooli?" she said.

I followed her eyes and found only a blank wall opposite her.

"How are you...?" she started.

The others were sharing similar looks of confusion.

The veins pulsed again as if to remind me where we were. This whole house was filled with illusion magic.

"Is it really you?" Tigala said again. Tears were coming to her eyes as she continued to stare at the wall.

Tigala took a step forward and then broke out into a sprint.

She jumped onto the table and then charged out a doorway opposite of us. I ran after.

The next room was a dead end, something like a large storage closet, and Tigala was alone in the room.

"Illusions," she said, angry and hurt by the revelation. "I just watched her disappear through this wall"

I gave her a moment to recover from what she had seen. When she turned back to the kitchen I did too.

"The house is playing tricks on us," I said to the others. "For whatever reason, I think we're seeing the illusion magic. And it's playing off of our own memories somehow."

Again, there was the added aspect to the magic. Maybe this land was imbued with mind magic or something, giving the treants their personalities and altering these illusions to use our memories.

"Ah, interesting," said Klaus. "This island continues to impress."

"Let's just stay together, just in case," said Sillius.

"Yes, I think that is a good plan," said Kesq.

"Sounds like they are targeting one person at a time," said Lolan. "So if you do see something, you should be able to point to it to make sure it's just magic."

"Good plan," I said.

We continued as a tight group looking throughout the house. Even if they were just illusions, it was scary. What would be around the next corner? What kind of memories was this old house going to stir up? Did it have access to all of our memories or just the strongest ones?

Through the next door, we finally found the stairs. The purple veins climbed up them, making it hard to find flat footing.

"Watch your step," said Sparr, now leading us forward. "There!" he shouted, pointing a feathered finger at the top of the stairs.

Others looked around the giant Avian to see what he was pointing at. I couldn't see anything but an empty hallway.

"I just see a wall," said Klaus.

"Me too," I said.

Sparr's pace slowed as he continued up the stairs. He didn't take his eyes off the spot he had pointed at until right before reaching the top. And after that, he looked more shaken than I had ever seen him.

We crept into the upstairs hallway, passing more bedrooms than it looked like they could fit in the house.

"Does anyone see that?" said Kesq, staring into the first room.

"No, nothing," said Sillius.

Kesq spoke slowly. "Okay." She continued down the hall.

"Over there," Lolan said quietly.

"Nope," said Tigala. Lolan was stuck, staring into the empty room.

"You okay?" asked Tigala.

Lolan gulped. "Yeah. Yeah, I'll be fine." His eyes moved from the illusion, whatever it was, and then back to it a few times. Then, he too continued.

The next room was my turn. I knew what to expect. I knew it was playing with our emotions, but nothing could have prepared me for this. In the room was a Gnome with a long white beard and a patchwork coat. Zef stared back at me with a sad smile on his face.

I was paralyzed and barely breathed out his name. "Zef." Lolan and Tigala stopped and looked too. "Oh," said Lolan. "I see him."

"Yeah," said Tigala.

"Zef," I said, louder this time. "I'm sorry. I'm sorry it had to be you. I wish you were here." I took a step toward him into the room. My emotions overtook me. "We could really use your help now. It's like there is no way to fix this. I can't help but think you would have something up your sleeve. You would know what to do—how to fix this."

"I'm trying. I really am. But I don't know how we're supposed to stop something that big—that powerful. I don't know how to unite everyone against it. Not without you."

The others had all stopped and were looking into the room that I now stood in with Zef. I knew he had to be an illusion. There was no way he was actually here, but I couldn't help myself. There was so much more to say to him. So much I wish I could have said before that day when the doom drake woke up. I didn't care if the others listened.

I took another step forward, and then another. I reached out to touch Zef on the shoulder, but just before I did, I saw a smirk show on his face—like a message to me, whatever it may have been. I paused, and then touched his shoulder. My hand went through it and the illusion dissipated into a cloud of fading purple sparks.

I stood there for a few moments, mourning the loss of my friend again. Then I felt a hand land on my shoulder. It was Tigala. I turned and saw her and Lolan right behind me. The rest of the group still stood silently in the doorway, watching.

I took a deep breath, and said, "Let's do this." We walked back into the hallway and continued into the room at the end, where the veins were at their brightest.

"This must be it," said Klaus.

"Yes," said Kesq. "It is. Let's see what we can do with this." The memory of Zef still floated in my head and I felt off balance. Even if this worked, even if we could try and convince people to join the fight, I was even less sure now that I could change anything. I missed Zef. I missed my family. I missed Chipry. All of them were casualties of hatred that spread like a disease through the world—no longer in my life.

And now, I have to tell everyone how important it is that we work together, even just this once. But how could I?

How would Zef do it?

He would look for the best in everyone, enemies or not. He would give the benefit of the doubt. He would continue on regardless of how his message was received.

I was lost in my thoughts as I thought of my lost friend. Then I heard someone say something. The words weren't clear. Then they came again.

"Are you ready to give this a try?" asked Sillius.

I looked up at the group. All eyes were on me as they formed a half-circle around the central point of the veins. I looked at Tigala, and then Lolan, who gave me an assuring nod. I looked back to Sillius and a subtle and unsure smirk came to my face.

"Yes," I said. And the smirk became just the faintest bit stronger.

20.6 Ash

We stood in the room staring at the center of the purple veins pulsing with magic. In the corner was a dead Human, rotted and decayed from the years spent lying here after she made this magical beacon.

I looked at Kesq. "So what do we do now? I guess Sillius should try using it, correct?"

"Yes, but we have to be careful," she said.

"Right," I said.

Sillius looked up to Kesq. "Do you have any pointers?"

"Yes," she said. "Magic flows like a liquid. These veins will have much more 'liquid' than when you're doing magic on your own. It's more concentrated, so it's harder to control. I suggest you try moving with it."

"What does that mean?" asked Sillius.

"Have you ever found it easier to do a certain type of spell on a specific day? Or do certain types of illusion magic come easier to you than others?"

"Yeah," said Sillius. "So I can only use those types of illusion magic? But we need to specifically create copies of Kaia. I'll need to do a very specific thing with it."

"Right, you will. But instead of just trying to force the illusions the way you know how, try and follow the stream to the spells you need. Whatever you do, don't push directly against it."

"And what happens if I push against it?"

"I can't tell you for sure. Magic, especially this concentrated, will do what it wants to do. It could be catastrophic. It could result in the kind of things Tigala was talking about."

That kind of made sense based on my previous experiences with the veins. Did I push against it? Is that how I created the wandering forest—by forcing it in a direction it didn't want to move?

"Okay…" said Sillius. "So I just have to figure out what that all means as I go?"

"Unfortunately, yes," said Kesq. "The best way to improve at this is through practice. I can give you analogies, but none of it is going to be useful until you have experienced it yourself."

"Alright," said Sillius. "I guess we'll give this a try then. Glad there's no pressure or anything," he said, glaring at the ground in front of him. He looked up at me. "Are you ready?"

"Uh, yeah," I said, unsure of what the actual answer was to that question. "I guess I better be. We don't have a lot of time."

"Right," said Sillius. "Here we go then."

Sillius began focusing on the magic. The purple magic swirled in the room as he worked. The veins pulsed and Sillius's forehead creased. The magic sparked and crackled around us. One behind Klaus, another by Tigala. And the room filled with a dull noise like the wind was picking up, but there was no wind.

I looked back at Sillius. He looked like he was struggling. His brows were knit together with concentration. Would he be able to do this? Or was this going to turn into another wandering forest incident? I really hoped it wouldn't.

Next, there were whispers circling around the room. As if one person was running circles around us and taunting us, too fast to be seen.

Should I ask how it is going? Or would that throw off his concentration? I don't want to push it.

I looked at the others. Everyone was fairly calm. Lolan and Tigala had been through worse than this, and Kesq was supposedly used to this kind of thing. Sparr looked like he had been through some pretty nasty fights. Klaus was the only one of us that looked a little more uneasy with the current situation. He held his book tightly to his chest.

A ghost appeared just past him. It shimmered with purple magic and then disappeared a moment later. Another appeared on the other side of the room. Then another.

"What are you doing?" asked Tigala.

"I'm trying to go with the flow," said Sillius through grit teeth.

"Good," said Kesq. "Now try and nudge the flow of the magic towards our illusion."

"Yeah," he said. "Working on it."

The images continued around the room. Then they stopped, or so I had thought. A moment later I saw a flash outside the window of the room. I strained my neck to see and saw a ghost about three or four times the size of a normal tallfolk. But this one was more defined than the previous ghosts. She wore a rough shirt and skirt, with a bag over her shoulder. Her hair was tied up in a messy ponytail and her face was mine. It was me.

I looked down at my arms as I moved them and then back at the image. It mimicked my motions, and then sparked out of existence, only to show up fifty feet away.

Each image that Sillius managed to create was bigger than the last. Finally, the storm stopped and out a window on the opposite side of the room, I could see a purple glowing illusion, but it was so big that I couldn't make out any details. I could only guess that I was looking at the bottom half of my leg. I moved to confirm, and the illusion moved as well.

"Alright, so should I start?" I said.

"I don't know," said Sillius, straining to maintain the image. "I can only make that one."

"Oh," I said. "Will anyone see it from here?"

Klaus chimed in, "No, unfortunately. I think not. The nearest town is Guardlew, across the ocean to the east. They may be able to see you on a clear day, but that would probably be it."

"I can't push it anywhere else," said Sillius. "My range isn't improved at all, or I'm doing it wrong maybe."

"You probably will not be able to push it any further either," said Kesq. "There is only so much we can do about that. Beacons will only boost magic in specific ways. Maybe we could extend it another way though..."

"How would do that? I don't like the sound of it," said Sillius.

Kesq looked at Klaus. "You are good with sight magic, correct?"

Klaus looked around, curious. "Yes. What do you have in mind."

"You can join your magic to his."

"Join my magic? Is that possible?"

"I don't know. It is possible when I use a beacon of a different kind of magic. I can mix illusion with water, so why wouldn't you be able to mix in sight magic?"

"And how would I go about doing this?" asked Klaus.

"I am not sure. When you are using a beacon, it is fairly simple. You just send your magic through the magic that you are sensing. So maybe try and do that through what Sillius is already doing."

"Alright. It's worth a try," said Klaus.

I looked at Tigala who I figured would be the most against tampering with magic. The look on her face showed that I was probably right.

"Just be ready for anything. Try to cancel it if things get out of hand," said Kesq.

"That's easier said than done," I said. "I know from experience. The rest of us should be ready too, just in case something goes wrong."

There were nods all around, even from Sillius as he strained to maintain the illusion of the giant purple version of me outside the window.

"Everyone ready?" asked Klaus.

"Just do it already," grumbled Sillius. "This isn't exactly easy."

"Right," said Klaus.

He focused on the veins of magic at the center of the room with his eyes turning white. The white glow stretched to join the general purple glow that sparkled about the room. Together, the two made a glittering swirl like a wind stirring leaves in a small tornado.

Klaus now joined Sillius in looking like he was concentrating on the task at hand.

"The same goes for you Klaus," said Kesq. "Do not push too hard against the veins. Try and ride with it. Follow it, and guide it. Do not subvert it entirely."

"I'm trying," Klaus said.

The magic was a lot harder for me to see. Sight magic was mainly only visible to the user, from what I heard. They saw things, past or present, near or far, and it was only in their own minds. I couldn't imagine what was going through Klaus's head, but for the moment at least, it didn't seem to affect the giant Kaia illusion outside.

We all waited there in silence for several moments, ready for anything, or nothing at all. Then all of a sudden, Klaus spoke. "I think I have something. I'm trying to combine it."

A moment later, "I see something," said Sillius. "A lot of things... places."

"Try and push the illusion to those places," said Klaus, struggling to maintain his concentration.

"I'm trying."

The purple energy surged throughout the room, colliding with Klaus's white magic. The giant illusion outside flickered and then reformed. White magic now swirled through the illusion, creating moving stripes that circled my limbs and body.

"I think we have something," yelled Sillius.

"Are we sure?" I said. "Should I begin?"

"I'm not sure. But this is as good as it's going to get. It's now or never."

"Right," I said. I looked down, trying to center myself. I had thought about what I was going to say, but at that moment, it had all left me. How was I supposed to convince the world to join our fight? I didn't have to consider the different options. *Who knows how long this is going to work? Now or never.*

"Hello," I said, speaking to the room of swirling magic. "M-my name is Kaia. I'm a Treek." *Ugh, like they couldn't figure that out.*

"And I know, you may not want to be seeing a message from a Treek. I know my people are hated. But that's why I am here. We are all the same, in a way.

"Just like you, I have lost my family and friends. I have lost people I cared about in the name of grudges—grudges that I personally gave no contribution to."

"I know, my people did a horrible thing. We all have though. We have all broken families apart. We have all hated each other for nothing other than the way we look and the traditions we were raised with.

"I came to Daegal to try and find my people, but through the time I spent here, I learned that it is possible to work together. It's possible to learn to care about people of a different race. I've learned to trust a Beastfolk with my life. I've learned to care about my friendship with an Elf. I've grieved the loss of Gnomes and Dwarves. And it's not because I am trying to take advantage of them, or them of me. If that were the goal, it would have ended a long time ago.

"I know this sounds weird. It is weird for me to even say it. A few months ago, I wouldn't have believed that I would say things like this, but it's true. It's all true. We are capable of living in peace. We are capable of coexisting.

"But there is a threat to that future right now. If you haven't seen it yet or heard of it, there is a giant on the loose —the doom drake. It is the abomination created by Shayde Mortem in the book *The Dangers of Magic*, and one of

Shayde's descendants figured out how to wake it up. He plans to control it, but so far, the monster has resisted. It destroys one city after another, even as we speak. And if left alone, it will not stop until we are all destroyed as well.

"But there is another way. If we all work together, we might have a chance. We might be able to stop it once and for all, and keep it from being used as a weapon, or worse, continuing on its rampage. We need every able person to do their part to stop it. We can't beat it separately. We all need to attack it at once if we're going to have any kind of chance at surviving.

"Count this as your first test, to see if what I'm saying is true. If we do nothing, we are all dead anyway. The doom drake will come for all of us sooner or later. But if you help us fight this monster, you will see first hand whether or not we can coexist, and we all may just be able to build a better future. The first step is to put aside your differences and join us in the fight."

I wasn't sure what else to say. Was that enough? Should I say more? Would people believe me? Probably not. But what was next? How would they join us? I hoped Amara saw the threat for what it was now and would be okay with me mentioning their ability to teleport.

"If you are able to help, we'll find a way for you to join our final battle against the colossus. The Gnomes have a way to move you in quickly, and we'll find a way to signal you in the next day or so. If you can help, please, be ready to join the fight. Say your goodbyes to your loved ones in case this doesn't work, and thank you for your help.

"I'm not going to pretend that the situation looks hopeful. It doesn't. We have already gone against the doom drake and were barely able to affect it. But if we don't try, there is no chance any of us survive. So please, ignore your differences, and help us save the ones we love."

20.7 Ash

In an instant, the magic in the room flickered. Sparks of purple and white shot out in random directions. Images of people from my memories appeared, making no noise, and disappearing just as quickly as they came. Portals appeared in random locations. A table leg fell through the floor where a portal opened. Another created a hole in the wall to some field.

"What's going on?" asked Lolan.

"I'm losing control!" yelled Sillius.

"Me too," said Klaus.

"Try and direct the magic. Point it out the window, away from us if you have to let it explode," said Kesq. She was visibly panicked, like the rest of us.

"I don't know if I can direct it," yelled Sillius. He stood in a horse stance, focusing with all of his might on the magic he was wrangling. The streams of glowing magic coming from Sillius and Klaus swirled around more violently throughout the room.

"The hill, there," shouted Klaus, pointing his beak to a hill out the window.

Sillius yelled as he threw his arms forward. The magic followed his arms and whipped out the window toward the hill.

"Now try to let it go slowly!" yelled Kesq.

"Trying!" said Sillius.

Klaus looked like he was having as much trouble, but he looked less panicked.

The magic still poured through Sillius and Klaus from the center point of the veins on the floor. It whipped violently, coiling around itself, like snakes preparing to strike.

"Everybody get out! Now!" yelled Sillius.

I looked around, and we all started moving at once, heading for the stairs. Sparr stayed behind with Klaus. But other than the three of them, we all sprinted down the stairs and out the front door.

I could still hear Sillius yelling from the upper room.

"What do we do?" I asked.

"Hope that they can let it go without it doing too much damage," said Kesq.

The magical streams swirled around the room, through the walls, and high above the building as well.

Then, with a final yell from Sillius, the magic exploded out of the room. The sky flashed purple and silver, then faded back to its usual blue.

We all stood there for a few minutes staring at the mansion. Did it work? Were they dead? Could illusion and sight magic kill someone?

Then, there was a crunch as someone appeared in the doorway. Sparr, with ruffled feathers, stepped out carrying both Sillius and Klaus. Neither of them looked up to even trying to stand. They were worn out. The look of exhaustion was clear on both of their faces. But they were alive.

After a minute, Kesq asked, "So did it work?"

"Heck if I know," said Sillius. "Sure doesn't look like it."

"You never know. Did it feel like you were creating the image?"

"Yes. It felt like a lot of things."

"And were you able to show him where to place the images?"

"I believe so," said Klaus. "But as he said, it's hard to tell."

"Hey, did you guys see this?" asked Lolan. I looked over to find him peeking around the side of the house towards the hill where they had tried to release the magic.

I ran over with Kesq and Tigala. On the hill was now a large storm of some kind of illusion magic. It was a swirl of purple and silver, similar to that which we saw in the room. Except this one had a key difference. It would flash, like lightning striking the ground, and with each strike, an illusion of a location was shown.

"What is it?" I asked.

Sparr had managed to drag Sillius and Klaus with him to take a look.

"I have no idea," said Sillius.

"Me neither," said Klaus. "Maybe it's now showing different locations from our memories." He looked at Kesq. "Is this normal?"

"None of this is normal," said Kesq. "This is not how I have tried using the beacons in the past. At best they were just a boost to my own magic. Never something that could bring a type of magic to extreme levels. It could be anything."

"It looks stable, at least," said Lolan. "Should we just hope it doesn't cause any major problems?"

"I don't see what else we'd do," I said. "We have bigger problems to worry about. We don't even know if our message was seen by anyone, and we can't beat the doom drake unless we have everyone's help."

"Yeah, we need to get back to the others," said Tigala. "I can carry Klaus on my back." She began to transform. Her body took the shape of a horse this time. Sparr put Klaus on her back and continued to carry Sillius, who still looked like he wouldn't be able to walk even if he wanted to.

"Are we ready to head back then?" I asked, taking one last glance at the magical storm of memories.

The others nodded in response and we began our slow walk back. It was too bad we didn't have more Beastfolk with us. It would have been nice to have some form of transportation other than walking. But not the wyverns. They were a gamble from the start.

We walked for a long time across the land. It was amazing how many details stood out when you took the time to walk through the landscape rather than fly over it in a fraction of the time. There were hills that I hadn't even noticed. Up ahead there was a tall mountain with the opening of a volcano at the top. I had seen the volcano, but what I didn't notice was the lava field that spread out around it. There were porous black rocks that littered the ground and made it hard to keep good footing. The rocks were sharp, cutting through skin without much effort. I wished I had something on that covered my feet better than just sandals.

When we could finally see the end of the lava field, Klaus spoke up. "There are people coming," he said from on top of Tigala's back. "It looks like a lot of them. The wandering forest too."

"What?" I asked. "Why would they be coming out here? Is there something going on? Klaus, can you sense anything with your magic?"

"My magic is exhausted, unfortunately," said Klaus. "And Sparr is good with immediate future or distant past, not location sight magic."

We watched the group approach us as we continued doing our part to close the distance. It was a lot of people. It looked like it could be the remainder of our battle-ready forces here on Daegal. The wandering forest walked in a perimeter around the group, as if protecting them. But it didn't make sense. Why would they all be traveling toward us across Daegal. Were they running from something? Did the doom drake attack Birdsbane? Were we too late?

The questions raced through my head as we all picked up our pace, trying to get answers more quickly.

Then, I could make out someone approaching us quicker than the rest. He rode on top of a large bird with orange-red feathers.

"Who is that?" I asked.

"Geralt," said Klaus, still riding on Tigala's back.

"Geralt? I thought he was still gone trying to convince the Humans to join the cause."

"That's the last I heard too," said Sillius.

"Why would they all be coming this way?" I said. "What happened to Birdsbane?"

"Maybe it's fine," said Lolan. "We can't know until we talk to them." "But why would they leave?

"We'll figure it out," said Tigala.

I was impatient. I didn't want to hear the bad news that we were no doubt about to receive. Luckily the oversized bird that Geralt rode on was fast. It reached us in a couple of

233

minutes and landed with a skid. The bird stood taller than any of us and stared with an intimidating gaze. It then bowed its head and let Geralt hop off in his full golden armor.

"What's going on?" I asked anxious to hear what was wrong. "What happened to Birdsbane?"

Geralt looked flustered, unsure of how to answer the question, or maybe preparing us for the worst. "Birdsbane is fine. We still have our injured there getting treatment." He paused, trying to figure out how to say what he needed to.

"Then why is everyone here?" I asked.

"Well, good news and bad news," he said with a nervous chuckle. "We think your message worked. We saw it at Birdsbane, and some of the Avians confirmed that it was seen around the world."

"Oh," I said, unsure of how to process that. I was expecting Birdsbane to have been wiped off of the map, and instead, my call for reinforcements worked. "What's the bad news then?"

"Right," he said, with another nervous chuckle. "The doom drake also changed its course. They think that it saw the message as well. We think it's heading straight for—"

Just as he was about to finish the sentence there was a loud explosion of magic. Purple-blue magic to be exact. It swirled behind us at the base of the volcano. It started small, but gradually grew to the size of a building, then the size of a large tree. But it didn't stop there. The magic stretched into the sky and now competed in size with the volcano itself. Finally, it stopped, reaching up into the clouds. A large portal now swirled in the air between us and the volcano.

I already knew what Geralt was about to say, but I didn't want to believe it. We weren't ready for another fight. Maybe my message worked, but we needed more time to get everyone together. We needed to control the next battlefield, but this? This put all of the cards in the hands of doom drake. There was no way we could get out of this one unscathed, if we got out of it at all.

As soon as a large black scaly foot stepped out of the portal, I knew my assumption was right. The doom drake came to Daegal, to destroy us before we became a real threat.

21 Banyan

21.1 Banyan

This couldn't be happening. How did it know where we were? And how was it possible that it traveled so fast? This monster was always one step ahead of us, mostly just by being infinitely more powerful than us. This did not look like a battle we could win.

"Fallback to the others!" yelled Tigala, as the monster gained its footing after the teleportation.

No one discussed it. We all just ran to join the others.

The monster began its attack by setting the battlefield. It conjured up a massive storm. Clouds stirred above us and the wind swirled. The sky flashed with lightning as the clouds hid the sun.

Small localized tornados formed and charged in our direction.

"Watch out!" I yelled. I dove at Kesq, pushing her out of the way just before one of the small tornadoes touched down where she was headed.

We kept running. No time for gratitude. Next, the ground began to rumble, making it harder to keep our footing. Luckily we were out of the lava field. At least, I thought we were lucky until I realized what the doom drake was doing. The ground rumbled behind us. I snuck a glance over my shoulder to see several pillars push up from the ground. Each one shot up from beneath the lava field. After a moment, the sharp black rocks landed all around us, pelting us with jagged debris that tore through skin. I stumbled, but Lolan was right there to catch my arm and keep me on my feet.

Geralt was just ahead of us on the large bird, slowing down occasionally to make sure we were all okay.

When we finally reached the group we had only a moment to catch our breath before the monster continued the onslaught.

Rodrigo was there, and I was very glad to see him. "This is our final stand," he yelled to everyone. "This is all that we've got. The best we can do is hurt this monster so that others can come together and stop it."

There were cheers and yells all around. We couldn't have had a battle plan for this fight, but we had been preparing for this mentally. We always knew this could be the way it ended for us. It wasn't a good thought, but at least maybe our sacrifice would help others.

"Spread out!" Rodrigo yelled. "Work with each other in any way you can. The only advantage we may have on this thing is that there are more of us, and we all carry different magic. Overwhelm it, and—"

He didn't get a chance to finish that sentence. Fire blasted out of the monster's mouth, enhanced by its magic, and possibly the volcano behind it. A red glow brightened behind the beast and smoke began to pour out of the volcano.

Humans stepped forward and blocked the blasts of fire. Rodrigo joined the effort as soon as he realized what was going on. He turned his head as he held back the flames and mouthed a strained "Go!"

We all broke up, giving the monster more than a single target to go after.

I stayed put looking up at the members of the wandering forest in our ranks. At the very least, maybe I could work in tandem with Grollock and the others with my magic. I had no concrete ideas, but it was worth a shot.

I charged through the chaos, through the army of different races, and through the rubble of the already destroyed battlefield. The treants surrounded the group and were beginning to spread out like the rest of us. I had to get closer.

Where is he? I thought.

There was an explosion of water in front of me, a tidal wave that swept away twenty or so people, slamming some of them into large pillars of earth that were recently created by the Dwarves as cover.

This wasn't working. I looked around to see a wyvern charging my way.

"What are you looking for?" asked Tigala. Lolan was already mounted on her back.

"Grollock," I said. "I was hoping I could work with him somehow." There was a loud noise in the distance. "Get on!" yelled Tigala.

I climbed on her back and we lifted off just in time for a large boulder to roll beneath us.

She flew in a tight circle, gaining altitude. We joined the ranks of several Avians hovering in the air as they tried to use their sight magic as a warning system for others below them.

"Are you guys okay?" I asked Tigala and Lolan.

"Yeah. Let's stick together this time though," said Tigala. "We might not make it out of this one. Might as well go down with friends."

"Yeah," said Lolan. "Besides, we work well together." He gave me a friendly pat on the shoulder.

"Okay, do you see Grollock anywhere?" I asked.

"No, not from here," said Lolan. The battlefield was chaos. Smoke rose. The wind whipped around us.

"Do you see that?" asked Lolan.

I looked up at the doom drake. It stood tall above us, on the side of the volcano. And through the rain and smoke, I could see a faint glow near its head. It was a pink glow. "Did Malcolm already get control of it?"

"I don't think so," said Lolan. He pointed to show what he was talking about. I followed his finger to the silhouette of a dragon, appearing through the clouds as lightning jumped from cloud to cloud. It was Malcolm. He was here, and not too far behind the doom drake.

"Why is he still trying?" asked Tigala, mostly to herself. "Help us, or at least give up already."

"He sure is determined," I said. I watched the silhouette, only visible when the lightning struck. Then Tigala took a hard dive to the side. A large vine shot up from the ground and clawed at the air where we had just been.

Once she recovered, I said, "I'm not seeing Grollok. Let's go up to the doom drake's head. Maybe we can do some damage to its eyes or something."

"Sure," said Tigala. Her wings took deep flaps and we began to raise into the air. The time it took to reach the monster's height showed just how big it was. Our friends and allies stood below us, small enough that it was hard to make out who was who.

When we reached the creature's head, Malcolm was still trailing behind the colossus on his dragon. It would be another minute or two before he arrived. This might be our best chance at doing some damage without Malcolm trying to stop us.

"To the eyes," I yelled. "Let's blind the beast."

Tigala turned us toward the eyes. They were enormous, each one was about the size of that ogre that Lolan and I ran into our first day out in Daegal. I didn't know if we had it in us to take down something this big and powerful.

As we got close, Lolan began nocking arrows. He let them fly, one by one. The monster's eyes flashed white for a moment, and before each arrow would have landed, its head twitched and turned, letting the arrows fly past it or bounce off of the monster's scaly hide.

"Keep trying that," I said. "It's bound to make a mistake at some point. We just need some kind of advantage."

I grabbed a pocket full of dirt and yelled, "Hold!" as we hovered close to the doom drake's head.

I ran and jumped off of Tigala, landing at the back of the monster's head. I climbed my way up and threw the dirt down where I stood, pouring my magic into the small amount of fertile soil. With the magic started, I ran back to Tigala. She anticipated my return and was already slightly lower than the top of the montster's head. I jumped and Lolan threw out an arm to keep me from overshooting and plummeting to my death.

I continued the growth in the small handful of dirt that I left behind. Maybe I could actually do something this time. I made the plant grab the clump of dirt like a bird's talon clutching a fish. Then I grew the limbs out of it. Two touched down, and then two more. A body grew, thickening as I fed more of my magic into it. The plant creature stood up at my bidding and continued to grow. I thought of my family, my new friends, and the good we could do. I thought of the people we would save from these terrible fates if we could stop the doom drake, and the small sapling grew to a small treant. It wasn't much compared to the towering colossus, but it was something.

"I'm sending it in," I said.

Lolan readied another arrow in response. And we held our position next to the monster's head.

The monster's eyes flashed white again. It was expecting something. It raised a massive claw to swipe at the treant. I told it to duck at the last second. The claw still ripped off one of its limbs, forcing me to spend my time regrowing it. But I didn't have a chance. Tigala swerved to dodge the claw as well, leaving us struggling to hang on as we were jerked through the air.

"How are we supposed to have any kind of success when it's ready for every attack?" I asked feeling defeated.

"It's not ready for everything," said Lolan. "Look." He was pointing down toward the base of the monster. One of its feet was now trapped in stone. Others were preparing alternate attacks as well as a result of the distraction we caused. "Now let's take advantage of it being distracted by them!"

He readied another arrow and took a shot. The arrow slammed into the eye this time, with a squishy impact.

The monster howled in a way that shook the air around us.

"Keep your eyes peeled, Tigala!" I yelled, anticipating an attack.

I stood my plant creature back up and dug its remaining arm into the scales at the top of the doom drake. Then it jumped off of the drake with its arm still connected. It swung down and landed on the monster's eye, next to the arrow. The drake was trying furiously to blink away the arrow, and now my treant, but it was unsuccessful. It began to flail its head around, releasing a deafening howl.

I told my treant to yank on the arrow before Tigala had to fly us out of range of one of the doom drake's arms, coming up to swat us from the sky.

We rolled through the air. Lolan, who was already hugging Tigala to stay put, used one arm to hold onto me.

It wasn't enough.

I fell from his grasp, unprepared for the quick maneuver, and started my plummet toward the earth. The wind rushed past me, but it was a great view of the battle below, beautiful in its own way. The glow of all of the different types of magic made a rainbow light show. Smoke and dust billowed out diffusing the lights. With the wind rushing around me, it almost didn't even feel like a war. It looked like a colorful cloud that I would land on.

Reality snapped back as Tigala swooped next to me, diving at the same speed. Lolan grabbed me again and Tigala pulled beneath me to catch me. She tried to ease my landing on her, but it didn't really work. I hit hard on my stomach, with my arms hanging off of one side of her and my legs off the other.

"Ow," I gasped when I finally caught my breath.

"The ground would have hurt more," said Tigala.

I looked back up at the monster's head. The dark shadow of the dragon and the glow of pink magic showed that Malcolm had caught up.

"Malcolm's back," I said.

"Should we go back up? Maybe we can get his help?" asked Lolan.

"No," I said. "I've talked to him enough times to know that he's never going to help us stop the doom drake. He stops when he controls it, or when he dies."

"Where to, then?" said Tigala.

As I stared up, I saw that the drake had managed to shake my plant monster from its eye. The plant creature fell from the sky and disappeared into the cloud of colors below.

"Let's go back down. Maybe we can work with others or find Grollok," I said.

Tigala changed course, heading for the chaos of the battle below. I looked up at the monster's face as we descended. Malcolm wouldn't give up, and we could use his help most of all.

Just before we entered the cloud, I saw something on the horizon. A flash of color in the dark stormy landscape. But what was it?

We were swallowed up by the cloud before I could make any guesses.

21.2 Banyan

Everything was hazy as we entered the cloud of debris above the battle that was raging at the monster's feet. It looked like an apocalyptic land, which may not be far from the truth. The ground was shattered and covered in ice and bouts of fire. Animals attacked the feet and served as a form of fast travel across the battlefield, while purple flashes moved people to and from crucial spots.

The Avians were doing their part as well, shouting orders, and trying to search the monster for weak spots. It was chaos, and the doom drake still seemed like it was fairly unscathed. Even the arrow to its eye didn't seem to be affecting it much.

No one said anything. We flew down to the closest group of Dwarves and Saurians that seemed like they had some kind of a plan.

The ground was a solid sheet of ice in front of one colossal foot, while behind it, the Dwarves created a large spike of stone sticking out of the ground. Humans charged the foot trying to antagonize it. Flame poured out onto the large black scales.

The doom drake howled and retaliated with its own attack. Purple glowed from above and the howl became ear-splittingly loud. Everyone stopped what they were doing to cover their ears, including us. Tigala lost control and we slammed into the ground.

The scream stopped a moment later, but the pain was still there. I brought my hand away from my ears and saw blood on them.

"Lolan," I yelled. My voice was an echo in my own head. "Tigala!" I pulled myself to my feet, feeling all of the fresh cuts and bruises with each motion. The world spun around me.

A loud crunch caught my attention behind me. I turned to see a Human get squished under the massive talon of the monster. The doom drake had dodged the patch of ice and killed many of its attackers in the process.

This is it. I thought. *There is no recovering from this. We lost.*

The other foot lifted and headed toward me. I stumbled forward, trying to get away, but what did it matter anyway. This is where we die. All of us.

Dirt and stone fell from the clawed foot as it pulled free from the earth.

"Kaia!" someone shouted. They slammed into me dragging me along. I struggled, trying to get my footing, but I was moving sideways, and whoever was pushing or carrying me was also struggling to keep up. They dove and we hit the ground a moment before the doom drake's second foot touched down, just behind us.

I spit the dirt and blood from my mouth and turned to look at my rescuer. It was Lolan, staring back at me. He groaned, holding his waist.

"Tigala?" I asked, starting to panic.

"I don't know," he said. "I'm sure she's fine. She can fly. Right?"

"I don't know!" I said, mad at the assumption even. "That thing is pretty big. She might need more than flying to keep safe from it."

"Let's look for her then. Can you walk?"

"Yeah," I said. I pushed myself to my feet, groaning. We started looking for her, making sure that we stayed clear of the monster's feet. All said and done, we weren't very effective against this monster. Lolan had fire magic, I had nature. But none of us had been in a war before. None of us knew how to work with teams of allies in such a large-scale fight. We could hold our own in battles against smaller enemies, but against the doom drake, it was like throwing rocks at a mountain.

I tried to find Tigala, but the world around us was a blur of destruction. The smoke and debris clouded the air and made it hard to breathe. Blasts of magic erupted all around us, and we did all that we could to stay out of the way of the attacks. But there was no Tigala.

"Tigala," I yelled. Tears started running down my face. I couldn't lose her too. After Zef had died so recently, I couldn't handle it. I needed to at least end this fight with the people who got me this far. "Tigala!" I yelled again.

I fell to my knees. *What are we supposed to do? And why do I keep surviving these situations while people die all around me? Isn't it time? Isn't it my time? How do I participate in a fight of this scale?*

Then, I heard something. In the distance, there was a blast far stronger than any I had heard so far. I looked up to see a large cone of ice stabbing out of the doom drake's leg and a cheer erupted from the Saurians and other warriors. It was quickly drowned out by the howl of the monster. They had done damage. They had actually hurt it. But how?

The group of Saurians looked bigger than what had shown up to the battle. As I looked around, it almost looked like our army grew. Was it just an illusion to make us look stronger that was put together by the Gnomes?

Then I heard wings flap behind me, and something skidded on the ground. I turned to find a wyvern looking back at me. It stood, favoring its front right foot, and wore a scar on its face.

"Tigala!" I yelled. I ran to her and gave her a hug. "I—I thought you were dead."

"Can't kill me that easy," she said.

"How did you—" I heard another large crash behind me, followed by more cheers. We were making progress. "What is going on?"

"Reinforcements," she said. "It seems our message was seen by most of the world after all."

"But how did they get here?" I asked.

"Gnomes can teleport with their magic. Sillius can. Sounds like whatever went wrong at the end of that message created a ton of portals throughout the world and they all led to that giant shifting portal behind the mansion. The people that were willing to help saw the portal as the sign you mentioned. They stepped in, and are now walking to the battle from the mansion. These are the first of the reinforcements, but by the looks of it, there are a lot more on their way."

I breathed out, unable to believe what I was hearing. We had help! Not only that, but with more people, we were actually affecting the monster. We were hurting it. We had a chance at stopping it.

"That's not all," said Tigala.

"What?" I asked.

249

"I found something while I was dodging the drake's foot." She led the way, not far off from where we were. There on the ground were the remains of my plant monster. Some of the vines were smashed to a pulp, but many others were okay, usable even.

I looked up at Tigala and said, "Let's hurt this thing." I focused my magic on the mangled plants, but as I did, I had an idea. The plant monster always wrapped around itself to hold the soil at its core. What if I was the one to hold the dirt? I picked up its core and let the magic flow out of me, through the vines. They coiled around me, around each of my limbs, and grew thicker and stronger. I pushed more from the root ball to cover my chest and head. I was still essentially creating a person-shaped plant creature, but instead of me controlling it from a distance, I was controlling it from within. I told the extended legs to stand me up off of the ground, with my long vine arms balancing me on the way up. I wasn't even done yet, and I stood at double the height of Lolan. I looked down at him and smiled. "Want a ride?"

"Woah," was all he said in response. I stretched out a vine arm and pushed more magic into it to stretch it closer to him. He stepped forward and put a foot on one vine, while he grabbed another with his free hand. I lifted him up and set him on my shoulder, like when the treants let me ride on theirs. But this time, I was the treant.

I used my magic, to loosely bind Lolan's legs to me, so he could get out if he wanted to, but also so he wouldn't fall off by mistake.

"Ready?" I asked, looking down at Tigala.

She nodded and we ran for the creature's legs.

As we did, the battle became alive around us. So quickly after I felt like all was lost, I now could breathe again. There was hope. Every attack from our side was more powerful. We were finally pushing the doom drake back, instead of it destroying us with every step.

"What's the plan?" asked Lolan.

"I don't really have one," I said. I looked up at the monster as I ran in big loping steps. There were open wounds on its legs where previous attacks had done damage. "Let's get up there," I said, pointing to a wound on its thigh. "Maybe we can dig that wound deeper. Break its legs or something."

"Sounds good to me."

Tigala flew above keeping an eye on us. We reached the monster's leg, but before we started our climb. I took one vine limb and threw a mound of dirt at the wound. It was slightly wet due to some of the Saurian attacks, so it held together in a ball fairly well. The ball of mud hit the wound and covered much of it. *Good.*

With the other arm, I grabbed another scoop and buried it in the tangle of vines near my actual legs—the lower body of my vine monster.

Then we began our climb. It was easier as a vine monster. My vines slithered around the monster like an army of snakes, digging into the scales and finding good grips. And it wasn't just my arms either. My legs were made of the same stuff, so I used them in the same way, like prehensile limbs. In no time, we were up to the wound.

"Keep an eye out for me," I said. "I'll tear it open. Then you can use your fire magic on it."

"Are you sure," said Lolan. "I still can't really control it well."

"You don't need to," I said. "We *need* fire and lots of it." I used my vine creature to start tearing into the doom drake's

251

open wound. It was nothing like cutting into the flesh of an animal. It was more dense—harder to move. Maybe that was a result of just how big the muscles had to be to carry its own weight, or maybe it was something else. I still was able to dig into it, it just took some extra work. I was glad to have the added strength of my vine body.

I tore at flesh, digging the wound deeper and deeper. The monster screamed as other attacks bombarded it. Still, it was overwhelmed, just at less of an advantage than before.

"Watch out!" yelled Lolan. "From the right!"

I shot one of my vines to the left, it grew longer and wrapped around the leg. I let go with the other arm and we swung around the monster's leg, landing on the back side of it just in time for its arm to swing by our previous location. We dodged a potentially fatal blow.

"Thanks," I said. We looked up to make sure the monster was done swatting at us, and then swung back to the front.

"Your turn," I said. "Blast it!"

Lolan paused for a moment and then threw his hands forward. Torrents of fire blasted out of them, charring my vine suit around him. I didn't mind. I could grow it back, and for all of the damage he was doing to my vines, he was doing more to the doom drake. It was worth the trade.

"Okay!" I yelled. Another arm was coming at us. This time though, the leg lifted to try and make the two meet quicker. I slipped out on my vine swing with only a small gap to escape through. The claw clipped my free arm and sent us spinning as we swung. I had to latch on with both arms to steady us again. That was a little too close.

"You okay?" I asked.

"Yeah," he said. "We need to be careful though. It has sight magic, and even without that, it's getting closer to catching us."

"Right," I said. "Maybe Tigala can get in there while we guard." I searched the skies for her and saw her circling around near us. She was transporting a Gnome who, when they got close enough, jumped off of Tigala's back and into a portal. A moment later another portal opened on the doom drake's back and then Gnome climbed out.

"Tigala!" I yelled. She turned and saw us so I waved her down. "We opened a wound on the front of its leg. Anything you can do to it?"

She nodded and flew around to the front of the leg. She landed on the wound in her wyvern form and used her large claws to tear at the flesh, digging the wound even deeper. Then, her tail readied and she stabbed it several times with the scorpion-like point of it.

"Here it comes," yelled Lolan.

Tigala jumped off and began to fly away, but she wasn't quick enough. I swung on one anchored vine arm and grabbed the incoming claw with the other. I couldn't do much against a monster that big, but hopefully it was enough to slow it down. All she needed was a little help. So I tangled up the arm, slowing it for just a second or two. Tigala took the opportunity to dip beneath it and out of its range.

We were making progress. We were hurting the doom drake. Others saw what we were doing and added their own attacks to the wound. A flurry of ice shards slammed into it. Humans gathered together to throw a giant fireball at it, and Dwarves worked together to launch sharp boulders at it.

The monster screamed with each impact and wasn't reacting quickly enough to properly dodge or retaliate. It backed up further, closer to the volcano. There were cheers around us as others could see our progress.

I looked up at it and the volcano in the background. I saw something that I had missed before—veins stretching up toward the peak. The veins glowed red. That could be a really good thing or a really bad thing depending on how this fight turned out.

I didn't have time to dwell on it now though. I swung down the doom drake's legs so I could help the forces attacking from range. Lolan was suited to it, and maybe my vine monster would be too. I settled myself among the Dwarves.

"Break up some rocks for me," I said.

The look of confusion showed they were not used to seeing plant creatures like the one I used as a suit. But they listened regardless. I'm sure most people had seen the army of treants helping serve as mobile outposts and bunkers. Many of them too were throwing large stones at the monster. When the Dwarves broke up the ground in front of me, I joined in, lobbing handfuls as big as me at the doom drake. My stones only did so much against the monster's thick hide, but in conjunction with the attacks of others, we were breaking it down, bit by bit.

Scales were tearing free, blood ran down its legs, and the monster walked with less strength than it had before. It was weakening, and it was only a matter of time until a leg gave out and we could take it out for good.

Then, there was a bright flash. The clouds reflected the bright pink glow coming from the monster's head. I looked up, covering my eyes from the light, but still trying desperately to see what was going on. The light grew for a moment and then faded out just as quickly. Once it was dull enough that I could look at the source, I saw the pink glow at the temples of the doom drake, now brighter than ever. The dragon that held Malcolm flew closer and landed on the head of the colossus. But the doom drake didn't react. In fact, it had stopped moving entirely. It was eerily still.

I watched Malcolm step off the dragon's shoulders onto the head of the doom drake. The battle had halted as we all watched what was happening above us. Even from the distance, I could make out Malcolm's words.

"Ahaaahh! I have done it!"

21.3 Banyan

Malcolm stood atop the doom drake as it let out a devastating roar. The ground shook and all attacks stopped as we waited to see if the worst had actually happened.

The doom drake stood tall, still taking advantage of the momentary reprieve, with Malcolm commanding it. The drake raised its arms and a purple glow emanated from them. Everyone tensed.

"I control the doom drake now," said Malcolm. His voice was magnified by the doom drake's illusion magic. I was pretty sure everyone on the battlefield could hear him speak. "I am Malcolm Mortem, and I am a direct descendant of Shayde Mortem, the man who created this monster long ago. He made it as a weapon, a weapon to use against his enemies. With a creature this powerful under his control, he could have ended the wars long before they started. He could have forced the feuds to end."

"I too seek peace—peace for my people. We have attacked and killed for far too long, and this is where we put that to an end. This is a tool for Humans, and Humans only. So, for all of you fire-wielders, join my side. Help me clean the world of these other races that seek to destroy us—to destroy our families. And in turn, I will show you how to truly use your magic, and magics that you have never dreamed of using before. Join me and help me save our people from destruction.

"As for the rest of you—those who stand in my way will not be tolerated. You have seen the doom drake's power. Combined with my own, you don't stand a chance. This is your end, and I advise you to give up and make this easy. I don't have to make you suffer, but I will if you oppose me and the rest of the Human race."

A silence hung in the air. I looked around the battlefield, looking for other Humans. I hadn't talked about Malcolm in my message to everyone. I hadn't mentioned that someone was trying to control it to better the Humans only—that he would wipe out the rest of us if given the chance. *Did his success in taming the drake also mark the end of our tentative alliances? Is this where it all falls apart, where people stop looking out for each other and turn back to only looking out for themselves?*

There was silence on the battlefield as Malcolm's words sunk in. A few Humans talked amongst themselves. I didn't recognize them. They were probably from the group that joined us recently. They must have come through the massive portal at the illusion veins.

Others looked tense, afraid that a fight would break out among the warriors. Some prepared, covering their backs in case things turned for the worse.

"Hey scumbag," said a voice. I looked over to see Geralt standing on one of the eruptions of stone scattered about the battlefield. He yelled as loud as he could to make sure he was heard. A nearby Gnome used his magic to boost the sound as well, broadcasting it to the rest of the warriors and no doubt Malcolm as well. "I kind of like these people," Geralt said.

257

"And you've killed more Humans than I can count. You're not doing this for us, you're doing it for yourself. You want glory and power.

"But I don't think you fully get what's happening here. Your greatest mistake in waking that thing is that you gave us all a common enemy. You taught us to work together, and whether or not you are stronger than us, we'll survive. Maybe not me, or the others in this battle, but there will always be other races. There will always be more of us. And we'll fight for *actual* safety as long as we breathe. So, you want to destroy the other races? Then get ready for a war."

There was another brief silence as Geralt finished his speech. And then, a cheer erupted. It was small at first, but it grew to a thunderous roar that rivaled that of the doom drake. The other Humans joined in with the cry, and it was clear that we were not shaken. We already knew that we could hurt the doom drake, so if Malcolm wanted a fight, we'd give it to him.

Malcolm was too far away for me to see any features of his face, but I could imagine how angry he must have been at the response, and the doom drake echoed that anger. Malcolm raised his arms and pink magic flew into the monster's head. In an instant, it roared and threw its massive arms forward while it flexed its wings. Red glowed from the doom drake, and the earth shook. But this wasn't an attack with earth magic. Red meant fire.

The ground started to split, showing small cracks. There was a loud explosion from the mountain behind the drake—the volcano.

Smoke billowed into the already cloudy air, and more red glow showed at the peak of the volcano. Another boom came and red lava began shooting from the volcano's mouth and bubbling down its sides. Like a trebuchet launching boulders, fiery rocks flew through the air and slammed into the ground around us, taking down large portions of our army. I watched as one of the lava rocks slammed into a treant's shoulder. It knocked the treant's arm clean off and lit the creature's foliage on fire. It fell to the ground as Saurian's rushed to its side to douse the flames.

But that wasn't the extent of the attack. The doom drake clawed at our people and directed lightning at them. Those who were trying to douse flames were now being electrocuted in turn.

That's when I heard the flapping of wings. Malcolm's dragon, now free from ferrying him after the doom drake, swooped down to join the fight. It flew by, grabbing an Elf and a Dwarf, one in each claw. It flew higher into the air and then dropped then. A Gnome was able to catch the Dwarf, but there was no one close enough to catch the Elf.

What do we do now? I looked over the battlefield as all of our advantages were removed from play. Malcolm was right, he had the upper hand now, and it showed in how much damage he was doing to our army, whether or not it was growing.

But I couldn't dwell on it. We had hurt the doom drake, quite a bit even. Maybe we could get back to that point and take it out for good. Maybe we still had a chance, somewhere, somehow. I couldn't think of anything that would get us back to a level playing field, and then I heard the dragon roar. That was something I could help with at least. I had stopped it once before, and maybe I'd have a better chance now with my vine armor.

"You up for taking down the dragon?" I asked.

"Let's do it," said Lolan, as he pulled an arrow from his quiver.

I ran across the battlefield to where the dragon had landed. It was attacking a unit of Saurians, who were having trouble pinning it down.

"Coming through!" I yelled as I charged toward the giant lizard. In my vine armor, I was about half of its size. It wasn't great, but at least it was better than me taking it on with just the small plants that I used to grow. Lolan dove off of my shoulder before I got up to speed, and then I slammed into the dragon, grabbing its head and slamming it into the dirt. The dragon screamed and sucked in a deep breath. I remembered what that meant, but I thought I had disabled its fire breath.

The dragon released a puff of flame that blasted the back of my vine armor, burning and snapping several of the vines. I was quick to try and replace them, but it exposed my back. If it got another hit off in the same spot, it would not be good.

I wrestled the dragon's head, trying to direct it to somewhere less dangerous if it did shoot fire again. It was stronger than me though. I heard it take in another breath, and I was terrified. I did all that I could, punching the monster in the throat. Instead of another puff of fire, the dragon choked and coughed up smoke. I was safe from that one at least.

The dragon then pushed off of the ground, standing on its hind legs. It swung a claw at me and tore through most of the vines that protected my torso. I fell to the ground in my torn vine armor and was sure it would attack my back next.

But the attack never came. Instead, there was the cracking sound of ice and a wave of cold air that passed by me. I picked myself up to see the dragon held just out of reach by several ice spikes. It screamed and started slashing through the spikes.

"Get out of there," shouted a Saurian.

I listened and backed up to join their ranks. Lolan fired arrows at the dragon and Tigala flew above, circling, waiting for an opportunity to strike. The dragon was angry. It looked at me, and I swear it saw me through the vines. It remembered me. The one to take away its flame.

It crashed through the remaining ice spikes and charged me. I ran toward it to keep it from reaching the Saurians that had just protected me. I began growing more vines as I ran. When I was about crash into it, I ducked down and slammed into the lizard's throat again. With the impact, I unwrapped the extra vines that I had been building and wound them around the dragon's neck as I swung up onto its back. The Saurians added to the fight with their own ice attacks.

The dragon breathed in again, and I tugged as hard as I could on its neck. It choked back the fire again, spouting smoke. The dragon saw it was losing and flapped its wings, picking me up into the air with it.

I grew more vines, snaking them around the lizard's neck and torso, but it wasn't enough.

There was an impact and the dragon screamed. I looked down and saw one of Lolan's arrows stuck in its shoulder. We were hurting it, but the dragon had the upper hand as long as it kept me in the air. It could fly, and if I somehow lost grip of it, I might not be as lucky as I was last time.

My vines were beginning to reach its wings, so pulled trying to steer it. It wasn't as simple as steering the wyvern though. The dragon screamed and reached its head back, snapping jaws bigger than me. It snapped a few of the vines near my right arm, and I had to regrow to ensure my grip.

What do I do now? I thought. I didn't have any of my normal resources.

Then there was a cry below. It was familiar. The cry of the Dwarves. They lobbed stones into the air that pelted the dragon and the doom drake too. The dragon roared down at them and continued to climb higher.

I needed to do something before we got too high up if I wanted any chance of survival. I focused on my magic, the only thing I had at my disposal. Vines were a staple of my magic, and to make them more dangerous, I had always given them thorns. So I did exactly that, focusing on the extensions of my body rather than the part where I was held. The thorns stretched out of the limbs, scraping against dragon scales, but not breaking through. So I squeezed.

More rocks pelted the dragon. Another arrow flew at it. Ice slammed its hide. Flying Beastfolk swarmed it. I wasn't sure if it was all to save me or to collectively take out at least one of our opponents. The reason didn't matter though. We were working together. We were overcoming our differences. That was what mattered.

And to top it off, the squeeze proved helpful. My thorns began to slip between scales, eating into flesh. The dragon began to falter. It screamed and puffed out more fire breath, but its recovered fire attacks had no distance to them and dissipated before they put anyone in danger.

The dragon tried to keep its altitude, but it was too much for it to handle. The beast roared and plummeted toward the ground.

I didn't let up. I couldn't let up now. We couldn't afford to fight Malcolm, the doom drake, and a dragon. I held on as tight as I could and the dragon fell.

We slammed into the ground with a violent crash. The dragon's body hit first, taking most of the impact. My longer vines snapped and catapulted me across the ground ahead of the lizard. I tried to get up but found myself too weak to stand.

I opened my eyes to a swarm of warriors on a mound behind me. I tried again to stand, and couldn't move any of my limbs. I searched frantically around me with just my eyes and remembered I was bound by my vine suit, even if it was in a sad state. I pushed out with my magic and told it to put me on my feet. The vine limbs were mangled and smashed, but were still strong enough to support me and give my actual body a small amount of protection.

I slowly found the energy to walk myself toward the swarm of people, and found beneath them the dragon, breathing its last breaths. We did it!

But there was no time to celebrate.

The scream of the doom drake behind it shook me to my core.

We had defeated the dragon, but we had only just begun.

21.4 Banyan

The dragon fell, but the battle raged on. The battlefield was even more destroyed than before. It looked like an unknown subterranean land. Smoke and storm clouds blotted out the sky. Rocks stabbed up into the air, some so high that you couldn't see the tops of them. The earth was cracked and charred and frozen. Gnome machinations joined the fray. A few still fought, but most now littered the landscape, lifeless and still. The lava was starting to make its way around our warriors. And through the smoke, was the massive silhouette of the doom drake, shown by flashes of lightning and fire.

It was a lot to take in at once. The dragon had served as a nice distraction from the real problem. How do we stop the giant with Malcolm at its side? The two of them were far more powerful than any thousand people from our army.

The doom drake roared above us and threw a torrent of fire at a group that I could only make out as shadows through the smoke. When the flames let up, those shadows were gone. We were back to losing again.

I pushed myself back onto my feet and searched around for Lolan. He was still amongst the Saurians that were helping in our attack on the dragon.

I stumbled over in my damaged vine armor, repairing it as I approached.

"Thanks for the backup," I said to Lolan and the Saurians.

"Same to you," said a green Saurian I didn't know. "We were losing until you showed up."

"Do you think we survive the two of them working together?" asked another Saurian with red scales and bone jewelry.

I looked up at the looming silhouette. "I don't know," I said. "We don't have any other choice but to try."

"We do," said another Saurian. "We could give up. But what fun would that be? I will at least do some damage on my way out."

A morbid way to look at it, but probably also a realistic one.

"We don't have much time," I said. "I'm going to try and figure out some sort of game plan. If I make it that far, hopefully, the Gnomes will be able to let everyone know."

The blue Saurian nodded. "We'll do as much damage as we can in the meantime." With that, the lizardfolk headed off in the direction of the doom drake.

"You okay?" I asked Lolan.

"Yeah," said Lolan. "Are you? That was insane!"

"Yeah," I said. "A little battered, but when am I not? I guess all of those dire situations taught me how to improve my magic quickly."

"Hah," said Lolan. "Maybe I should be a little less careful with my fire magic."

I smiled. "No, definitely be more careful with your fire magic. You could burn down a house in no time with that stuff."

He smirked back at me. "So no plan yet?"

"No. Not yet. I don't know how we win against someone who knows all of the intricacies of magic and an ancient dragon that's been stewing in magic juice for the past five hundred years."

"Well I'll let you know if I come up with anything," he said.

"Thanks. Let's see if we can find where Tigala is helping. Maybe we'll think of something on the way." He nodded and climbed onto a vine arm that I extended toward him. He sat back down in his perch on my shoulder and we headed out across the battlefield.

There were cries all around us. Some were of adrenaline, some of pain, and others of despair. The doom drake stood still and seemed to be using earth magic to destroy the ground in front of us. After a moment, the magic dissipated and it was clear that he hid his movement with an illusion. The warriors that stood where his foot now was were squished into nothing beneath its weight.

There was nothing we could do. Those people had just sacrificed their lives in hopes of the world being a better place. Thousands of others in this fight alone had met the same fate. We had to make this count. We had to put everything we had into this fight. This was the final one. If we lost this, there was no surviving. Malcolm would destroy us all—all except the Humans.

But how could we stop him? I still couldn't think of any answers as I ran. I used my vine arms to slingshot Lolan and me over streams of lava. Rocks still fell from the blackened sky as torrents of rain poured and lightning cracked above.

I searched and found the shape of Tigala's wyvern form through the clouds. There was a group of Avians working with Gnomes to disperse tactics to the rest of the warriors.

The doom drake must have discovered them and wanted them to stop. It threw up an arm and giant thorned vines pulled out of the ground, slamming into several of the Gnomes. Avians took flight, some with a Gnome clutched between their legs or hanging on to their necks. But the doom drake was continuing its attack.

One Gnome, in particular, was struggling to hang on to its Avian ride. Tigala saw the Gnome and swooped in, ready to catch him if he lost his grip. The Gnome's fingers slipped a moment later and Tigala dove. She flew with such speed toward the ground that it looked like she wouldn't be able to stop. She caught the Gnome and quickly changed her direction, slowing her descent.

But the doom drake, or maybe Malcolm, didn't want to see the Gnome survive. A bolt of lightning struck through Tigala.

"Nooo!" I yelled. I ran as fast as I could toward her. My eyes took a moment to adjust after the bright flash, but when they did, I saw Tigala crash into the ground and skid thirty or so feet.

I charged to her side and knelt down next to her while the doom drake's lightning attack targeted the other Avians.

I knelt in my vine armor and reached out to her. I frantically watched her chest. She was breathing. I put my head close to her, which left the shoulders and head of my vine armor hanging far past her.

"That's a weird look for you," Tigala coughed out.

"Are you okay?" I asked. I looked up and saw the Gnome several feet away. He was burnt and black.

Tigala lifted a wing and showed a burned hole through the skin of it. "Just hit the wing," Tigala said and she began transforming back into her Beastfolk self. The wound in her wing showed on the back of her shoulder. It was a deep charred and gooey wound.

"That looks really bad," I said. "You need to get out of here."

"No," she said. "If we're going out, we're doing it together."

"Right," I said. "You're not able to fly anymore though, are you? I don't know if I can carry you both."

"I can walk," said Tigala.

Just then I heard the clacking of hooves. I looked and found Palem riding over on Bubba. It was good to see them, even though the situation was so dire.

"That's a nice wound. Let me patch you up," said Palem. Without hesitating, he hopped off of Bubba and created a green growth on the earth. A plant pushed out with wide leathery leaves. He reached down, bit the end off of a leaf and chewed for a moment, then spit it back into his hand. "Comfrey," he said, before repeating the process. "It'll plug up that wound, help stop the bleeding."

Once he had a good handful of chewed comfrey leaves he walked over to Tigala and shoved the mush into the wound. She winced at the pain, but let him do it.

Next, he grabbed a length of ripped fabric from a pouch slung around Bubba and proceeded to wrap it around the wound.

"That should hold you over for a little bit," said Palem.

Tigala rolled her arm to test it and winced again. "Thanks," she said.

I wasn't sure what we were supposed to do. How do we stop this thing? My thoughts couldn't stop wandering back to the doom drake.

Palem nodded and climbed back on Bubba's back. "Stay safe," he said. Then he looked at me. "There aren't many of us left."

I nodded. "You too."

With that, he traveled on to the next area of destruction in search of more wounded.

"Wait, that's it," I said.

"What's it?" asked Tigala.

"Nature magic," I said. "The answer. How we beat the doom drake and Malcolm."

"I'm not following," said Lolan.

"Grollock," I said. "Kesq said you can use beacons outside of your own magic. We just saw Sillius and Klaus do it with the magic veins of illusion magic. Grollock is a walking beacon that we can all use! It's dangerous, but it may be our only chance at taking down the doom drake."

"Oh," said Lolan. "Isn't that a beacon too?" He pointed up to the volcano behind the drake."

"It looks like it," I said. "If we can get people to channel their magic through those two beacons, we might have a chance. One of us using a beacon is extremely powerful, but what about all of us?"

"Sounds like a giant killer," said Tigala.

"I need to find Grollock. But first, we need Kesq to tell everyone how to use the beacons." I searched the battlefield for her and couldn't see her through the destruction and smoke. I did happen to see someone who always stood out though. Gold shining armor gleamed even despite the air conditions.

"Geralt!" I yelled. He looked our way and I ran to meet him halfway.

269

"How can I be of service?" he asked. Soot marked his face, and he looked worse for wear.

"I need you to find Kesq," I said. "Remember? The blue Saurian that we met in the wandering forest."

"Yes, alright. What for?" he asked.

"I think I know how to stop the doom drake. You need to tell her to get help from a Gnome to tell everyone how to use beacons."

"Beacons?" he asked.

"She'll know what you mean. Tell her I said that it might be our only way to win this fight."

"And if... if I can't find her?" he asked.

"Have a Gnome tell everyone to try and funnel their magic through the magic on Grollock's chest and the veins at the top of the volcano."

Geralt looked up to the top of the volcano and then back to me. "Alright. I'll make it so!" He raised a fist in the air as he disappeared into the battlefield.

Now to find Grollock. I searched the horizon for the glowing green chest in the shadow of a tall treant. It was so hard to see. I found a group of the smaller trees and shrubs attacking the doom drake's tail and headed in that direction.

"You good?" I asked Tigala to make sure she was keeping up.

"I'll be fine," she said, working to keep pace with me and Lolan riding in and on the vine suit.

In the distance behind the small trees, I could see a few of the full-size treants attacking as well. It looked like some warriors rode on them to try and get a better vantage point against the doom drake.

"I think he's over there," I said, pointing where we were heading.

A lightning bolt struck just in front of me, and then someone flew down to block my path. It was him, Malcolm.

"I know what you're doing," he said. "And I'm not going to let you slip out of my grasp this time. It's time we end this." He pulled his hands back and they glowed red. I braced for the impact.

But it didn't connect. I felt the heat, but it wasn't as hot as it should have been. I looked down to see Rodrigo holding the flames at bay. The fire formed a half dome between us and Malcolm.

"Go," said Rodrigo sparing a moment to look back at me. We'll hold him off.

Alejandra joined him in redirecting the flames and several other warriors joined the effort with their own forms of magic.

I ran as fast as I could from the fight and trusted them to keep Malcolm occupied. We needed to get to Grollock now.

There were more warriors ahead, working in tandem to cripple one of the monster's feet. I ran through them, seeing the green glow showing on one of the treant silhouettes now. He was just ahead of me.

"You don't deserve to survive this!" yelled Malcolm. I looked back and saw him blasting toward me. His hands glowed again, this time with yellow magic. In an instant, another lightning bolt struck down just to my left. I wondered why he missed and found a trail of yellow magic leading to Tallesia.

"Tell me you have a plan," she said.

"I think so," I said.

She nodded and swung her arms back, sending a powerful gust of wind behind me. We kept running toward Grollock. Almost there.

"Have a boost," shouted someone else. I looked to find Amara, almost hidden amongst the other warriors. Her hand spun in a circular motion and a purple-blue portal opened in front of me, big enough for my whole vine armor suit to fit through. The three of us dove through it, and it spit us out about a hundred feet closer to Grollock. I raised an arm as thanks.

"We've go this," I said to the others. "We can do this." I looked back and saw Malcolm, further behind than before, but still steadily making his way toward us. We didn't have much time.

We ran through a group of Dwarves, and I realized who they were. Marv was in his rock form rescuing injured from the battlefield, while Dunnel and Abigail launched boulders at the doom drake.

Grollock was just ahead of us, but I couldn't afford to convince him to help from the ground. I needed to get to him quicker than that. Quicker than Malcolm would catch up to us.

"Can I have a lift?" I yelled to Abigail and Dunnel.

"Where too?" shouted Dunnel.

I pointed at Grollock, and the two Dwarves stomped and went into a horse stance. The ground beneath me and Tigala erupted and we were launched into the air. The air blew all around us, and I was afraid we might not make it. I reached back with one arm and grabbed Tigala, while I reached forward with the other, extending my vines toward Grollock. He saw us flying toward him and slowly reached up a hand. It was enough. My vines connected to his wrist and pulled us in. We swung beneath the arm until he was able to use his other arm to pull us up.

"WUUUTTT DOO YEEWWW NEEEDD?" he asked.

"I need you to get close," I said. "We're going to use your magic to take it down."

21.5 Interlude: Geralt

Kaia lumbered off into the battle sitting at the center of the awkward, leggy vine suit, with Lolan sitting on her shoulder and Tigala just behind them.

Man, they sure are cool, thought Geralt. It was hard not to be excited fighting alongside them. They were innovative, and somehow their purpose didn't waiver. Even when it did, there was always a core understanding of what they needed to do, they just might need a little push here or there.

Fire roared in front of Geralt as the doom drake blackened a whole swath of the battlefield. Geralt was brought back to the present. He had a task to do. It was up to him to save the day, and that started by finding Kesq.

He scoured the landscape and couldn't spot her anywhere in his immediate vicinity. He could make out a few Saurians mixed amongst other warriors nearby, but the air was too hazy to make out any identifying details. The group was working in tandem to create giant mud pools to slow the monster.

"It's time to save the day," Geralt said, raising his sword to the air.

He ran for the group keeping his eyes peeled for the blue spear-wielding Saurian.

The battle roared on as he did. It was so different than he had imagined. In his stories, they always talked about fighting. They talked about the epic duels, the catapults being launched, and losing or gaining ground. But what they didn't often talk about was the horror of it all. War was not adventurous. It was not exciting in the sense that he had always thought of it growing up. There were people torn apart. Lives were snuffed out in the blink of an eye. Many bodies were so mangled that you couldn't even tell who they had once been. And being a warrior with a sword and no magic, there wasn't much that Geralt could do to help their side win. All he could do was help the wounded. He could pull the brutally injured off of the battlefield and hope that they'd survive their wounds. He could carry the broken.

It was a painful job. It broke one's resolve. And trying to be more sincere with himself, Geralt was beginning to admit that he was losing hope. He was afraid that this all would be for nothing. He believed that stopping Malcolm, stopping the doom drake, was the right thing to do. The two would destroy whole nations together—people that Geralt had begun to respect—people that respected him. Hatred was not the answer. He understood that now. But he couldn't help but think that those thoughts would die with him and the other warriors on the battlefield. Every time he thought they were gaining ground, they were put back in their place—not outnumbered but greatly outmatched.

But he couldn't think about those things now. He had a task to perform. Kaia seemed to have hope, so maybe he could borrow some of hers. He could tell himself that this was going to work out because someone he trusted seemed to think it would. It was all he had. It was all he was able to do.

So he ran for the group of Saurians making mud pits. As he reached them, he realized that Kesq wasn't among them.

"Kesq," said Geralt, panting after the run in his full gold plate armor. "Blue Saurian with a spear. Have you seen her?"

The group looked amongst themselves and shook their heads.

There was a loud crash off in the distance. It was Malcolm, trying to catch up to Kaia.

Geralt's heart skipped a beat. What if Malcolm catches her? He watched intently as the Human flew after the group. He was getting harder and harder to see through the smoke as he moved slightly away from him, but Geralt thought he saw a white glow coming from Malcolm. Malcolm stopped mid-flight and turned, his eyes glowing with the Avian's sight magic. Malcolm's head turned again as if searching for something, then it stopped. Geralt tried to follow his line of sight and found a group of warriors with a tall blue Saurian standing in the middle of it. Malcolm knew what was going on.

The white glow faded from Malcolm's eyes and a pale green glow came from his hands. It stretched out in a sickly way. But what was pale green? Was it some form of nature magic?

The tendrils of pale green magic reached out not to the earth, but to the bodies that littered it. The light crawled into the corpses, and in a moment, the dead began to move. They twitched and convulsed with the magic, slowly pulling their arms beneath them to stand themselves up. The magic faded from Malcolm's hands, but it remained in the corpses, pouring from their eyes, mouths, and any open wounds they had. The dead climbed to their feet and began to shamble in Kesq's direction.

Geralt wasted no time and took off sprinting toward the same destination as the shambling dead. But they were closer. They reached Kesq's group well before he had a chance and began attacking. Humans stepped forward with blasts of fire, Gnomes with simple illusions and teleportation. Beastfolk in animal-form tackled the undead, but they were outnumbered ten to one. And the corpses had no fear, no self-preservation. They attacked like it was all they could do. It was all that they knew.

"Run," Geralt yelled, but he was drowned out by the groans of the dead.

The corpses had overtaken most of the group that Kesq was in. She was now at the center with a Beastfolk in gorilla form, an Avian, and an Elf. They fought, but they were surrounded and it was only a matter of time.

The dead were just ahead of Geralt, and he didn't hesitate. He knew what needed to be done. This was his chance to live out the stories that he had read so many times as a child. He had to save them. It was up to him and him alone.

Geralt charged into the horde with his blade drawn. He struck one zombie along its shoulder blades, cutting deep. The corpse fell apart and the magic faded from it. He stabbed another through the back of the skull, sending it in a heap to the ground. Another met its end with a golden bracer smashing its skull. But he was not exactly quiet in his entry. The ones closest to him turned at the sound of metal clanging on bone. They lunged at him clawing and biting. Geralt did everything he could to stay standing, but they were too many. He was forced onto one knee.

Geralt still fought, throwing his sword into the chest of another corpse. With a second push, he drove his fist through its chest and his blade into a second corpse. But they had all begun to pile on. The weight was oppressive, pushing him further and further down. It was only a matter of time now until the monsters tore him apart.

Or so he thought. As he waited for the end, it didn't come. He paid more attention to what was going on around him, and though he was surrounded, the monsters were trying to bite and claw him. But with his golden plate armor on, there was nowhere to bite. And with the sheer amount of them that had piled on, there was no space to pull him to pieces. He was alive, for now.

It felt like minutes that he had been under there with no reprieve. Was he running out of air? Were the dead getting heavier? Weighing on him?

There was a sudden jolt, and the load resting on him lightened. Then there was another, and the army of corpses seemed to be moving in more of a frenzy than before. They continued to lighten, breaking up the pile that had formed on top of Geralt. Enough had moved away that he was able to push to his feet. Through the crowd of zombies, he could see vines attacking, like those of Kaia. But she was supposed to be finding Grollock.

It didn't matter. Geralt needed to do his part. He raised his sword and began chopping down the zombies that surrounded him. He sliced his way through the horde in the direction where Kesq had been previously. Knowing that he was safe against their attacks, he targeted legs and knees, each swipe sending more of the dead to squirm on the ground. One after another, they went down, and with the nature magic covering his back, he was making progress.

Then he saw her. She had survived behind a wall of ice, along with the few remaining warriors that Geralt had seen her with among the walking dead. Geralt stabbed another zombie through the shoulder and caved in another's chest with the pommel of his sword, the bone turning to dust.

Those who had been surrounded joined in the fight, but Kesq stayed where she was, not moving. The Gnome teleported out of safety and twisted a head from a zombie's shoulders, while the Avian stepped forward predicting the actions of the dead. In a few moments, the corpses had all been dispatched.

Geralt ran and knelt down next to Kesq. "Are you alright?" he asked, but he could already see the answer to that question. She had been pushed onto a broken Gnome machination. A sharp mangled edge of the metal was stabbing out of her stomach, pinning her in place. Her life was draining out of her. He had arrived too late.

"I do not think I am," said Kesq. "However, I would not have survived this long without your distraction." Geralt thought back on the distraction that he had created. He looked behind him and saw dead vines and an old Treek riding away from the scene on an elk. That must have been how he had gotten out. He had almost gotten himself killed, if it weren't for the armor of the Grandsome Glories, that is. And here was Kesq, torn to pieces when she was needed to stop the doom drake.

He turned back to Kesq. "I'm sorry I couldn't get here in time."

"You did what you could, and for that I am grateful," she said, coughing up blood.

He had moments to talk to her, and he needed to make them count. "We need to tell people how to use the beacons," he said. "Kaia sent me. She said it might be how we win this."

279

"What?" said the Saurian, her surprise was laborious. "I told her, this information is too powerful to hand out."

"We don't have any other options though, do we? We are going to lose without some kind of advantage. We need to turn the tide of this battle."

"Yes, but if we kill ourselves in the process, what is the point?" asked Kesq.

Geralt wasn't sure what to say. He knew too little about the situation and magic in general.

"We are dying anyway," he said. "At least with beacons we have a chance at survival." Her face was expressionless as she thought. The doom drake roared above them, shaking the ground. "This is dangerous information," she said. "You cannot let it into the wrong hands." Geralt nodded. "Of course."

She looked him over one last time. "You need to send your magic through it. Each kind of magical beacon will feel different. But the key is not to fight its whims. Let your magic flow through the beacon. Don't try to tell the beacon how to express itself."

"Right," said Geralt.

"They will change your magic and make it stronger. Be careful where it is directed because there may be unforeseen effects." Kesq gave a slight nod and then winced at the pain in her abdomen.

"Thank you," said Geralt. He tried to keep the details in his head. There was a reason he didn't know fire magic. He was never good with the details. He always hoped it would just happen naturally, that he shouldn't have to practice something innate to his people. But it never happened for him. And now it was up to him to relay the message—to teach the magic users how to use a new kind of magic.

"You can do this," said Kesq, her voice noticeably weaker. "You have to. It's up to you now."

"No, I can bring you to someone first. Or I can get you help," said Geralt.

Kesq looked down at the blood-soaked metal stabbing out of her torso. "No. I'm already fading. Do what is right with that knowledge. Protect it. It's powerful, and others want to know about it."

Geralt nodded and tried to find the words to say. He sat with Kesq as she took her last breath.

"Thank you for your help," he said, once she had passed. He placed her spear in her arm and laid it over her chest. She looked like a warrior.

Geralt wiped the tears from his eyes and stood. He glared up at the doom drake that towered above him and knew it was time for all of this to end. He searched the battlefield again, this time not looking for anyone, in particular, just the purple glow of illusion magic. He found it and ran to the Gnome wielding the magic.

"I need your help," said Geralt.

Porthos turned to look at Geralt. "What is it?"

"I have a message that everyone needs to hear. We might have a way to take down the doom drake. Can you amplify my voice? Just to our warriors though, not Malcolm."

"Of course," said Porthos. He pulled his hands up to his ears and pulled the purple magic from them. A translucent horn shape came out, pointing toward Geralt. "You're on."

"We may have what we need to stop the doom drake," said Geralt. "Beacons. They are large concentrations of magic. There is a nature beacon on Grollock, the green glowing treant, and the other is a fire beacon at the top of the volcano. You can use these beacons even if you don't use that

281

type of magic. You can feed your magic through the beacon. Just whatever you do, don't push the magic in a certain direction. Let it lead the way."

There were looks of confusion across the battlefield. Would it work? Did Geralt's words make any sense? Or did he get it wrong? Was he not clear enough? Did he not get enough of the correct information from Kesq? He had so many questions and no way of answering any of them.

Then, there was a bright orange light off in the direction of Grollock. It mixed with the green of Grollock's beacon and out of the battlefield rose a monstrous lizard. But it was no normal lizard. It was covered in leaves and vines. Large thorns stabbed up from its tail like an oversized mace and vines hung from the creature's back as it crawled on four legs toward the doom drake. Its large jaws clamped down on the drake's leg and blood sprayed as a result.

More magic flashed across the battlefield, swirling together. This was their chance to win the battle.

21.6 Banyan

I clung to Grollok's arm in my full vine armor. Lolan climbed up onto the treant's shoulder and Tigala held onto the top of his forearm as the tree walked toward the doom drake. Even at the top of his canopy Grollok only stood a little less than half of the doom drake's height. It was no match if the two of them were to go head to head, and Grollok made a pretty big target.

I scanned the battlefield, wondering if I could see Geralt. Had he made it to Kesq yet? Would the message get delivered? I didn't have time to wonder about it anymore, as I saw someone familiar speeding toward us. Malcolm was still trying to stop us, having seen what we were planning. Would he use the beacons instead? Or was that something outside of the vision he saw with his sight magic? I hoped it was.

"Malcolm's headed this way," I said. "We need to protect Grollok. Can you two focus on keeping him safe?"

"Where are you going?" asked Lolan.

"I'm going to do what I can to help," I said. I dove off of Grollok's arm and reached out to the beacon that glowed on his chest. It might not have been the smartest move, but it looked cool, and it kept me from weighing down Grollok as my vine armor expanded rapidly from the beacon-boosted magic.

The vines shot out beneath me, meeting the ground before I fell half of the distance to it. They caught me and I stumbled slightly, getting used to the new leg length. But I didn't just grow my legs. I fortified the entire armor. New vines coiled around others, making the armor three times as thick. My vine arms extended to almost the bottom of my legs. Vines weren't enough though. If I was going to fight Malcolm and dodge attacks from the doom drake, I would need something tougher.

I focused on the magic inside of Grollok's beacon, and funneled it out and into my armor. I worked on hardening the exterior of my armor. Dark bark began to grow on the outermost layer, forming large panels that resembled rough-cut plate armor. They were wiry and gnarled, but they were as thick as a brick wall. They covered my arms and legs first, and then my chest, back, and head in various plates.

Malcolm was on us in an instant. He flew straight to me and paused for a moment.

"You couldn't just die when you were easier to kill, could you?" he said. "Now it's going to have to get messy."

He pulled both arms back, and like he was lobbing a large rock at me, he threw them forward. A giant blast of fire materialized from his hands and barrelled toward me. I threw up my arms, crossing in front of my torso. The flame hit me with a force that pushed me back, with the feet of my vine armor scraping trenches in the ground. The heat wafted over me, even through the thick armor. But I was still intact. I had weathered an attack from Malcolm.

However, it wasn't something I wanted to keep doing. I reached forward and shot vines from my already abnormally long arms, reaching for him. He was too quick, dodging out of the way. I threw the other arm and met the same outcome. I was too slow compared to a single Human that was able to fly.

I swung again with my left arm, while my right worked on something else. I swiped a little high, and Malcolm flew low to dodge. When he did, the other vine I had grown behind him slammed into his back, swatting him at the ground. He hit the dirt, rolled, and skidded.

I didn't waste a second. I needed to tell everyone what was going on. I needed help. I couldn't hold Malcolm off all on my own. We needed Grollok if we were going to do this. I acted without thinking. I started speaking, but as I did, either by luck or some strange technique handed down from my ancestors, I used my plants to try and amplify my voice.

"Protect Grollok," I said, pointing at the treant behind me. The words were echoed by vines and twigs rubbing together in strange ways. It was muffled and hard to hear at first, but trying gave me a better idea of how to improve. I tried again. "Protect Grollok. Protect him," I said, still pointing my armored vine arm at Grollok. I moved the vines and branches intentionally now, and my words carried further.

Others began to join the fight. A thick fog rolled in behind me, obscuring the walking tree. An Avian flew up to my side with glowing eyes, ready to predict Malcolm's next move. Dwarves and Saurians below began pelting Malcolm with rocks and blasts of water as he stood to his feet. It wasn't much against someone with as much power as him, but it was enough to slow him down at least.

Malcolm dodged most of the attacks, only taking a few small hits from the rocks and water as he pushed himself back into the air. He centered himself on me and began flying forward again. The Avian flew to intercept, but Malcolm's eyes glowed white as well. The two clashed in what looked like martial arts, but Malcolm was almost free of gravity, while the Avian could only use her legs since her winged arms held her aloft. Malcolm struck the Avian, and she plummeted to the ground. Without even waiting to watch the Avian fall, Malcolm continued his flight toward me.

Then, the announcement came. A voice was in my ear like it was my own thought, but it wasn't my voice. It was Geralt's. What happened to Kesq? Was she alright?

"...don't push the magic in a certain direction. Let it lead the way," said Geralt as he finished his instructions. It was clear now that he knew more than what I had told him. So Kesq wasn't alright. Did Malcolm stop her? Did he kill her?

Malcolm continued toward me like nothing was happening. He met my eyes and smirked. Could he not hear what we were hearing? Maybe we actually had an advantage here that he didn't know about. Maybe we could use it against him.

I reached out and tapped into Grollok's magic behind me. My arm shot at Malcolm at a speed he wasn't even ready for. The vines wrapped around him and I could see the look of surprise in his eyes. He had no clue how I was doing this.

I wound up, ready to throw him at the ground, but just before I could, a heat overwhelmed me. I pillar of fire shot between me and Malcolm, burning off the end of my vine arm. When the flame dissipated, I couldn't find Malcolm anywhere. The doom drake was still watching out for him. Then, an impact hit my leg, shredding vines and making me unstable. I used my unharmed arm to hold myself up and Malcolm followed up with illusion magic. The purple magic covered my vision and the battlefield faded away. Malcolm faded away, and I was left in darkness. I searched for the light, but it was so dim. I looked up and found a grate letting in a small amount of light. I followed the light down to where it highlighted crude metal bars. Was I in another jail cell? No, this was illusion magic. But why was I seeing *this*? Then something moved behind the bars. It was a hand, cracked and skeletal. It grabbed the bar. Then a face followed it. The face was gaunt with starvation, but it was familiar. It was a Treek. The dark brown bark-like skin matched my own. I looked closer. The Treek had her hair in dreads, now wiry and frayed from lack of maintenance. It was my mother.

"Mom," I said, trying to scramble forward to the bars, but everything felt weird. I could see my hands move but not feel the motion. She was so thin and emaciated. How could anyone do this to another person? I pushed my face closer to the bars. "Mom, I'm so sorry," I said. I grabbed the bar and found she wasn't alone in the cell. Behind her, curled up on the floor was my father, even thinner than my mother. He was wasting away on the floor, looking like a skeleton draped in a thin cloth.

"I can get you out," I said. "I'll get you out." I reached for my magic, but it wasn't working. Then, the darkness faded and I returned to the battlefield. Malcolm was just in front of me with a yellow glow coming from his hands.

There was a flash and a sudden excruciating pain that ripped down my back. My body seized and I fell toppled to the ground, vine armor and all. My face slammed into the mud, unable to do anything about it. I writhed there and wondered when Malcolm would finish the job.

Then there was a sound above me that I didn't quite understand. It was a roar, like a large animal, but none that I had ever heard of.

I tested my strength again and managed to get the vine arms under me. I relied on the magic to lift me to my feet again and face the creature that I had heard. I found the source was a large giant lizard covered in vines, thorns, and flowers. *How did that happen?*

I watched closely wondering if I had one more enemy to fight now, but the creature began attacking Malcolm. Malcolm sparred with it until he knocked the lizard off its feet with a well-placed pillar of stone, but then there was a flash of energy. Yellow mixed with a green coming from behind my back, and a tornado of vines and branches spawned out of the sky. It headed directly for Malcolm, sweeping him up in the mess.

I looked behind me and found Grollok was the source of the green magic. *They are using the beacons*, I thought, *and it is actually working!*

There was another flash of energy as a Dwarf launched a boulder covered in a thick layer of briars. It hit Malcolm, but instead of launching him, the thorns caught on his robes and he sailed through the air with the large rock.

This was working. We might have a chance.

Malcolm, seeing that the situation had changed, managed to pull himself free of the ensnaring boulder and looked us over. There was clear confusion on his face. He was frustrated and for the first time, unaware of our abilities. After a moment, he fled back to the shoulder of the doom drake.

21.7 Banyan

We finally had it. We had an advantage. It was a gap in Malcolm's knowledge, and we had to do everything we could to use it while it was still unknown to him. I stared up at him as he landed back on top of the doom drake's head. He looked back down at me. But I had bigger things to think about now.

I surveyed the battlefield. It was filled with people who had come together here. We had overcome our past and chose to live in the present. There were no more Treeks, Dwarves, Avians, Beastfolk, Gnomes, Humans, and Elves. We were just people trying to protect those who couldn't protect themselves. We were here, united for the sake of ending the hatred and destruction. And it was up to us to do just that.

I set my jaw and raised a charred vine arm at the doom drake. "ATTACK!" I yelled, and the warriors all around me joined with their own voices. Flashes of green mixed with a rainbow of other colors exploded all around me so fast that I didn't have time to figure out what the original magic was supposed to look like with each attack. Regardless of who cast it, there was a tinge of nature to everything that happened. Vines, branches, bushes, carnivorous plant maws. They all slammed into the doom drake.

And it was working. The doom drake was starting to falter. We focused on the wounds created before Malcolm took control and we dug them deeper, with the tag-along plants adding to the damage of each hit.

I couldn't let them do all of the work though. This war started with my people and I needed it to end with my people too. Though we were few, we had our own part to play. I reached back to the beacon on Grollock's chest, and this time I didn't hold back. I used all of the tricks I had learned along the way. I focused on the hope of winning this battle, defeating the doom drake, and getting to enjoy the company of the people who helped me do it. I let the magic go where it wanted to go, and I let my body do what came naturally to it. Maybe there was still some muscle memory somewhere deep in my being that would let me use my magic the way my ancestors did.

I let the magic wash over me and my vine armor stretched and pulled me upward. It grew exponentially, pushing me to a height just above Grollock now. I was a small Treek at the center of a massive goliath of plants, vines, bark, and thorns, and my magic controlled it all as naturally as if it were my own body. I closed my eyes and let the vines and bark protect my head. I saw through my plants. I could feel what they felt and see where they were. But it wasn't just the plants in my armor. I could sense all of the plants around me, even the ones created as a secondary effect of the spells created by others. All of it formed a three-dimensional map in my mind of what was going on around me.

I had come so far, and now was the time to use it.

I charged at the doom drake and slammed into its leg. The monster brought down a giant claw to scrape me off of it, but I was no longer so easily swatted away. I wrapped vines from my arms around the leg and used my free arm to dig into the exposed flesh of the monster's leg.

Our attacks came faster than the doom drake could retaliate, pushing it back onto the foot of the volcano. It had never stopped fighting us or turned its back on us, but it was now stumbling backward up the sharp lava rock.

However, the doom drake wasn't alone anymore. Though we had it on its back foot, Malcolm was the perfect ally for it. There was a glow of pink magic from above, and when it stopped, the doom drake turned its backpedaling into attacks. Each footstep turned into a wave of rocks spiking up into the warriors still on the ground. Many were thrown into the air, others were pinned in the cracks in the earth and crushed to death.

The doom drake used the opening to smack a few of the falling warriors back into the ground with its tail. It was just so powerful, and even with our concerted effort, if it had Malcolm thinking for it, we were still outmatched.

I had to get Malcolm. Somehow, I needed to separate him. I needed to take him out of the picture so the others could defeat the doom drake. I thought through as many ideas as I could all at once. Was there any other way to do this? To take on Malcolm might be incredibly dangerous. Even though I managed to make him slip up earlier, there was no guarantee that I could do it again. If I were to make one mistake, that would be the end of me. But if I could win, if there was some chance that I could get him away from the doom drake, the others might be able to take it down.

It was worth the risk. It might be the only thing I could do to let us win this war. I couldn't take down the doom drake myself, but I could at the very least lure away Malcolm.

I began climbing the doom drake, still in my tree-height body armor made of vines, bark, and thorns. I sent my vines up, latching onto the limbs and fins of the doom drake, higher and higher. The weight of my plants pulled the monster off balance, making it adjust its feet to support me. It swatted at me, but I bound its claws in vines before it could impact. It pulled them free tearing the vines and tried again, but I was able to stop it each time, growing more vines. The doom drake was then pelted with attacks, distracting it from me once again. I swung to the back to avoid any major attacks and used its back fins as handholds on my way up.

I could see Malcolm well now. He stood just above me, looking down on the battle. He fed instructions to the doom drake when he saw weak points and used his sight magic to predict our attacks. But he was focused on the warriors below and didn't even see me coming as a result. I reached the doom drake's upper back and whipped my vines into Malcolm, curling them around him. I knew I wouldn't be able to hold him long, so I threw Malcolm higher up the slope of the volcano, away from the battle and the doom drake.

He recovered quickly and began to use his flight before he even impacted the black volcanic rock. I threw vines close to where he would have landed and wrapped them around a rock outcropping. I used the anchor point to pull my full armor in his direction. Malcolm dodged me as a sailed toward him and slammed into the side of the volcano. It was a rough landing, but I could handle it. I had forty feet of vine cushion between me and the ground.

Just as I landed, Malcolm slammed into me like a comet. He blasted a hole right through the vine armor's shoulder.

"You want me dead?" I yelled to him, doing my best to amplify my voice with the aching and rubbing of vines. "Come get me!" I had to keep him distracted as long as possible to give the others a chance.

I stretched out an arm further up the volcano still and found another anchor point to latch onto. I jumped and used the anchor to pull me forward, climbing the volcano quickly.

Malcolm didn't seem to care. He was so much faster than me. He did another attack, like the first, but this time through the lower abdomen of the vine armor. He was getting closer to hitting my actual body.

I closed the holes as quickly as I could, but it wasn't very fast now. I was outside of the range of Grollok's beacon. But there were veins all around me, climbing and converging further up the volcano. They pulsed with red magic. It was fire magic. I considered tapping into it, but I was scared. I knew others were tapping into nature magic from Grollock below. I knew it must have been uncomfortable for them. Nature magic killed so many when the plague hit so many years ago. It was the whole reason my people were hated so much. And many were looking past that correlation so that we could win this battle and defeat the doom drake once and for all.

But I had a similar issue with using fire magic. It was the magic that stole my family away from me. It was what Malcolm started out with. It had caused so much pain for me and the people I loved. Even though others were no doubt facing the same dilemma below, I wasn't sure if *I* could overcome it.

Malcolm flew back toward me and this time used his own fire magic to create a pillar of fire, slowly making its way to me. It reached the bottom of my vine legs and I could feel the moisture being sucked out of them. The flames ate at my plants and charred them, sealing them and making it hard to regrow from their ends.

But instead of backing away from it, I grabbed a large column of volcanic rock. I tore it from the mountainside and used it as a shield against the flames. The rock heated, but it was a thick black glass that was made with heat. It wasn't going to fall apart due to some fire magic. I jumped through the pillar of fire with the rock breaking an opening for me, and swatted at Malcolm again. My attack landed and I launched him further up the volcano. He slid on the glossy black earth.

Malcolm yelled with a ferocity I hadn't quite seen from him before. He was always so controlled and sure of what he was doing, but it seemed I was starting to really get to him. *Good*. He stood and used earth magic to glide down the mountain toward me, riding a wave of cascading stones.

I hunched down, preparing for a hit, but it was harder than I expected. The stones jutted out of the mountain and slammed into me, sending me and my whole vine suit spinning.

A flash of orange magic had him transforming into a dragon himself. He looked eerily similar to the one we had just killed below. Malcolm, in dragon-form, breathed in deeply and my heart leapt. I knew that sound, but could he...?

Flames blasted from his throat at me. I dove out of the way, charring more of the vines that made up my left arm as I did. I didn't wait for him to strike again.

I threw a torrent of vines at him, adding exploding seed pods to each. They erupted, and Malcolm flapped his wings as fast as he could to escape. Spines stuck out all over him, but he was still intact in his dragon form. I followed up by launching myself at him. We crashed into the mountain in a tangle of vines and scales. He let out blasts of fire and bit through vines as I grew more, trying to immobilize him.

Then, there was another flash of orange magic, and the dragon faded away, turning back into Malcolm. In his smaller Human form, he slipped through my grasp, flying just beyond my reach at the top of the mountain. For the first time since I had first met him, he looked like he was struggling. He breathed heavily and sustained injuries all over his body.

"We need to stop it," I said, hoping there was some ounce of sympathy left in him for the other races. "You can't kill so many just to keep your race safe. They will always find something to fight—"

"I don't care what you think. You're the dirty Treek. Your people killed hundreds of thousands once you found out how to use your magic well. You have no right to talk to me about other races," said Malcolm.

"That wasn't me. That was you. You tricked the world into believing it was the Treeks to get revenge for what a few Treeks did to your mother."

Malcolm looked shocked, taking a step back toward the volcano's mouth. The red lava glowed and lit the edges of his silhouette. Sparks of red danced in the air around him. He gave an evil smile. "Ah, so you've learned Sight magic. I must say, that was rather quick."

I had just watched in on Klaus's sight magic, but I wasn't about to tell Malcolm that. "We don't want to hurt you. We just want to stop the fighting." I said.

295

Malcolm's smile widened as he broke out into a mocking laugh. "You still think you can hurt me? After all of this, you think that you can do anything about what is going on? You don't even know how outmatched you are."

Malcolm leveled his gaze at me, the shadows accentuating his brow line. He took a step toward me and threw one hand forward at a time. From each, a blue glow produced sheets of ice so thin they were hard to track as they flew out at me. I tried to dodge, but the ice came too fast. One sheet sliced the entirety of my vine leg clean off. The other sliced off an arm from my armor. I fell to the ground, kneeling on my one remaining vine knee and holding myself up with the opposite arm. I looked up at him, trying to regrow the vines before he could send a follow-up.

I wasn't fast enough. Before I knew it, two more sheets came at me, aimed for my remaining two limbs. I couldn't grow the vines fast enough, but just before they hit, I reached out to the veins that surrounded us and centered somewhere in the mouth of the volcano. I used the beacon and vines shot out in front of me, covered in flames. The ice hit hardened bark, shattered, and melted instantly, pelting my body with droplets of water instead.

Malcolm wound up again. I continued reaching out to the beacon. I didn't extend my body this time but instead grew branches out of the volcanic rock around him. They all were covered in flames. They would last a much shorter time than normal due to the heat, but they were also a heck of a lot more intimidating.

Malcolm looked at the branches, unafraid, with a quizzical look. "How are you doing that?"

"It doesn't matter. The fact is I can hurt you, and we will stop you. Stop this so we don't have to," I said.

Malcolm reached out at the vines. His hand glowed with red magic, but it was a slow unprovoking motion. The red glow touched the flaming branches. He stared at them, and then looked down at the veins, following them to where they met inside the volcano. "Ah, I see," he said. "You're not as smart as you think."

He reached his hands back and I saw the red glow reaching for the magic in the fire veins.

"No! Don't!" I yelled. But I was too late.

Malcolm erupted in flames. They engulfed his body without burning him up. He used his flight to lift himself into the air as a flaming beacon of a man. Then, with a thrust of his arms, a torrent of fire as wide as the doom drake's legs shot at me. I dodged, but with my limited mobility, there was only so much I could do. The flames burned over half of my vine armor in an instant, shrinking vines around me, and trapping me inside of them.

As I fell to the ground, I looked up at him one more time. He was laughing with corrupt power. He reached back for more fire magic from the beacon. But this time, when he went to unleash it, there was a rumble and cracking from within the volcano. Globs of lava shot high above him, but they were just the precursor of what was to come. Lava spewed from the mountain, and a look of terror showed on Malcolm's face. Whatever was happening, he was no longer in control. Malcolm tried to let go of the magic and run, but before he had a chance, the lava consumed him without even giving him time to scream. He was gone in an instant, and the rumble of the volcano wasn't stopping. The volcano was erupting and all of the people I had come to care about were just below.

21.8 Banyan

There was no time. The volcano was in full eruption now, and I was too close to it with a broken body of vine armor. The lava rocketed into the sky like a geyser, and I had only seconds before it would consume me too.

I used the veins. I couldn't see them, but I could feel them. I grew vines as fast as I could, but not to rebuild my vine armor. This time, I grew them just on my arms. I reached out with them as soon as they had some length and grabbed onto the strongest rocks I could find within range. With something like a slingshot motion, I catapulted my crippled vine armor body down the volcano with me in it.

I tumbled down further and further, occasionally taking an impact so hard that it knocked the wind out of me, but I used the time to regrow, as much as I could manage. When I had finally stopped spinning and sliding down the mountain, I pushed myself up. The world spun around me, but I could see the red glow of lava creeping closer and closer, even still, despite my quick descent. The doom drake fought on above me, but the pink glow had disappeared from its temples.

It screamed and thrashed. Some of the warriors were beginning to look around, wondering if they should run from the volcano or keep fighting. I needed to do something. This was our chance to stop the doom drake.

I pushed myself up. Nearly half of the vines that made up my vine armor hung off of me, limp and charred, but I was still a giant among all but the doom drake.

I yelled, amplifying my voice as well as I could with the creaks and rubbing of vines and bark. "Keep the doom drake pinned! We need to trap it in the lava!"

The people below looked up at me with renewed confidence and doubled down in their attacks.

"Gnomes, keep it from teleporting if you can. Use the beacons," I said.

I joined the fight, pinning its leg in place. My vines wrapped around it and coiled until they reached the ground where they took root. I squeezed, doing my best to crush the wounded leg of the monster. It wasn't enough, but it would help.

The lava came closer. Globs of lava and molten rocks fell from the sky, no doubt killing some of us instantly, but we couldn't let up. This might be our only chance to stop the doom drake.

"Hold!" I yelled.

We were more numerous now than we had been throughout the whole fight. More and more had poured in from the illusion beacon not far off, and now we were a force to be reckoned with, but so was the doom drake, unfortunately.

A stream of lava came barrelling down the mountain toward the doom drake. It was almost there. It was almost close enough to melt the monster into nothing. I continued to grow my roots and hold the creature in place. The doom drake screamed, but we were now making progress. Its arms had been frozen over several times. Each time, it broke free but had less mobility. The tail too was being pinned by mountains of stone.

The lava reached the stones holding the monster, and let out a sizzle as it flowed through the stone and began to eat at flesh. It let out a ferocious roar and turned its head to find the source of the pain. The doom drake breathed deep and a red glow formed in its chest. But instead of fire coming from its mouth, the lava began to pull back out of the crevice that held its tail. Globs of molten rock were raised into the air, floating for a moment.

I tried to yell a warning, but I was too slow. The monster's magic launched a spray of lava across the battlefield. Hundreds fell, but the lava was still rolling down the mountain.

The doom drake took another look over its shoulder and saw the lava continuing toward it. It glowed a purple-blue now.

"Gnomes!" I yelled as I held the drake's leg. The magic flickered and lit in full force. There was a flash and then I was in a different location, still attached to the doom drake. We were about 100 feet from the volcano now.

I looked around for the warriors that were no doubt being engulfed in the lava now that the doom drake wasn't in the way, but I couldn't find them. Where had they gone? Then I heard the war cry from behind me. Everyone involved in the battle was still behind me, further from the lava than the doom drake. The Gnomes must have tapped into the teleportation spell and brought us all with the monster. It was something, but if the drake teleported further, we might miss our chance to kill it.

The lava was now further away, but the Humans in our ranks ran forward to pull the rivers of fire closer to the colossus while the rest of us focused on grounding the monster again. Treants surrounded the drake's feet and legs. Saurians worked together to freeze as much of it as they could. The Elves repeatedly struck it with lightning and clouded its vision. We might be able to do this. Just a little longer.

The volcano shook harder now than before, spewing lava at an alarming rate. The Humans sped up the process even more, pulling large waves of the molten earth toward the doom drake. I could feel the heat now, and I was sure the doom drake could too. So what was the next move?

The creature roared. It was almost entirely immobilized, with vines and bark and thorns in every nook and cranny of each spell. They were doing damage with Grollok as our mobile beacon.

The doom drake glowed purple-blue again, and I knew this could be it. The doom drake could escape, recover, and then kill us all once and for all. It was up to the Gnomes to stop it.

The purple glowed and lit the sky. It grew brighter and brighter as the doom drake got closer to completing the spell. I didn't dare say a word this time. I had to trust that the Gnomes had this under control. I had to believe it. The purple flickered and dimmed, and then grew again. It was so bright that I was surprised we hadn't teleported yet. Then all of a sudden, like a bucket placed over a lamp, the glow disappeared.

I held my breath, and after a moment, dared a look around. We were still there, at the foot of the volcano. All of us were there.

A cheer erupted among the people. We had done it. We had kept it there. The cheer was interrupted by sizzling as the lava flows hit the tail of the doom drake again. The drake tried to redirect it, but we had too many Humans on it and a fire beacon close enough to use.

The drake tried to claw at us, but the sustained ice magic held its arms in place. Some would break, but it was being replaced faster and faster.

My roots held it to the ground along with the rocks of the Dwarves.

Plant-covered giant animals tore flesh from bone.

Avains flew and attacked with spears, and found weak points in the armor of the creature.

Then, all of a sudden the ground shook harder than anytime before. The volcano growled with anger. Boulders of fire began raining from the sky and rolling down the mountain toward us. The Dwarves dissolved several of them, but there were too many to block them all. Some rolled through our ranks, erasing people in their wake.

We needed to hold. We were so close. We needed to keep the doom drake there. It was our best shot.

Then, like a gift from heaven, a boulder fell from the sky with lava dripping off of it. The boulder slammed into the doom drake's back and the smell was worse than the sound of melting flesh. In a moment, I saw the red glow in the monster's chest, but this time, it wasn't of the creature's own doing. No. The lava boulder was melting all the way through it.

"GET BACK!" I yelled along with many others. I cut off all of my rooted vines and ran, scooping people up in my vine arms as I did. The doom drake was going down.

People scattered in every direction, and the doom drake stopped fighting. Its body slowly went limp and began plummeting to the ground, where all of our warriors began trying to escape.

We ran. I thought about all of the people I cared about. I thought of Tigala and Lolan. They were with Grollok last I knew, but were they safe? Would they make it out? Would the people of the colony get out in time? I grabbed people without hardly looking, holding them in my arms crossed across my chest as I ran. The shadow behind me grew darker and darker, and I used my last moment to dive.

I threw out one last flush of vines to grab as many people as I could, and the doom drake slammed into the earth, shattering it beneath him. The colossus was down and we wasted no time in keeping it there. I used my vines to wrap around it. Others did the same with their own forms of magic.

But it wasn't dead yet.

An orange glow came from the monster, and the wound slowly began to close. But before it could make any progress, the lava caught up to it, now engulfing its feet.

We continued our attack, slowly making our way toward the monster's head, which was the furthest part of it from the volcano and the lava. More lava rocks littered the battlefield, taking out some of ours, but the Dwarves were now doing their best to redirect the molten earth into the doom drake instead of us.

The monster screamed, but it wasn't as forceful as before. It came out in a gurgled puddle from its throat. It continued desperately trying to claw its way free, but we had the upper hand. We outnumbered it by the tens of thousands now, and our magic kept pouring into the restraints. The lava flowed further and further up its body.

As the lava progressed, and the doom drake lost more and more strength, people began fleeing the scene, putting as much distance as they could between themselves and the lava. Gnomes began opening large portals for hundreds of people to go through at a time. I held as long as I could, waiting for the lava to even start eating into my vine restraints on the monster, and then I joined the others.

I scooped up stragglers as I ran in my severely battered vine armor. Our people were gathering past the reach of the volcano, and those who had already made it stood silently watching the doom drake as it was slowly consumed. I was among the last to join them, and when I did, I set the people down that I had been carrying, and turned back to look at the monster. It was now nothing more than a pair of shoulders and a head, with the lava still creeping forward and slowly devouring it.

We all watched in silence, unbelieving of what was actually happening. I half expected the doom drake to lift its head any second and stand, unscathed by the lava. Each moment that went by I hoped it wouldn't happen, but I expected it all the same.

The lava made it to the monster's head, and no one looked away. The lava crawled over the creature, returning it to the earth that it had so recently awakened from. And the more I stared at it, the more I thought I saw more colors than just the orange-red glow of the lava. Maybe it was just my mind playing tricks on me, or maybe it was the release of all of the magic that was trapped inside of the doom drake, but a glow in all colors seemed to rise up and fade into the sky above it.

The lava crawled over the tip of the monster's face, and it was gone. There was still silence. I couldn't believe it. Was it really gone? Everyone else must have been thinking the same thing. No one moved. We were all collectively terrified it wasn't over yet. But when the lava leveled back out to show the shape of the land instead of the giant hill that marked where the doom drake had laid, it was clear we had won.

A cheer erupted all around me, and tears came to my eyes. We had done it. We had defeated the doom drake. And even bigger than that, we had done it together. We did what our ancestors couldn't, putting an end to the problems of the past to spare our children the same fate.

22 Methuselah

22.0 Methuselah

One month later…

The trek back to Birdsbane wasn't easy. So many were injured—so many people had died. It felt wrong to leave the bodies behind to be consumed by the flames, but we didn't have much of a choice. We barely had the time to get the injured out of harm's way before the lava reached us. There was no time for the dead.

Once the doom drake had been consumed by the flames, and the rains had stopped, we all took a deep breath, gathered any who were still alive, and walked back to Birdsbane. There, we took a much needed break, letting people recover. Tigala, with Nadira's help, started learning to heal with transformation magic. I focused mainly on feeding everyone with *my* magic and had some extra help from Grollok's mobile beacon.

The newcomers, those who joined the fight after using the portal on the other side of the island, were a bit afraid at first of eating Treek-grown food. I couldn't blame them. It had been programmed into everyone for so long. But they all saw me fight. They knew I had almost sacrificed my life for theirs, so the uncertainty didn't last very long.

Everyone did their part to help. Dwarves built temporary infirmaries and stretchers. Beastfolk did what they could with healing and shaping splints and tools. Saurians made sure everyone had plenty of fresh water for drinking and cleaning wounds. Elves kept the weather clear to lighten our moods. Avians helped in diagnosing injuries and looking into possible reactions from the rest of the world once the news got out of our victory. Humans helped cauterize wounds and cook. As for the Gnomes, they moved people from place to place without disturbance. They also kept our spirits high with illusions and tall tales.

Honestly, it was a magical time. There was so much hurt —so much pain and destruction. So many had lost people that they deeply cared for. But at the same time, there was a giant sense of relief that strung it all together. We all knew that the sacrifices made were to make the world a better place. We had gotten past the hardest part, and now it was just up to us to make the most of those sacrifices. We needed to continue what we started to honor the people who died fighting Malcolm and the doom drake.

We stayed at Birdsbane for a few days while people recovered, but after those few days, some of the Avians were advising that we do something to represent our combined effort against the doom drake. The rest of the world was waiting to hear what had happened. Some may have already found their way back to the mainlands and started telling the tale of the doom drake's fall, but we needed to be ready for people to come and see it for themselves. More than that, we needed to be ready to tell the world *how* we defeated the doom drake. We did it through cooperation, and that cooperation needed to continue. It was no longer an option to continue as we had been. Our hatred had created this mess, to

309

begin with. We couldn't allow that to happen again. It was time for change, and as the Avians said, we needed people to tell our story and exemplify it.

So, Tigala, Lolan, and I, along with many others, traveled to the shore to build a new colony. We picked a spot that hadn't been touched yet. The old colony had been mostly burnt down from the dragon attack, and Birdsbane was too far from the shore to make it a good port on Daegal, so we picked a spot with a river that fed the waterfall we had swam at not too long ago.

We all used our magic together to rebuild. I focused on building living structures with willows and other trees. The branches weaved together and continued to live and grow and change. For things that needed a little more structure or cover from the elements, the Dwarves were able to use their earth magic. Beastfolk aided in construction by shaping other materials that the Dwarves and I couldn't work with. And the colony itself came together rather quickly. The walls to protect us from the monsters on Daegal went up in a couple of days, and from there it was all buildings. We built houses, a market, and the Saurians helped us find good places for wells.

It was a strange feeling, looking around at the town we had built, but it was a good feeling. It was something I never thought I'd see. Unlike the original colony on Daegal, in our new colony, I was accepted, without question. People knew me, they even seemed to enjoy my company. They were happy to eat any fruits and vegetables I provided for them. And when people did finally come to our colony from the mainlands, I had no doubt that the locals would make sure that no one was being treated poorly because of their skin, their ancestors, or whatever else people might blame them for.

As the buildings went up, we grew more and more comfortable in our new home. Those injured in the fights with the Doom drake, the dragon, and Malcolm, slowly recovered and made the trek from Birdsbane to the new colony. The Gnomes also worked on creating a teleportation gateway in the town, and once it was ready, we could connect to Losterious and any other gateways throughout the world. It gave us a chance to become a new nation in a sense. We were small compared to the others, but we were strong. We knew who we were and what we wanted. We wanted peace. We wanted to be able to enjoy each other's company, regardless of what we looked like. And we wanted to spread that ability to others.

Of course, I didn't expect the rest of the world to be fully on board with our new way of living. But there were enough of us that we could be an example. And having defeated the doom drake, people would be afraid to challenge us. So we would use our position in the world to help others.

Once we had the colony established and running smoothly, we decided to send out groups to the various towns and cities that had been destroyed. It didn't matter what race each city belonged to, or how they felt about us. We just wanted to help those in need and rebuild. Some would stare at us. Some would be hateful. But we won't stop.

The fire glowed in front of me, crackling and popping at the air pockets in the dry wood. It was mesmerizing to watch while I thought. And I had a lot to think about. The past few months felt like years. We had been through so much. We had come so far.

"Where should we start?" asked Rodrigo.

"There's a lot to choose from," said Klaus. "The doom drake destroyed many large cities, a few towns, and even a handful of villages."

"Is there anyone that needs it most?" asked Lolan. "Anyone who was hit harder than everyone else?"

"I don't believe so," said Klaus. "Obviously, the cities sustained more damage because there was more to be damaged. But every race lost multiple cities."

"We should go to a Human city first," I said, coming back from my trance. The others watched me, waiting for my explanation. "We need them to know that we don't blame the Humans for what happened here. The actions of one can no longer be paid for by many. Malcolm is gone. I watched the volcano swallow him. So I think it would be a good gesture to help the Humans first. We'll show them that we mean what we preach."

"I think that is wise," said Palem.

Tigala and others nodded as well, showing their approval.

"Then we'll go to Brighton. They were one of the first to be attacked by the doom drake, and it is a rather large city with plenty in need."

I looked over to Amara who had also been quiet. "Are there any gateways close to the city?"

She looked up. She had also been lost in thought while staring at the fire. "Yes, we'll be able to get you close enough."

"Thanks," I said.

"Speaking of which, the Avians are seeing things with their magic," said Klaus. "They believe there is at least one ambassador on the way to our shores within the next few days. They're coming to hear news of the doom drake, but they will undoubtedly want to hear about our colony as well. We are going to have to represent our colony to the world. And not just the colony, or the people of it, but we need to represent our way of life. Unity, cooperation."

"I'm happy to help with that," said Rodrigo. "I know my track record isn't perfect, but I have experience with nobles."

"I'm here to help as well," said Geralt, cocking his head upward as he spoke.

"I don't have experience with that," said Marv. He was sitting with Abigail by the fire and Crag was nestled up against his leg. "But I would like to help as well. We owe our lives to cooperation." He looked down at Abigail and she leaned on his shoulder.

"Good. That's a start," said Klaus. "I believe we'll need people from each of the races as representatives. We need them to know that we are united and this is not just some idea that is going to fade away if we want to be taken seriously." He looked at me, Lolan, and Tigala. "We think you three would be good people to be involved with those kinds of talks too."

I looked at the others, and then back to Klaus. "We're happy to help."

Klaus nodded. "Well, that's all I have for tonight. I'll let you all rest, you deserve it."

"Thanks, Klaus," I said.

The crane-like Avian stood and disappeared in the dark of the colony.

It was a beautiful night. It was just cold enough for the fire to make it more comfortable. The stars shined bright above us and I couldn't help but think of Zef. The twinkling was like the one in his eyes when he smiled.

"You okay?" asked Tigala.

"Yeah," I said. "I'm just thinking about Zef. He would have been so proud to see us now."

"You're right. He *would* have been proud," said Tigala, echoing my words as she looked back at the fire.

"Do you remember the waterfall?" I asked.

Lolan and Tigala nodded.

"I wish we had more time there," I said.

"You mean before the water tried to drown us, right?" asked Lolan with a smirk.

"Yeah, before that." I smiled back. "The time we spent here, it always felt like we were against the clock—always running from one situation to the next—always trying to keep ourselves, or others, alive. But that day, just swimming in the river, that was the first day I've ever spent where I felt safe with people I care about."

"It was a nice day," said Lolan.

"We can go back sometime," said Tigala. "Pay our respects. Maybe he'll still be there in some way or another. We've got time now. The doom drake is dead."

"I'd like that," I said. I looked at the two of them. They were two people I never thought I would have any kind of relationship with. Lolan was a half-Elf half-Human and over the course of the last few months, I grew to trust him, and rely on him to back me up when I had a crazy idea. We had saved each other's lives countless times and shared things that I only thought I could experience with another Treek.

And Tigala. The first day I met her, she attacked me. She wanted me dead just for being a Treek. Now she was the most fearsomely loyal friend I had ever known. No matter what, she would be there to back me up. She would give her life to protect us, and she had proven it multiple times over.

She had been scared like me. She was alone. But together, we found a friendship that I didn't think was possible.

"How do you think it's going to go, talking to these other nations?" I asked.

"Piece of cake," said Lolan.

"Oh yeah?" I asked, smiling.

He shrugged. "No, but I'm sure we'll figure it out."

"Yeah," said Tigala. "We've handled worse situations than this." I nodded. Through it all, Zef was the one that guided us. I just needed to remember what he had taught us. I had no clue where things would go, but they were right. With them by my side, I knew we'd figure it out.

I looked up at the night sky as I thought about the future. I didn't even know where it could lead. Everything was so different now than when I scrounged for clues of my parents' whereabouts in Brighton. None of this was what I had planned on, but it was good. The fighting was over. The war had ended. Now it was just up to us to show everyone else the way.

I saw something flutter past the moon and was reminded of another friend I had said goodbye to so long ago. Something landed on a tree just above me. I looked up and heard a familiar chirp, and a smile grew on my face.

A Note from the Author

Writing *Sprig* has been a journey. This was my first real foray into writing publicly, and I am so proud of how far it has come from the day I sat down and said I was going to write a story. This story encapsulates so many things in my own life, and I hope it does the same for you.

I especially want to thank you for giving me a chance. Thank you for investing your time in an unknown author and trusting me to provide you with a story that is worth your while. I can't express how exciting it is that other people might resonate and maybe even learn and grow from the words I have written. So thank you for going on this journey with me.

And if you are wondering, yes, there will be more books, though I don't have any specific dates yet. But I have other books currently in the works, and I think they are even better stories than this one. I believe they do a better job at focusing on real life issues and dissecting them so that we can grow from them. But, you'll have to wait and see for yourself.

If you want more of my stories, please subscribe to my mailing list via the link on the next page. There, you will get exclusive *Sprig* content as well as updates on future stories. I make the first draft of my stories available online for free, so it's easy to try it out and see what you think.

Again, thank you so much for going on this journey with me. If you have thoughts on the story, or even just want to say that you read it, I would love to hear from you. Send me an email at me@houstonhare.com. Aside from that, dream big, and I'll see you in the next one!

Adventure awaits!

- Houston Hare

The Adventure Continues!

Subscribe now to be notified about future releases and promotions! In addition, you'll receive the following:

- Exclusive **3,500-word bonus chapter** about the original Treek colony on Daegal
- Digital copy of the **map of Daegal**
- Printable *Sprig* **bookmarks**

Sign up at the link below!

HoustonHare.com/subscribe

A Quick Favor

If you are enjoying the story so far, please consider rating and reviewing *Sprig* on Amazon and/or Goodreads. I'm still starting out as an author so every review makes a big difference.

Thanks for the help!

Amazon:
https://www.amazon.com/review/create-review/?asin=1734298073

Goodreads:
https://www.goodreads.com/book/show/203687539-sprig

Acknowledgments

Special thanks to all of the following people who helped make *Sprig* what it is today!

Meghan Hare, Rosie, Willow, Daisy, Garrett Wood, Tyler Baldes, Carachel, Claire Rouleau, Landon Stoner, Elise Stoner

Thank you to all of my patrons for their help in funding new chapters and this book!

Josh Gore, J. C. Weston, Novagirl93, and others

To read chapters in advance, fund more chapters and books, and get eBooks early, visit my Patreon at the link below.

Patreon.com/HoustonHare

Made in the USA
Middletown, DE
12 September 2024

60792439R00183